A Death at St. Anselm's

By Isabelle Holland

A DEATH AT ST. ANSELM'S
THE LOST MADONNA
COUNTERPOINT
MARCHINGTON INHERITANCE
TOWER ABBEY
THE DEMAURY PAPERS
GRENELLE
DARCOURT
MONCRIEFF
TRELAWNY
KILGAREN

A Death at St. Anselm's

ISABELLE HOLLAND

DOUBLEDAY & COMPANY, INC.
GARDEN CITY, NEW YORK
1984

All of the characters in this book
are fictitious, and any resemblance
to actual persons, living or dead,
is purely coincidental.

Library of Congress Catalog Card Number 83–11668

Printed in the United States of America
First Edition

Library of Congress Cataloging in Publication Data

Holland, Isabelle.
A death at St. Anselm's.

I. Title. II. Title: Death at Saint Anselm's.
PS3558.O3485D37 1984 813'.54
ISBN 0-385-18332-1

A Death
at St. Anselm's

PROLOGUE

THE WATCHER crouched behind the wet bushes at the top of the low hill above the road, knowing the car would soon be along because the driver was always punctual. Once the car came into sight, the watcher would have several options as to what to do next but, characteristically, preferred to leave any final decision to the last minute. The main purpose was the clearing up of an ugly situation. It was a terrible secret that the watcher carried, and the burden could no longer be endured. Something had to be done, and the time to do it had arrived.

The watcher, intent and determined and getting wetter by the minute, had no eye for the magnificent fall coloring, brighter than ever this year because of the early frost, and vibrant even in the gray drizzle that had been descending all day.

Below the hill curved the road, sleek with rain, as was the surface of the shallow apron built out from the road on the south side of the curve so that cars could stop and admire the view. Far below that ran the river, descending here in a great arc of water where the riverbed dropped thirty feet beneath the overhanging rock.

Past the apron, but still on the curve, the stone wall gave way to a limp and rickety fence, hardly strong enough to stop a determined wheelbarrow, let alone a car.

Thirty years before there had been a much stronger fence. But that had disappeared one night when a car, propelled by a teen-ager, exalted with his first bout with alcohol, had plunged down the side of the hill to the river. Immediately afterwards, the present fence had gone up, sturdy at first, but the worse now for many winters of bad weather, snowdrifts and careless cars.

If the current dispute wrenching the nearby community had taken place then, the proponents of extending the stone wall protecting the apron to cover the entire curve would have won, hands down. But the mutilation death of the terrified youngster was a generation old. Only the older citizens remembered it. To the younger members, it was simply another version of the modern dispute over the priorities governing the spending of public money: whether the funds should go towards extending the apron wall (built since the accident) to benefit those who owned and drove cars or to the almost nonexistent public transport in the adjacent town.

On a much-traveled road the sound of a car meant nothing. The watcher, though, knew well the particular noise made by the right car, and suddenly stood up. But before anything else could take place, there was a screech of tires as the car, going much too fast around the long, dangerous curve, skidded and slid, lurching out of control past the sturdier apron area, and, before the horrified stare of the watcher, went through the guard fence as though it were paper.

Paralyzed with shock, the watcher stood for a moment, then started down the hill, only to be stopped a few seconds later by the explosion from below the road. A minute or so after that came the roar and crackle of fire.

The watcher made a terrible sound, then jumped down to the road and ran across, staring below to where the huge fire enveloped the car and reached hungrily for the trees.

After what seemed a long time, a figure, lying at a distance from the inferno as though flung from the car, sat up, then gave a cry and sprang up. But there was nothing that could be done.

The watcher saw the figure finally limp away down towards the river and then along to where the banks were lower.

The watcher stayed for a long time, feeling the beginning of a numbness that in time would obliterate everything.

Nothing after that would ever be the same.

1

MONDAY MORNING was always the worst. It was not just that, being a member of the clergy, I found the day after Sunday a letdown. Partly it was memory: my late husband, Patrick, also a member of the clergy, needed more wifely reassurance and general affirmation on Monday morning than on any other day. Sunday, the busiest day of his week, he woke up exalted, ready to do the Lord's work, the parish's work, and to be father, husband, brother, son and all-purpose friend to a vast number of people who would turn up at the ten-thirty service to tell him (1) how wonderful he was, (2) that their problem (whatever it was) had come to a nasty head and they needed to have a private conference with him immediately or (3) they didn't wish to be negative, but felt that he, Patrick, would want them always to be honest, and with that in mind they (or he or she) felt called upon to state that his (Patrick's) sermons were not as good as they used to be.

Patrick took all that in his stride as he shook hand after hand. He always had two comments that he felt could cover any contingency (excluding personal tragedy): "Thank you very much for letting me know how you feel" and/or "I'll take it up with the vestry."

Which makes him sound cynical—which he wasn't. Far from it. A product of the sixties, Patrick came to the Episcopal priesthood out of the civil-rights and anti-war movements. He was an idealistic activist, and he remained that, more or less, for all of his short life. Becoming rector of a parish did not dent his idealism, but it did bring him up short behind tiresome and depressing details, such as trying to pay the heating bill for the church and parish house and having to draw up an annual budget when people felt it against their principles to pledge.

"Jesus Christ did not have to work within an annual budget when he fed the five thousand, Mr. Aldington, so I don't see why the modern church is so taken up with money. That's one of the things that's wrong with it . . ."

But none of these pinpricks really bothered Patrick till Monday morning, when he invariably woke up feeling like an accountant with books that didn't balance and an overdrawn bank account, rather than a priest dedicated to the propagation of the Gospel. At which point I would resort to much soothing wifely murmur and extra amounts of T.L.C.

But that was five years in the past, I thought, that Monday morning, pushing open the door of the main entrance of the great parish house on East Sixty-second Street off Park Avenue. Patrick was dead. I was the ordained member of the family, and Monday morning was still an anticlimax, although to what I wasn't sure.

As I passed the reception desk I noticed idly that Josie Beardsley, the receptionist, was in, evidenced by the unopened container of coffee on her desk and her typewriter minus its cover. But she must have been delivering some mail or powdering her nose, because her chair was empty and she was nowhere to be seen.

I also noticed a few shabby figures coming up the stairs from the parish room below, bringing with them Styrofoam cups of coffee and some of them still holding buns. These were members of the homeless, a growing army of men and women who lived on the streets of New York for reasons ranging from an inability to pay rent, to failure in coping with contemporary society, to mental illness. Most were despairing and desperate. Some were profoundly disturbed. A few were criminal, their victims most often their fellow sufferers. Both sexes and all ethnic groups were represented, though a heavy majority were black and Hispanic. Most were middle-aged or older. But a surprising number were young.

The financially overburdened city struggled to give them food and shelter, but it was always too little. St. Anselm's, among other churches, had started a program to feed as many as could be accommodated twice a week, and to allow up to twenty to sleep at night on cots in the parish room downstairs. The wretched recipients had to be got up, given breakfast and urged out as early as possible so the premises could be cleaned and readied for the usual day's activities.

In a sense, Christ's statement "The poor ye have always with you" was becoming true in a literal and immediate sense. To care for these discarded members of society was the project closest to the heart of St. Anselm's rector, the Reverend Norbert Shearer.

I picked up a handful of telephone messages from my mailbox behind the reception desk and was walking towards the wide stairs at the back when I saw Josie come out of the ladies' room.

"Hi," she said, and looked surprised.

"I still work here," I replied in a feeble attempt at Monday-morning humor.

"Yes, but—" The phone on her desk buzzed, and she went off to pick it up.

When she put down the receiver she said, "That's funny. I was sure I'd seen you—or at least your back. I was bending down picking up some papers that had fallen on the floor and when I straightened you were walking down the hall. I thought it was odd you didn't say anything."

"Who was it?"

"Like I said, I thought it was you. So I don't know who it was. I wonder if I was having a hallucination."

"Where were you last night?"

She grinned. "At home, watching television."

"Norbert back yet?"

"No. He's coming in around eleven-thirty or so."

"He was at the anti-poverty rally in New Haven, wasn't he? There was a big piece in the paper about it yesterday."

"Yes. He was supposed to be the lead speaker last night at the closing ceremony or march or sit-in or whatever."

"Who's going to take Morning Prayer?"

"Johnny McKnight, I think." Josie consulted a book. "Yes."

"Where's Larry?" Larry Swade was another clergy assistant.

"Out on an early call."

As I walked upstairs I reflected that it was entirely in character that Norbert Shearer should be the lead speaker at an anti-poverty rally in New Haven. Except that he was handsome and commanding, he reminded me in many ways of his Yale classmate, Patrick. He shared the same social theories and had the same instinct for activism and passionate advocacy. His installation as rector had been a triumph for the 55 percent of the congregation that felt that the Church's main role lay in renewal and outreach. The 15 percent who were new or unsure at the time of his installation, and had sat out the fracas, were fast coming around to his side. The 30 percent who had lobbied and politicked within an inch of their lives to keep Shearer out, and had lost, now bore the look of those who were biding their moment not too patiently, waiting for Norbert to make his first major goof. As a Norbert fan, I thought they'd have a long wait, although he did add fuel to their bitterness by undergoing a second divorce after his induction as rector, a step that drove the division in the congregation even deeper.

Reaching the top of the stairs, I walked back along the hall and fitted a key into a door bearing the nameplate "The Rev. Claire Aldington." After two years of seeing my name preceded by "The Rev." and adorning that particular door, I should have become used to it, I thought. But I wasn't. It was still a shock. It wasn't that there weren't by now plenty of ordained women in the Episcopal Diocese of New York. It was just that I still found it astonishing that I was one of them. Of the two of us, Patrick was far more a feminist than I.

Not long before he was killed he said idly one day, "You know, you really ought to do this work in the Church as an ordained member of the clergy." By "this work" he was talking about the therapy group sessions that I was running as part of my master's degree in clinical psychology.

"Come on, Patrick," I replied. "I'm not one of those women."

"What women?" Patrick asked ominously. He was always catching me up on what he considered my knee-jerk reactionary response.

I sighed. "All right. I take it back."

"And it's not as though you'd even met one of 'those women,' is it?"

"No."

"We don't even have them in this benighted diocese, do we?" We were not then in the Diocese of New York, but in a regrettably (to Patrick) conservative diocese west of the Hudson.

"I said I take it back."

"I've long had the revolutionary idea," Patrick said patiently, "that the Church is where the psyche, as in psychology, and the soul meet. *Vide* Jung. The tragedy is that for a hundred years the Freudians and the ecclesiastics spent most of their time and all their energy throwing brickbats at one another. Now, at long last, they're beginning to see that they are dealing with different aspects of the same problem. And some of the more liberal, not to say progressive, bishops are putting trained psychologists who are also clergy into large parishes. Naturally, nothing as wild or off the wall as that would cross the mind of our own dear bishop."

"All right, Patrick. But he won't live forever."

"Is that a guarantee? As coming from a member of the family?"

I grinned. The Right Reverend William Fitzalan, bishop of our diocese, was my uncle. He was also one of the Church's most ardent advocates of Holding the Line against the liberal hordes bringing the new prayer book, folk masses and the ordination of women.

"He's rising seventy," I said. "That's your guarantee."

"But all the Fitzalans are very long-lived." Patrick spoke with such genuine and heartfelt gloom that I had to laugh.

"Cheer up," I said. "I may have a fatal accident long before then."

Patrick looked reproachfully at me. "You know I didn't mean that," he said.

I loved him dearly for his idealism, his warm heart and a teddy-bear comforting quality that seemed to embrace the whole world. As I reminded myself frequently, one can't have everything, and Patrick's sense of humor was not his most highly developed characteristic.

"Don't talk that way," he said.

"Sorry, I'll try not to die young."

It was a joke and a casual smart-aleck comeback, not to be taken seriously, for all that Patrick frowned slightly before turning away. When I thought about it afterwards, it brought pain, because it was Patrick who, two weeks after that conversation, was killed in a car accident.

Sighing now, I turned the key and went into my office.

It was a small and delightful place, with a window looking out onto the square garden entirely enclosed by the parish house on one side, by the back of the church on another, and two rows of town houses, at right angles to one another, occupying the third and fourth sides.

More, much more than my apartment, this was a haven and a refuge, and I fought against becoming so fond of it that I would suffer when I had to move, which sooner or later I would have to do. Clergy, especially junior clergy, whose main function is that of pastoral counseling seldom stay long in one parish. But, I told myself, when the time came to move, then I'd move, and that would be the end of it.

It was curious, I thought, putting down my bag and my ever-present tote bag containing book, papers and reports, that of all the rooms I had ever occupied, professional or domestic, this was more truly my own than any other. More than my room in the home where I grew up? I wondered, sifting through my phone messages. More than the big master bedroom that I had occupied with Patrick during our marriage? More than my own apartment now, where I lived with Martha, my stepdaughter, and Jamie, our son?

The answer to all these questions was "yes." Which was both astonishing and disturbing. Did it mean that all those other rooms contained something undesirable that was not here? Or did they lack something desirable that I found in my church office? Either answer was full of traps and barbs, so I decided to think about something else—such as the business at hand.

I glanced at my watch. It was eight o'clock—more than enough time for me to look through whatever had accumulated for me to do, to attend an abbreviated Morning Prayer held the five working days of the week in the chapel and to meet my first appointment at nine-fifteen.

But I discovered as I looked at the messages that, early as it was, there was an even earlier call from Martha's school, St. Julian's. Would I please call the headmistress at my earliest convenience?

My heart went down with a familiar "thunk." The temptation to return the call at any time other than my earliest convenience was so overwhelming that I picked up the receiver immediately, dialed nine, then dialed the school. "Miss Webster, please," I asked when the school operator answered.

"Her line's busy," the operator said. "Would you care to wait?"

"No. Just tell her that Mrs. Aldington returned her call." I hung up in a burst of cowardice and relief and went back to the other messages.

One member of the parish had called to break an appointment. Another had called to make one. I took care of both of these, looked over the day's schedule, noted (with once again a sinking heart) that I was slated for an appointment with the church's business manager, then decided it was time to make tracks for the chapel.

Fishing a comb out of my top drawer, I swept it through my freshly washed hair. Slightly waving, heavy and thick, it was a dark reddish brown that, fortunately for the time I had at my disposal to spend on it, looked best in a simple cut. As for the rest, underneath a square forehead, I had hazel-green eyes, a white skin that had to be kept away from beaches, freckles, a body that was slight and rather flat, but nice feet—my one real vanity. I looked down at my triple A pumps, the heel a little too high to be in perfect taste with my gray skirt, black blouse, round clerical collar and gray jacket. "From the ankles down," Patrick had once said in an unusual flight for him, "you have a tendency to look like a chorus girl."

I powdered my nose, put some lipstick on my large and frequently indiscreet mouth, decided that I looked every day of my thirty-five years and went down to chapel.

Johnny McKnight, an assistant rector and the head of Christian Education, winked at me as I wiggled into the choir stall beside him. He had won his major battle, which was to abandon the old-fashioned Bible-oriented texts in the church school in favor of ecumenical booklets emphasizing social problems, and was moving (he told me) slowly and steadily towards a still newer concept, about which, however, he was still most secretive.

Jennifer Riddle, our seminarian, was busy finding the right collect for the day.

"O Lord, open thou our lips," Johnny began, when in walked Brett Cunningham, banker, leading vestryman, former treasurer and business manager and a pillar of the conservative contingent.

"And our mouths shall show forth thy praise," the congregation murmured in response.

I heard Brett mutter, "Sorry to be late," as he slid into one of the pews near the front of the small chapel.

A Christian is not supposed to hate, I reminded myself, listening to Johnny's rather stilted reading of the opening prayers. Even less is a Christian minister supposed to indulge in prejudicial attitudes, uncharitable judgments and malicious fantasies. Nevertheless, if Brett Cunningham's foot found a banana peel and he fell flat on his pinstriped suit, I would get an unseemly pleasure out of it and laugh like anything. Luckily for the more progressive of us, after years of holding the post, he was no longer our treasurer and business manager. A well-planned coup, carried out by the liberal element in the congregation, had managed to relieve him of his job, held now by the much more up-and-coming Dick Grism. Unluckily, since the bank of which Brett was chairman of the board was a mere five blocks south, he was frequently present for Morning Prayer.

"Come on, Claire," Norbert had said once, when I was being particularly eloquent on the subject of Brett. "He may not be your cup of tea. He's not mine, but that doesn't mean he isn't a sincere and believing Christian."

"So was Torquemada."

"That's not fair," Norbert said. But he was grinning.

The supreme irony of all this was that Brett had emerged from the same Yale class as had Patrick and Norbert, and whenever I saw Norbert and Brett together, they seemed to exude the same quality of unchallenged authority, for all the vast differences in the ways in which they viewed the world.

When asked once by one of the newer clergy what Brett had done to enrage me, I had listed the following: He had insisted on such a close tally of the costs of my own particular pastoral counseling program that the whole thing had been delayed for a year; he had bullied the rector into reducing the feeding of the homeless from three times a week to twice, on the grounds that it was becoming too expensive; he had opposed the installation of air conditioning in the church for the same reason; he had maintained, in the face of Norbert's overriding enthusiasm, that we could not put up cots for the homeless in the basement of the parish hall until we were sure we had enough volunteers to sit up all night with them, both for their safety and for the church's; he had—

"All right, all right. I get the picture," the assistant had said. "But isn't that his job as church business manager?" (He still held the post at the time of the conversation.)

"It's the job of the executor to execute, of the bill collector to collect, even if it means harassing, but we don't have to love the person who does it."

The assistant had sighed. "I withdraw the question."

We were well into the psalm when it occurred to me that we were short of our usual complement for Morning Prayer. My eyes ran over the figures sitting in the front pews: Mike Ferrare, the sexton, and George Hearn, Matthew Pearson and Pedro Gonzales, the custodians, were in the front row. Susan Bailey, parish secretary, was behind them.

On the other side was Miss Leila Something, who worked in the area and who was there as faithfully as Norbert himself—more faithfully, as a matter of fact, because the rector was so often away, as he was this morning. Then there was Mrs. Reynolds, a librarian from the Public Library down the block, and Mr. Frank Rainey, an accountant with one of the large department stores. Rain or shine, they and Brett Cunningham, laypeople of the Church of St. Anselm's, worshipped at Morning Prayer. Then, according to the season and the weather, they put on their coats, put up their umbrellas and left to conduct their daily lives. Whenever I saw them I was haunted by the strong feeling that they were a lot nearer to God than I was. Because if I were not actually and physically *in* the church, but were in, say, a therapy clinic somewhere, or in private practice, would I get up early and leave the house every single workday to attend Morning Prayer?

No, I wouldn't. Or perhaps I was simply afraid I wouldn't.

And then, as we launched into the final prayers, I suddenly realized who was missing: Dick Grism, our current business manager. Despite his considerable disability—he was a paraplegic—he was usually in very early and nearly always attended Morning Prayer. The miracle was that he did not miss it more often. Getting himself out of his specially made car and into his wheelchair and then into the church undoubtedly cost more in effort than the rest of us would ever know. His only concession to the usual working day was to avoid the rush hours by arriving often before seven and leaving before four. When he couldn't do that, he'd come in at ten or eleven.

I was still thinking about Dick when, incongruously, I saw in my mind my stepdaughter's face. It was extraordinarily vivid, almost as though she had walked in front of me, and the incident shook me, even as it continued. I became overwhelmed by the fact that in some way Martha was *present* with me. Why had I thought of her? Or, put another way, why had she visited me at that moment?

The reason, I decided, was most likely the phone call to Martha's headmistress that I would have to make again and that I dreaded so much. Martha, now fifteen, was seven when her father and I married. She barely remembered her mother, who had died when she was four. Then, when she was ten, her father died. Other than her grandmother, there were no near relatives on either side of her parents' families, and, anyway, it was her father's wish, expressed in his will, that she should live with me. So for the five years since his death, she and I and Jamie, Patrick's and my eight-year-old son, had lived in uneasy peace. That is, Martha had lived in uneasy peace with Jamie and me. Because Jamie and I got on splendidly, largely because whatever was on his mind was on his tongue less than a tenth of a second later. Repressed anguish was not Jamie's thing, which kept the *tessitura* of the household a little high, but it also put things out in the open. Martha was the exact opposite. If she'd ever had a genuine blowup, I'd have lit bonfires, not because I was of the "let it all hang out" school—despite my therapy-oriented viewpoint—but because her alternative layers of passive compliance and passive rebellion were the most effective barrier I had ever encountered. It was probably because of reasons involving something related to that that Miss Webster had called me . . .

"Amen," Johnny said.

"Amen," we all murmured.

I replaced the prayer book and slid out of the choir stall.

"Good morning, Claire," Brett Cunningham said, as pleasant as though he were totally unaware of how much I disliked him—which he wasn't.

"Good morning, Brett," I replied, determined to match civility with civility. I glanced at his rather worn raincoat. "You look as though you thought it was going to rain. Are you a good weather prophet, or is it just natural pessimism?"

"Probably a little of both. I hear you're trying to sweet-talk Dick Grism into letting you lower your lowest-fee bracket. As you know, I think it's a poor idea."

"Why? Natural parsimony?"

He smiled a little, his eyes very blue against the remains of a summer tan. "Partly," he said. "Coupled with a profound New England belief that people don't respect what they don't pay for. I thought all shrinks held that view in common if they believed nothing else."

"You mean we're moneygrubbers?" I asked amiably.

"No, I think I mean you don't give your services away, so why, in our frequent arguments, are you so indignant when banks and corporations hesitate about giving away theirs?"

"Ah, but what they're stingy with is profits. What I'm talking about is need. Medical help should be available to everyone. Even if they have nothing. Especially if they have nothing."

"Nobly said. Fortunately, perhaps, for the church budget, I don't entirely believe that. When you go into private practice, if you ever do, are you going to follow that rule of thumb yourself?"

"Whenever I can."

"Then I think you'd better marry a rich husband again."

"That was a rotten, dirty crack," I said.

"Why? I disagreed with Patrick Aldington about almost everything. But I will say this for him: he made no bones about being a rich man's son."

"True. But you implied that I married him for that reason."

"No. You inferred that from what I said. Why are you in such a fighting mood?"

Suddenly the whole thing struck me as funny and I started to laugh. The moment I did I knew how bellicose and provocative I was being. "Try, my dear," my father had once said. "Just *try* not to have more than one major battle a day . . ."

"I suppose," I said, sighing, "I'm cross because I have to phone Miss Webster, Martha's deputy headmistress. She left me a message, and I know this means trouble. Also, I have to go and see Dick Grism, who's been brainwashed by you to say no to everything I suggest."

"Yes," Brett agreed. "I did brainwash him as much as I could. Some of your projects are a little on the expensive side. I know we're a church and dedicated to aiding the poor. But we're not going to be much use to them if we go out of existence. And our annual deficit is getting larger, not smaller. Which is undoubtedly why Norbert would like to sell that monstrosity sitting on the heights above the Hudson."

"What you call that monstrosity has been the pride of St. Anselm's since Lackley's day in the last century. If Norbert carries through his intention to sell it, he's going to let loose a hornet's nest. That's *terra sacra.*"

"In that case there's going to be one unholy row when they hear what Norbert has in mind."

"What's that?"

Brett didn't say anything. As he continued not to answer, I burst out, "Well, what is it, for heaven's sake? Do you want me to die of curiosity?"

Brett grinned. "A California guru wants to buy it and make it into his east U.S. ashram. They—the guru and his staff—don't want the building. What they want is the land, which, as you know, overlooks the Hudson. They plan to pull down the house and put one up more in the Eastern style."

"Holy cow!" I resorted to a childhood expression.

"Most apt!" Brett commented. "Nevertheless, they're offering ten million dollars. Think what that would do for Norbert's outreach program!"

"Think what it'll do to the congregation!" I replied. "Polarized as they are now, it'll slice them right down the middle." I glanced at Brett. "Where do you stand?"

"Why do you want to know? So you can take the opposite side?"

I opened my mouth and then closed it, humiliated to realize that there was more than a little truth to what he said.

Brett grinned sardonically. "I wasn't far off, was I? It's a case of 'name yer givverment and I'm agin it,' isn't it?"

"You know," I said, "I find it hard to put together the Brett Cunningham who, rain or shine, turns up for Morning Prayer every day and Brett the stone-throwing urchin who takes such a pleasure in taunting me."

"It's a question of your urchin versus mine and who throws the first stone. Remember the lunch-box hubbub? Remember when you wanted regular theater-club subscription for some of your poorer clients?"

I could feel the blood surging up my neck. "Remember the feeding of the five thousand? Remember the Sermon on the Mount?"

"Yes indeed, but I don't think the Master had to contend with the caterers and the cleaning-up staff unions at the time. Furthermore, I don't believe that temples in the Holy Land had large heating bills."

By this time the bantering had developed an edge. Neither of us was entirely kidding. There was no longer a twinkle in Brett's Baltic blue eyes. They glinted, chilly as an ice floe.

"You know," he said, "there are moments when I think you're speaking less for yourself than for your late husband, Patrick Aldington. But I also think, from what I now know of you both, that it's what the shrinks call overcompensation. I can't help feeling you're making up for something."

I was now very angry—much too angry to think before I spoke. "Perhaps the same could be said of you and Pamela."

There was a silence. Outside on Park Avenue cars could be heard starting up from their wait behind a red light. A bunch of people passed below on the sidewalk, chattering. I stood, appalled at myself. I had forgotten what was common knowledge: Brett's wife had simply walked out on him. Since, for all his physical attractiveness, I couldn't imagine anyone able to live with Brett, my sympathies, such as they were, had always been on her side. Still, it gave me no right to make such a remark.

"My apologies," I said. "I shouldn't have said that."

Brett's brows shot up. "Why not? It's in the public domain by now. To revert to our original topic, I still think Norbert's biting off more than he can chew with this land sale. It'd be a lot better if he'd look around elsewhere for the funds to make up for the deficit."

"It's not just the deficit," I said stubbornly. "We have to remember that we need it for the outreach—the homeless, the mentally ill . . ."

"And the television program."

That was news to me. My curiosity struggled with my irritation. Then I saw the frost leave Brett's eyes. Once again they reflected amusement.

"Let me save you the struggle you're obviously going through and answer the question you're trying not to ask. Norbert has been approached by a local station about a half-hour program on the air on Sunday morning. The man who approached him is a member of the congregation and admires Norbert a lot, but it still costs the earth and then some."

"Oh." I paused. "I see."

"I knew you would. Well, on to the daily grind. Goodbye."

I watched his tall, rangy figure cover the length of the chapel in a few strides.

Such a show, I thought, as I wandered back through the chapel into the church and from there to the parish house, could split the congregation just as thoroughly as the projected sale of St. Cuthbert's. On one side would be those who thought that the word of God should have as much exposure as Archie Bunker, and on the other, their opponents, who would shudder at the whole idea as the height of tackiness—the kind of thing one associated with southern Fundamentalists.

I didn't know what I thought about it, and didn't have a chance at that moment to find out.

"Josie's been looking for you," Larry Swade said as we met in the parish house hall. The Reverend Lawrence Swade was one of the several clergy assistants at St. Anselm's. His specialty was Christian Spirituality and he was in charge of organizing retreats, Quiet Days, prayer groups and so on.

"Where were you instead of at Morning Prayer?" I asked severely.

"Out on a parish call."

"A likely story," I said, teasing him. "What does Josie want me for?"

"I don't know. She didn't say. But somebody's been burning up the switchboard looking for you. One of your crazier clients, no doubt, ha-ha," Larry said.

"Ha-ha. Not funny. How do you know I don't have a trio poised on the edge of suicide?"

"Sorry, I don't."

He bustled off, quivering in every one of his two hundred and twenty-five pounds.

Why, I thought, going up the stairs two at a time, did people never look the way they ought? Or why did I have such a problem with the visual vis-à-vis the conceptual? Spiritual directors should, my visual sense said, be thin and ascetic, the temptations of the flesh (if any) conquered well in the past. They should have hollow cheeks and a quality of sternly repressed desires. They would, of course, be celibate.

Larry Swade, happily married to one of the prettiest girls in the parish, was quite frank about his greatest temptation: it was a well-known and particularly rich ice cream, of which he yearned to eat a pint every night before he went to bed. If not a quart. Of all the forms of lust it undoubtedly had the least class. Scarlet sins, wild bouts of drinking—at least these were interesting. They had style. Gorging on a quart of ice cream was . . . well . . . common.

Yet Larry led the finest retreats of any retreat master I'd ever known. He knew more about the snares, passions and deceptions of the human heart than anyone since Brother Lawrence, and he was the one that I often sent people to when I knew they were beyond my help. Yet there he was, unheroic in every bulging inch, round nose, round face, round body, a walk that frankly waddled, but the nearest thing to a saint I'd ever encountered.

". . . moves in a mysterious way, His wonders to perform," I muttered to myself, thrusting open my door. The phone rang as I was halfway across the room.

I snatched up the receiver. "Yes?"

"Mrs. Aldington?"

"Yes. Is that Miss Webster?"

"Yes. I called because it occurred to me that you must have decided that the worst of some kind had happened. We couldn't locate Martha, who is usually here by seven-thirty on the mornings she closes the school paper. The other kids were gathered and waiting for her. It seems she and Polly Rhodes were across the street having a pizza and turned up a few minutes ago. Anguish over. Now I have to think of a suitable punishment. But I'm bound to say that I was so glad she'd *eaten* I was ready to forgive her anything."

"Where is she now?" I asked drily.

"I assume in her classroom. Why?"

"Because I don't think we can assume it. It would be nice if she were. But there's a good chance that she's in the nearest john with her finger down her throat making herself throw the whole thing up."

"Oh my God!" Miss Webster said slowly. And then: "I'm going to put down the phone and find out."

I heard the click and replaced the receiver. The phone rang again.

"Claire Aldington," I said.

"Claire? Josie here. Your first client called to cancel. She has a cold and can't make it in."

"Oh. Well, thanks. Any other messages?"

"No, not at the moment."

Suddenly I had forty-five minutes that I wasn't planning to have. There was plenty of paper work I could catch up with if I wanted to. The trouble was, I didn't greatly want to. I stared at my desk and then stared at the typewriter, which was still covered. The phone rang again. And again it was Josie.

"Have you seen Dick Grism this morning?"

"No. Why?"

"Well, I know he's here because he picked up his messages before I came in. But I can't get him on the phone and nobody seems to have seen him. I thought he might have been in the chapel."

"No. He wasn't. I remember being surprised he wasn't. Look, Josie, I'll go along to his room and see him now. I have to anyway, and I have the time to do it. I'll tell him he's being paged. Maybe he's busy and just won't answer his phone."

"He does that sometimes. But usually he tells me first that he doesn't want to be bothered."

"I'll call you back," I said.

Dick Grism's office was at the other end of the parish house and overlooked East Sixty-second Street rather than the gardens. In other words, it was as far from mine as it could be. I walked down one corridor, turned a corner and walked all the way down another. Grism's office was the last one at the end of the hall. As I got nearer, my steps slowed.

I had, quite justifiably, accused Brett Cunningham of brainwashing Dick Grism, training him to say, I sometimes thought, with increasing irritation, Brett's favorite word: No. No, you may not have extra money for your wackier and poorer clients; no, you may not buy a secondhand school bus so you can take your therapy group out for its weekly sessions to a rock on Bear Mountain, the better to exorcise their demons; no, you may not have a fund for setting up a psychology-oriented library; no, you may not . . .

When he was treasurer, Brett's tight-fistedness had made me furious. But I had, however grudgingly, to admit that he was neither pompous nor self-righteous. In fact, it was partly his matter-of-factness that drove me mad, turning down every request as though I were asking for an unearned raise, instead of badly needed help for the poor and disabled.

I said this once to Brett and he infuriated me further by saying, "I'd be much more likely to give it to you if it were a raise. I approve of raises."

"But not help to the needy?"

"Within limits."

"As long as it doesn't get out of hand," I said sarcastically.

"You sound like Patrick."

"Thank you."

"It was fine for Patrick to sound like Patrick, but I'm not sure that it's so good for you." He paused. "With him they came from his center. He was born to think the thoughts he did. But I don't think you are. You took on his world view to drown out your own. The two of you were very different."

Why that thought should have struck me at that moment, standing ten feet from Dick's door, I don't know. I was indignant at the time, of course, both at what it said and at what it implied as to why I married Patrick. I pushed my mind away from that. What did all this have to do with Grism?

What it had to do was the fact that I felt terribly uncomfortable around Dick; that when he said no, I sensed there was a reason beyond the reason he gave; that he delivered his refusals with an air of rectitude that could have turned whole congregations into pillars of salt; that the fact that he had wanted to see me meant he was about to turn down some other project I had launched. It was true that half the congregation was rigidly conservative and felt that the whole outreach program, of which I was a part, had gone too far and too fast, and that we needed to haul in our sails, pay attention to the deficit and tend to the spiritual state of the parishioners . . .

I snatched my mind back. What I was doing, maundering on like this, examining the bulletin board at that end of the hall, reading every single message pinned to the cork back, was postponing the evil moment.

"Get on with it," I said aloud to myself. I went to Dick's door and knocked. There was no answer. I knocked again, louder this time. There was still no answer. Odd, I thought, turning away. Dick's paraplegic condition was the result of a fairly recent accident, and he managed his mobility with such ease and speed that after the initial impression of a big man with a big torso and shriveled, lifeless legs, one was inclined to forget his disability. It was the single thing I liked best about him. So little did he appeal to our sympathy that most of us felt perfectly at ease getting angry at him. It was, in its strange way, a great compliment.

But the fact that Dick was in a wheelchair made it all the stranger that no one had seen him since he had arrived in the building and picked up his telephone messages. When he whizzed around the halls he was far from inconspicuous.

I was halfway down the hall when something—I could never afterwards decide what—made me turn back. Once again I knocked at Dick's door. Still no answer. I turned the knob and went in.

I saw the blood before I saw anything else. It ran down one side of his face, onto his shoulder and then onto the floor, as the heavy body sagged in the wheelchair. The light brown eyes were staring, their whites showing, and his lips were drawn back. There was a horrible feeling in the room. And Dick was dead.

2

WITHIN AN HOUR the police were all over the parish house and a detective had taken charge. A cameraman and TV person were sitting downstairs, waiting to interview someone—preferably the rector.

There were plainclothesmen taking photographs of poor Dick, of the desk and room and anything else that struck them as relevant, and what looked like an entirely different team were concentrating on fingerprints.

Since I had found Dick, a Detective O'Neill questioned me as to every detail of my finding him. He wanted to know how I felt about him, especially after the late treasurer had turned down, or advised against, so many of my pet projects, and he kept coming back to what had made me return to Dick's office, knock again and this time open the door.

"I don't know," I said. "I really don't. I just—" I spread my hands. "I don't know," I repeated.

"You just what?" he persisted gently.

I shook my head. "If there was anything else there in my mind I wasn't aware of it."

"Did you think there was something strange in the fact that he had not answered any of your previous knocks?"

"Yes, of course. The way Josie thought it was strange. Dick was a man of regular habits. He was always here early—earlier than anyone else. For that matter—" I stopped, remembering something.

"Yes?"

"Well, he was usually in chapel for Morning Prayer. Not always, but usually."

"What time was that?"

"Eight-fifteen. It's supposed to be so that most people can attend and still get to an office on time."

"But he wasn't there this morning?"

"No. But while it was unusual that he wasn't there, it wasn't *that* unusual. He was, after all, a paraplegic, a fact that, because of his enormous physical independence, most of us were able to forget. But sometimes there were things he had to be a little flexible about, such as chapel."

"Was he married?"

Somehow—it was now getting on for midday—this was a question I should have thought the police would have asked immediately. "I should think you'd know the answer to that by now."

"Do you object to answering the question?"

I cursed the fact that I hadn't answered it immediately. Now it sounded to my ears as though the detective thought I had a vested interest in Dick's lack of domestic attachments.

"No," I said sharply. "He's divorced. He was divorced some three years ago, and his wife lives out there somewhere." I waved my arm.

"Out where?"

"Out there. Somewhere west of the Hudson."

"That covers a lot of territory."

I was tired and upset. The shock of finding Dick's body was beginning to have its effect. One client had canceled, luckily, but I had had to put off another, something I didn't like to do, especially to someone as fragilely balanced as the one whose appointment I'd had to postpone. "You know, Mr. O'Neill," I said, "I'm not in the mood for the hallowed provinces versus New York wrangle. If Dick's *wife* had been living outside the metropolis, I'd probably know where, because I'd assume it was important to him, a colleague. But she was a former wife. I don't feel that my pastoral or collegial duty extends to former, ex- or late wives."

Unexpectedly he grinned. "Sorry," he said amiably. "You do understand, though, that we have a murder by person or persons unknown, and that finding ways of making them known is—er—a central part of my job."

"In other words, you were trying to trap me."

"A little. Are you going to fly to the nearest civil liberties lawyer?"

"It would serve you right, but no." And then I added, for no particular reason. "My father was a district attorney once."

"Oh? Where?"

I sighed, already regretting my disclosure. "Out there somewhere."

"Flyover country."

I gritted my teeth. "Illinois."

"So you should understand the problems of the frequently misunderstood arm of the law."

I was about to get up, but stopped. His comment swept me back to the early days of my marriage. When I married Patrick I soon discovered that one of his favorite places to be was marching with protest groups. The Vietnam War was over, but he and his co-protesters and marchers had switched much of their focus to the environment and the anti-nuclear movements. In the course of this they often collided with the police, and Patrick had been known to make less than charitable comments about the constabulary.

At the time I married, my sympathies tended to be with the law—natural enough, considering my district attorney father. It took Patrick only about a month to turn me around, partly, I think, because to live with him without such a metamorphosis would have been impossible. After that, my conversion to the anti-war, pro-peace, pro-environment, anti-government, anti-business (you can fill out the rest) was total. Like any new convert, I crashed to the opposite extreme. Patrick was very proud of me, which more than compensated for the nagging, messy little doubts (usually sounding just like my father's voice) that would assault me at vulnerable moments. The detective's comments about sympathizing with the arm of the law brought them strongly back.

I got up now. "I cannot have any sympathy for fascist repression," I said piously.

He rose, too. "You've got to be putting me on."

"Yes," I sighed. "I am. I don't know where Mrs. Grism is."

"You knew her?"

"No. But I heard him mention her from time to time."

"I see."

At that point Josie came up breathlessly. "That school has called about three times, Claire."

"Okay. I'm coming, I'm coming. Why are you away from the switchboard?"

"I'm on my coffee break," she said indignantly.

Murderers could murder. The church could be thrown into total disarray. But the integrity of the coffee break must not be breached.

"Okay," I said. "I'll go back and call Miss Webster."

The detective got to his feet. "What's this about a school?"

"Only that my stepdaughter sent her school into a paroxysm of panic this morning by not showing up. I had about three calls from the headmistress before I even arrived and then another after Morning Prayer. I don't know what the problem is now, because they found her. Miss Webster must have— But that's of no interest to you," I finished lamely. Why parade poor Martha's problems before the New York Police Department?

"Everything's of interest to me," Detective O'Neill said.

"This isn't," I replied firmly, and left.

"What's the trouble?" I asked Miss Webster when I finally reached her.

"Just that you were right. I tore down to the girls' cloakroom in time to hear some extremely explicit noises going on in one of the booths. In other words, she was vomiting." Miss Webster sighed. "I really thought her stay in the hospital had cured her of that. I waited until she came out and said as much to her. She just looked at me and said, 'But I'm getting terribly fat.' Mrs. Aldington, she's not a skeleton anymore, thank God, but she's thin. Which means she still has the obsession, doesn't it?"

"I'm afraid so," I said. Anorexia is an ugly disease. "What did you do with her then?"

"I sent her back to class. I didn't know what else to do with her."

"All right. I'll try and deal with it when she comes home tonight."

They took Dick away later in the morning. Everyone came out into the halls to see the two men carrying the covered stretcher. Under the blanket was Dick—or all that remained of him.

De mortuis nil nisi bonum, speak no ill of the dead, went the old phrase. Yet, though I felt great sadness seeing Dick's body, empty of whatever had made him himself, being carried out, I also knew that nothing had changed the fact that basically I didn't like him.

At ten to twelve, Norbert swung open the parish house door and came in. I was down in the hall checking to see if there was a message from one of my clients. Getting Josie on the phone was now impossible. The switchboard was permanently busy. Evidently others were having the same problem, because half the staff was in the hall plus a great number of police.

"What in heaven's name—" Norbert said. "What are all those police and reporters doing outside?" He eyed the various men who, though not in uniform, were fairly obvious policemen. "What on earth has happened?"

"You don't know?" I asked.

"If I did I wouldn't be asking."

"Sorry. Dick Grism is . . . is dead. He was murdered." It was astonishing how hard it was to get that word out.

Norbert just stared for a moment. Then he said, "Oh my God." After a pause. "When did this happen?"

Several of us were explaining when Detective O'Neill pushed his way through the crowd. "You're the Reverend Norbert Shearer?"

"Yes. Who are you?"

"I'm Detective O'Neill. I'd like to ask you a few questions."

Norbert mounted the last few steps up to the hall, towering over almost everyone there.

"Of course," Norbert said. "Anything I can do. What a horrible thing!"

Detective O'Neill checked his notebook. "Your receptionist, Josie Beardsley, told me that you were in New Haven over the weekend at an anti-poverty rally. I take it that's where you've been."

"Yes, until around nine this morning, when I started from New Haven, drove down here and went to my apartment to shower and change. I'd meant to start earlier, but there were people I couldn't see until this morning. As a result, I didn't get moving until nine."

I had heard the overused word "charismatic" spoken often in describing Norbert. It was one of the few times when I thought the term reasonably accurate. The quality was most visible when he preached or talked to groups. Even now, talking to the detective, Norbert's looks and his height were joined with an ability to project outwards some fierce power within him, and the result could be overwhelming. I glanced at O'Neill to see if he was showing the customary reaction. But O'Neill, wiry, dogged, notebook in hand, seemed unfazed.

"Tell me," Norbert said. "When was Dick killed?" He put his hand for a moment to his head. "What an awful thing to happen, and somehow worse for it to happen on church premises!"

"As far as we can gather, until an autopsy is done, we think he died between six-thirty and seven-thirty this morning. By the way, was he normally here that early?"

"Yes. Or he didn't come in until around ten or ten-thirty, but that was rare. As you know, he was a paraplegic and he had a specially made car which he could park almost anywhere. But even with those aids, he hated to have to cope with traffic, so he came early and left early to avoid the rush hours. If for some reason he couldn't get here by seven-thirty, then he'd wait until ten or ten-thirty. He certainly didn't stint the hours he gave his job. He worked hard."

"So almost everyone would know he'd be here then, between six-thirty and seven-thirty."

"I should certainly think so. He was known to be the earliest here." Norbert hesitated. "Do you have any idea at all who might have done it?"

"We haven't narrowed the list of suspects yet, if that's what you mean. Now let me ask you something else. I have learned that you feed a great number of the homeless from the streets and that you allow about twenty to stay here downstairs in the parish room at night. Is that true?"

I could see the slight stiffening in Norbert's neck. "That's true. But there's no more reason to suspect them than anyone else. Just because they're homeless does not mean they're criminal."

I heard the faint warning signal in his voice as he went on, "They are the victims of our injustices, not the creators of it."

"Maybe, maybe not, Reverend," O'Neill said skeptically, "but there are some real kooks among them, ex-mental patients and so on, and some of the older street people would be the first to point out that the criminal element among them has grown."

"Nevertheless, I will not have them harassed or bothered any more than anyone else."

Given the way Norbert felt about the poor and the abandoned, his attitude was almost inevitable. But it was as though he had drawn a line between himself and Detective O'Neill.

"We don't want to harass anybody," O'Neill said. "That's not our way. Now, can you answer whether there were people in the church last night, and how many actually spent the night here?"

Norbert looked coldly at him for a moment, then said, "Johnny, can you answer this?"

Johnny McKnight came forward. "Yes, we had twenty here last night."

O'Neill turned. "Can you tell me who they are?"

"I know the names of some. Some simply don't want to give their names."

O'Neill looked at him. "Can you give me the names you do have?"

"Sure." He paused. "But I can almost guarantee that none of them came up the stairs. There were two of us on guard last night."

"On guard. You mean you don't sleep yourselves?"

"Oh no. We sit up, walk around, read."

"And you can absolutely guarantee that none of the people sleeping downstairs ever came upstairs? Not even in the morning?"

I saw Johnny hesitate. Then: "I'm about ninety-nine percent sure. I can't swear that in the morning both of us were in the room with the cots every minute of the time. We have an urn downstairs and serve them coffee and a bun before they leave. Also, we have to get some of the stuff from upstairs in the cafeteria. When people finish they're supposed to leave immediately, and one of us is usually upstairs to make sure they don't—er—wander around. We've been doing this for some weeks, and we've never had any problems yet."

"You never had a murder either."

Norbert said in a stiff voice, "I trust that your inquiries have also included the staff, who are not, fortunately, homeless, but who are also in the building."

"Yes, Reverend Shearer, I have been questioning your staff ever since

I got here this morning around nine-thirty. Why? Do you have information I don't that one of them could be guilty?"

"Of course not! It's simply that I don't like to see people who are poor and frequently members of a minority immediately targeted for suspicion when something goes wrong."

"We only target people for suspicion, as you put it, when there is something suspicious about them," Detective O'Neill said. "By the way, I take it you can give me the names of people who talked to you while you were in New Haven?"

Norbert's angry expression relaxed, and he smiled. "Pages of them. All through the weekend and this morning. I can even give you the names of the four young people I brought down in my car. It was a squash, but we made it."

"Okay." O'Neill put away his notebook. "That's all for now. Please hold yourselves available." He went rapidly down the hall and the steps leading to the door. As he swung it open, the cacophony outside suddenly got louder.

Norbert made a face. "Has anybody done anything about those reporters outside?"

"They're like a bunch of hungry coyotes," Josie said. "Ready to spring on anybody who goes out."

"Well," Norbert said. "I suppose one of us has to give them something." He paused, and his eyes wandered around our group. "Claire, why don't you come out with me. You've been here all morning and can answer anything I can't."

"All right."

Norbert turned. "Josie, do you have a pad or something? If I'm going to be quoted in the papers and on television I like to have a script to go on and I can scribble on that."

Josie handed him a lined yellow tablet and a ball-point pen. He stood for a moment, thinking, then, bending down, rested the pad on the reception desk and wrote for a few seconds. "What do you think, Claire?" he said, handing it to me. "Will that cover it?"

I took the tablet and struggled through Norbert's large but eccentric handwriting.

We are all deeply grieved over the untimely death of our friend and colleague Dick Grism. We are, of course, giving the police every coop-

eration. As a Christian community we do not feel that vengeance or the punitive approach can offer any solution. However, we hope that the person, or persons, who have, for whatever reasons, done this fearful deed will be able to bring themselves to speak with the police.

"What do you think?" he said.

"I don't think it's giving way to the eye-for-an-eye approach to want the killer picked up, Norbert. And punished."

"But what possible good could it do to Dick?"

"Since I am no expert on what happens next in his particular journey in eternal life, I can't answer that. But I do think that to find the murderer and put him behind bars would be an act of signal mercy to the next person he's going to kill."

There was a short silence. Norbert's lips folded in that expression of disapproval that I was beginning to become aware of. "That is, of course, the very law-and-order response of all people who would like to establish concentration camps for the wretched ghetto youths who are driven to commit crimes of violence."

"Now wait a minute, Norbert."

"No—my mind is made up. That's the way the message is going out. I'm sorry, Claire. Perhaps we can have a talk about it some other time."

"Well, then why the devil did you give it to me to read?" I muttered inaudibly as I followed him down the hall.

Profile slightly raised, Norbert made his way to the front door of the parish house, outside of which a mike had been set up.

When he had finished reading his prepared statement there was a chorus of "Reverend!" followed by a babble of questions. A look of well-bred distaste flickered across Norbert's features. In the Anglican Communion members of the clergy are not addressed as "Reverend." It is either "Father Smith" (High Church), "Mr. Smith" (low and middle) or (in writing) "The Rev. John Smith." "Reverend Smith" is considered un-Anglican.

"Perhaps one at a time," he murmured.

"Reverend," one recognizable young TV person said, "you mean you think that whoever killed—er"—she glanced down—"Mr. Grism, should be let off?"

"That's not quite what I said," Norbert stated carefully. "I hold so strongly to the view that it is better that twenty guilty people should go free, rather than that one innocent should be falsely jailed, that I sometimes wonder if anyone should be behind bars. The flaw is so often in the system itself that we are all guilty."

"You think that prison is often a form of class oppression, then?" an intelligent-looking young black asked.

"Much too often, yes." Norbert was plainly glad to have someone who felt the way he did.

"Are you kidding, Reverend?" an angry voice from the back said. "What about all the victims—mostly women and old people—that your twenty guilty people are going to knock over and maybe kill while you're rejoicing over the one going free?"

"Tragic as it is—" Norbert started.

"That's not tragic, Reverend. That's *dumb.* And what's more, you're a snob. Fine for you to be so bighearted about other people being mugged. Where do you live? Queens? I bet!"

"I don't think there's any point in pursuing this any further," Norbert said, his fine nostrils flaring a little. "Good afternoon." And he swept back into the parish house with me trailing after him.

"It's that kind of thinking," he said angrily, striding along the hallway, "that is preventing us from selling that eyesore on the Hudson and getting much-needed money for our outreach programs. Thinking that is punitive, self-righteous, full of law and order. No recognition at all for the pressures that the really poor are suffering."

"Well, you don't have much sympathy for the muggees," I said, and then stopped, astonished at myself. I was sounding like the old, pre-Patrick Claire.

Evidently Norbert sensed the sea change, too. "That's not like you, Claire."

But there was something beyond all this that was bothering me, and it surfaced just as we passed Norbert's office door and he was about to go in.

"Norbert," I said suddenly.

He stopped.

"I suddenly realized what all this was about. You think some ghetto type walked in off the street and whacked Dick over the head."

"Don't you?"

Curiously, *what* had happened had completely pre-empted my attention. I could not remember thinking about who might have done it. How strange, I thought. And then, to my embarrassment, I realized that I was no different from Norbert. Like him, I had assumed that one of the many of the poor who were connected with our feeding programs, our outreach programs and our social welfare programs, had succumbed to sudden rage or temptation and picked up something and killed Dick Grism. "Yes," I said finally. "I suppose I do. I mean, who else could it be? I certainly don't think it's anybody who *works* in the church."

"Well, there you are."

"What happens now?"

"I suppose the police will do their thing and some wretched street person will be dragged off to the pokey."

"Murder *is* the ultimate crime, Norbert. And particularly in this case. Dick was a paraplegic. He could hardly have defended himself."

"I'm not defending his killer, Claire. My God! Dick was a friend. It's terrible and tragic. But I just don't see how society or the Church or anybody would be benefited by having whoever did it sent off to a jail where every destructive instinct he has will become worse."

"Better to let him go free where he can kill somebody else?"

"No, of course not. But put him to some socially useful work." He glanced at his watch. "I have to go now. See you later. I hope they clear this thing up soon." And he disappeared inside his office.

A client was waiting for me when I got to my office, and there wasn't time between him and the client following to snatch a sandwich, so I told my hunger pangs to wait until I had finished with the second. By that time I was ravenous. I glanced at my watch. A quarter to three. If I moved like lightning I just might make the parish house cafeteria before it closed. Breathing heavily, I arrived at the door just as it was being shut.

"Please!" I said plaintively.

Susannah, who runs the kitchens, is a trim black woman who could earn four times her salary anywhere in the country running a good, basic restaurant. But for a variety of reasons, one of them me, she stays with St. Anselm's Parish. Her daughter Clarissa is a client of mine in whom I have a particular interest: both she and Martha are anorexic.

"If it were anybody else," Susannah said severely, opening the door a crack, "I'd slam the door shut."

"Thanks for the dispensation."

Susannah closed the door and locked it. "Why couldn't you get here between twelve and two-thirty?"

"Well—you've heard about Dick Grism?"

"I have and am horrified along with everybody else. But what does that have to do with you?"

"It has to do with the fact that because Norbert wanted me to go with him to talk to the press, I missed my usual lunch period."

Susannah grunted. "What do you want to eat?"

I told her.

"I'll bring it to you. Where are you going to sit?"

My eyes roved round the dining room. There, rotund back bent over a book, was Larry Swade. "By Larry," I said.

"Three people have tried to sit beside him. He's told them all he has to study something and wants to be left alone."

"I'm still going to sit beside him. Or rather, opposite him."

I slid into the chair across from Larry. "Larry, I need to talk to you."

"Go away," Larry said. "If I don't get my lecture up for tonight I'll be fired and my wife and children will be left to starve."

"Come on, Larry. It's about Martha."

He kept his head down for a moment, then sighed. "You're an original, Claire. Everybody else wants to talk about poor Dick Grism and how awful it all is and you want to talk about your tiresome stepdaughter."

I knew he didn't mean a word he said, so I ignored him. "Forgetting Martha for a moment, who does everybody think killed Dick?"

"What they want to think, of course. That one of our many unprivileged people shuffled in, killed him, collected the dough and shuffled out."

"But you don't think that?"

"I'll admit," he said grudgingly, "it fits better than anything else."

"But you still don't think it."

He sighed. "It's not so much that I don't think it. But I can imagine how much aid and comfort such a conclusion would be to the Enemy in the Great Brouhaha. It'll be plum jam for them. I can hear them now. 'We told you what would happen when you let all those unsavory people into Our Beloved Church,' they will chant. And just you mark my words. The press is going to have a field day. It's going to do for them almost what Watergate did for the Washington press corps. Every time they mention St. Anselm's, they're going to rake up every single battle between the liberals and the conservatives this church has had for the past several years. In loving detail they'll run through the old skirmishes: outreach against anti-outreach; the Dear Old Prayer Book against the Horrid New Rite; the ordination of women; and descriptive passages about those who wish to Hold the Line against the Forces of Permissive Barbarism (heavily capitalized, you understand) against those who yearn for the Church to get at least a toehold in the twentieth century . . . it'll be the whole damn mess all over again, just when we thought it was dying down. And we can kiss goodbye any thought of selling the Monster on the Hudson."

"My, my," I said. "I didn't realize you got so worked up about all this." I put my head on one side. "Why does it bother you so much? I didn't think you were either a passionate progressive or an ardent traditionalist."

"I'm bothered because, shy-making as it may be to say so, I truly love the Church, and it drives me mad to see other people—such as the press—feeding every single little fire that can burn it down. I'm thinking of starting my own movement for the abolition of the First Amendment. Care to join?"

"No. And neither would you."

"Well, all right. What is it you want?"

"Why do I keep having the feeling that it is something else you're bothered about?" It was curious. Now that I had said it, I knew that it was true. Everything Larry had blustered about, he was indeed concerned for. But I had the odd feeling I was being led away from something.

"Because you're a shrink. That's your occupational hazard. Somebody says good morning, and you spend the next three hours trying to decipher the psychological code. What did he really mean when he said that? That he wanted to kill his mother? Shoot the President? Become a transsexual?"

"Larry," I said patiently. "I want to talk about my anorexic stepdaughter. I don't think she's getting better."

"Why do you say that?" He was looking at me in an intent way.

I told him what Miss Webster had said to me. "And not only that, I've seen signs of it at home. I opened one of her drawers recently when she was out—I know that's not nice but there was no other way—and found pats of butter lying among odds and ends of makeup."

"Why don't you send her to the hospital?"

"Because she has pleaded and begged and wept not to go. And because of her father's death, and having no mother, I didn't want to push it."

"You wouldn't let a client get away with that."

"No."

"And I don't think you'd let Jamie get away with it either."

I sighed. "Probably not."

"I have a really startling and innovative thought: Why not send her to a shrink?"

"I have. Three of them. She's walked away from all of them."

"Umm." He munched a bite or two of his sandwich. Susannah came over with a tray bearing another sandwich and some coffee and put it down in front of me. "Not that I wish to interfere or anything," she said ominously. "But the overtime for the kitchen help is adding up."

"We'll be out of here in a jiff," Larry said, cramming the rest of his sandwich in his mouth. "Claire will do far better if she eats alone."

"Thanks a lot," I said as he stood up, took a final swallow of coffee and said, "I'll give the matter of your stepdaughter my best thought. 'Bye."

"How's Clarissa?" I asked Susannah.

"She's getting better. I hardly dare mention it, but she's up to a hundred and five pounds and doesn't seem to be going into her usual hysterical declarations of being monstrously fat. I must say," she went on rather gruffly, "we have you to thank for that. And we're grateful. Therapy with you was a tremendous help. I take it," she said tentatively, "that Martha's not doing so well."

"No, she isn't."

"It's a pity she can't use you as a therapist."

I made a wry face. "I'm a major part of the problem, I think, although I haven't quite been able to figure out the dynamics. But thanks, anyway."

I was putting things away in my desk, preparatory to going home, when I looked up and saw Brett Cunningham in the doorway.

"You've heard the news, I take it," I said.

"Probably Inner Tibet has heard it by now." He held up an afternoon paper. MURDER AT ST. ANSELM's screamed the headline. Underneath there was a picture of the rector making his statement before a forest of mikes and, standing beside him, me, looking harassed.

"And I was hoping our newsworthiness was declining," he said.

"Is that all you feel about Dick Grism being killed?" I asked, and remembered some of the comments I had made.

"Much as you'd like to think so, no. You seem to forget that I recommended him for the job of treasurer."

"I thought you were shoved out when Gary Parkinson took advantage of your holiday to execute a coup," I said with brutal frankness. Gary was the leader of the New Church group.

"I know you did. And it gave you so much pleasure to think that that I never disabused you."

"Whereas you planned the whole thing—putting Dick in your place. A likely story!"

"If you don't believe me, ask Norbert."

"Norbert has never said an unevasive thing in his life, as you well know."

"Ah well, it's not important. There's something else I'd like to ask. How about dinner and a concert?"

I stared at him, totally astonished. "When?"

"Well—tonight."

What was surprising and unnerving was not that this representative of all I most disagreed with asked me. It was how much I wanted to accept.

I took a deep breath. "No, I can't. But thank you for asking me."

"Why can't you?"

Usually, I thought, when people are refused, they have the good taste to leave it at that.

"Because I can't. For one thing, I have an eight-year-old son and a fifteen-year-old stepdaughter, both of whom need dinner and an adult in the house."

"Well, that's too bad. Another time."

Of course, my Judas-like mind was prodding me, I could call home and suggest that Martha sit with Jamie, which she would do anyway, and that they get burgers from the corner coffee shop . . . One evening like that would hardly kill them. And it had been a long time since I had gone out with an attractive man, even though he might be the greatest reactionary since Louis XIV . . . What on earth am I thinking of . . . ? I reproached myself. Or I could ask him to dinner . . .

"I'm sorry," I said firmly. He was the camp of the enemy and I must not compromise myself.

"So am I. As I said, another time."

Martha, Jamie and I occupied an apartment on East Eighty-second Street between Fifth and Madison avenues, a roomy apartment in a good location made possible by the private means I'd inherited at Patrick's death. Every time I entered the well-appointed lobby and was greeted by the two doormen I felt both gratitude and guilt. On the salary I was making, the three of us would have had to live somewhere in the darker outreaches of Brooklyn or Queens. The guilt I had taken on from Patrick. He had called it the Puritan monkey inherited by rich Wasps who didn't approve of great private wealth, wouldn't have parted with a penny of it, but salved their social consciences by assuming a scolding attitude towards commerce and the profit motive (from which they so handsomely benefited). Coming from a thoroughly middle-class family myself, I did not carry the monkey and would twit Patrick about some of his less consistent opinions. But I became a convert, and with his death, a crusader for his causes.

"Good evening, Mrs. Aldington," Joe, our oldest doorman said. "Package for you."

He handed me a parcel, which obviously contained some books I had ordered, and took me up in the elevator. Although the elevators were self-service, one of the pleasant things about the apartment house was that we were often taken up.

"The children in?" I said.

"Jamie is," he said. "He got in about the usual time after school, took out Motley and is in again."

I looked up. "Martha?"

"I don't think so. Unless she took herself up when I was in the package room. She sometimes does that."

"Yes," I said. It was not a good sign.

"Mrs. Aldington," Joe said.

I knew what was coming. Joe's face had been bursting with a question ever since we got in the elevator. As the elevator door opened I said, "Yes, it was our church."

"That's terrible. Who did it?"

"We don't know."

"It'll be one of them homeless. Crazy they are, most of them. Terrible thing to have them on the streets."

"Well," I said, not up to making a case for unprejudiced thinking, "we don't know yet. Thanks." And got to my front door as fast as possible.

When I opened the apartment door Motley hurled himself at me, all forty pounds of him. His name was given him when he was a puppy after an evening spent deciding how many breeds had contributed to his small person. I claimed he was mostly German shepherd. Jamie held out for mostly yellow Labrador. Martha took no part in the conversation. After that he was just called Motley. And there were moments when such was his sense of the absurd, all he needed was the jester's traditional bells to complete his role. For example, as I took off my raincoat, he let me know by all the devices and cunning of the canine world that he had not had a walk, that no one had paid any attention to him, that he was deeply deprived. This came to a climax when he bounced up carrying his leash.

"Liar," I said, and went into the living room. The television set was on and Jamie was lying on the floor looking at the paper. I went and turned the set off.

"Mom!" Outraged, Jamie looked up.

"How much of a walk did you take Motley?"

"He's had plenty of walking."

"How much?"

"Round the block."

"That's not enough. While I prepare dinner, I want you to take him down to Seventy-ninth, up Fifth, across Eighty-sixth and then home."

"Mom, there's a super show just going on, specially for children."

"Which one?"

"This." He pointed to an item listed under Public Broadcasting's Education programming.

"You saw that last week."

"Yes, but—"

"Out! We have a contract, you know. He's your dog. Either he gets the food and exercise and attention he needs or we don't have him."

I knew I'd used the magic tool. Jamie adored Motley, even if he was inclined to rush back to a TV show he wanted to see. And, of course, it had been raining this morning, so Motley's walk had been brief.

"Oh, all right," my son said ungraciously. "Come on, Motley."

"Jamie!"

I heard his feet slide to a stop.

"Has Martha been here since you've been home?"

"No. Haven't seen her."

After a moment's silence, I heard the front door close.

I knew I had to start dinner, but I went first back to Martha's room. The room had a slightly schizoid quality. Usually it was tidy to the point of starkness. But from time to time it would start to look like the room of a five-year-old. Not only would there be garments all over the floor, but there would be crumbs and bits of food scattered about. When this happened, it usually presaged another attack of the strange eating disorder that had struck two years after Patrick's death. Martha would simply stop eating. If I made enough of a fuss, she'd eat, and then make herself vomit it up. Occasionally she'd take food off to her room swearing she was going to eat it, and then I would find it here and there in her bureau drawers. When questioned, she would claim to have no knowledge of it whatsoever. At the peak of her illness, about three and a half years after her father's death, Martha had reached sixty-nine pounds, which for a girl five foot five meant dangerous starvation. It was then she went to the hospital and stayed for three months of intensive treatment and therapy. At the end of three months, she weighed almost ninety pounds. Still far too light, of course, but almost within the light-normal range for a girl of her age and bone structure. The therapist, Dr. Adele Meitzner, wanted to keep her much longer.

"She has other problems, Mrs. Aldington," Dr. Meitzner said. "I think she would benefit from at least another three months. She'd be better physically, and we'd have a clearer idea of her psychological problems. Right now, we're not quite sure."

"Quite sure of what?" I said, trying hard not to sound defensive. As a therapist, I knew very well how difficult it is sometimes to unravel and define neatly the different strands of a complex psychological problem. Unfortunately for both of us, I was also Martha's stepmother, a relationship notably fraught with pitfalls and land mines. It had been many years since I had not winced at that hoary staple of myth and folk tale, the wicked stepmother.

Dr. Meitzner had hesitated. "I'm not sure enough even to answer that."

If I had not been her stepmother I might have hardened my heart. But I was, which meant, among other things, that I cared deeply for Martha, daughter of Patrick and his first wife. We had lived together since she was seven years old, when I had married her father. Even though her memory of her own mother, who died when she was four, was necessarily dim, Martha and I never pretended that I was anything but a stepmother. From the beginning she called me Claire. Our relationship was—I had thought—extraordinary and wonderful. She was a marvelously amenable child, good at school, fun at home, welcoming to Jamie, who was born when she was eight. She adored her father. She and I were good friends. And then, two years after his death, I looked up from the table one night and noticed that she had become a skeleton—like some mockery of a concentration-camp victim. How on earth could I have not noticed it before?

The answer was all too clear. Because I was busy studying for my degree and my ordination examinations; because the baby-sitter I had was much more preoccupied with Jamie, who was a toddler; because my guilt over my absence—and there was plenty of that—was more directed towards my own child, who was at the early stages where I believed and feared he most needed me, than towards Martha. I had convinced myself that she had weathered her father's death unusually well. No tantrums, no crying spells, no sudden rebellions, all of which I had expected. She went to school, she did her homework, she was on the school magazine, was in the drama class, was one of their best swimmers, was never, apparently, doing the various destructive things that working mothers of teen-age children had come to dread and expect. And then that night—I saw her, really saw her, for the first time in what must have been months. Since then it had been a long, painful struggle for us both, hampered on my side by guilt and—I had come to realize—resentment and anger.

So when Dr. Meitzner wanted me to commit Martha for an additional three months, I listened instead to Martha, who begged to come home.

"I promise," she said, "I promise I'm going to be okay. I see now what I was doing. The obsession's gone. I'm eating normally. Ask them!"

So I did, and it was indeed true that Martha's eating problems seemed to be under control. She ate three meals a day without too much fuss. So I gave in to her wish. She regained her weight. And everything for a while seemed to go well.

Twice before this morning she had been missing from school. Each time she'd gone on an eating binge with a friend, and then proceeded to vomit it all up. This was the third time. And her weight was down again from the one hundred and fifteen she had managed to attain to a little over a hundred.

I stared now at her room. The telltale bits of food were there on the floor, which meant that they were probably elsewhere, too. This time I found pieces of toast in her drawer. I recognized those bits; they were from some cinnamon toast I'd made for breakfast. I should have known when she picked up her plate to take back to her room with the contents half eaten that this was a danger signal. But—I was late getting to the church, I had work and clients to worry about . . . .

What you ought to do is stay home and take care of your children . . . All the ancient voices were there, internalized, combining with the severe, reproving voice of my own mother, who wanted me to marry and have a family. Period.

I couldn't even claim poverty as a reason for working for a living. My widow's mite, thanks to Patrick, was quite generous. What I had to remind myself constantly was that my relationship with Martha, already filled with problems, would not be improved if I added further resentment over having to stay home on her account.

Now, after a brief search, except for the toast there seemed to be no further food squirreled away. Everything else was in reasonable order. I prayed that this attack would be short. I was told that there would be periodic relapses, but that if the illness as a whole seemed to be getting better, not to worry too much.

My eyes slid around the rest of the room. In a way Martha's room was the nicest of the three bedrooms. Not the largest, it was the only one that faced the back and overlooked the gardens of the town houses on the next street. On a corner, it had two windows, though one of them looked into nothing more exciting than the wall of the apartment house next door. Pictures lined the walls and decorated the top of her bureau. Two were of Jamie and Motley. There was one of me, looking like something out of Anthony Trollope with the towers of the Cathedral behind me, and there were at least six of her father: Patrick had been a big man, with brown eyes and longish blond hair. Various studies of him showed him in a cassock outside of his church, in climbing clothes when the two of them were off on a climbing trip, in round collar, in open-neck shirt, with other members of the clergy, with Martha herself, one with Jamie and me, and one, bearded and looking very young, with Priscilla, Martha's mother. The latter was a framed snapshot. I picked it up and looked at the two faces, trying to see if anything there would help me to help their daughter.

In appearance, she inherited a little from both: her father's brown eyes, her mother's dark hair and features. It was Priscilla who had made an activist out of Patrick. She had marched and protested and sat in in the late sixties before Martha was born, and Patrick, whose social activism had been somewhat tepid until that moment, had caught fire from her. I looked at these two privileged children of gilded backgrounds, with their dedicated faces, their jeans, their long hair, their anger. Here, in this snapshot, they wore poverty like a badge. But Patrick was a graduate of Yale and Priscilla of a finishing school and Vassar, whereas I, growing up in a middle-class town, had gone to the local high school and to the state university . . .

"What are you doing with my pictures?"

I turned. Martha, looking astonishingly like her mother, was standing in the doorway.

3

"JUST LOOKING at an early photograph of your parents. It was on the bureau, out where anybody could see it."

"Is that what you came into the room to see?"

I had to remind myself, as I so often did with Martha, that hers was the deviant behavior, not mine. Since a year or so after her father died, I had become the villain.

I put the picture down. "No. I came into the room to see if you had hidden food anywhere. Miss Webster told me about your pizza blast this morning, and also told me she found you trying to get rid of it later."

Martha came in and put her books on the desk. "I shouldn't have had it in the first place. I'm not used to pizza, and it made me sick."

"Except when you ruin your own digestive tract, you have the digestion of a truck driver and you know it."

"But I *have* interfered with it," Martha said with sweet reason. "So it isn't like a truck driver's anymore. We both know that, don't we, Claire?"

"I found some of this morning's cinnamon toast."

"I was going to clean it out. I just couldn't finish it and I knew you'd make a fuss if I left it out."

"So you put it in a drawer. With the roaches practically taking over the city, do you think that's the smartest thing in the world?"

"But then I'm not very smart, am I?"

I opened my mouth to say that, as she and I and her entire school knew, she had a gratifyingly high IQ and some of the best grades in the entire student body. Then I realized I was falling into one of her traps: "Beat me, I'm no good!"

Instead I said, "That's my T-shirt you're wearing. I didn't know you had it. Where's it been?"

The shirt was instantly recognizable because of its brilliant red, on the front of which was sewn in white a handsome stalking cat.

My comment, of course, was thoughtless and stupid and sounded as though I were accusing Martha of stealing my garment. She and I were of the same height, and when she was eating like a rational human being, we were about the same size. Now, of course, she was somewhat thinner. But we still occasionally exchanged blouses and sweaters, and at times of peace between us, I was frequently amused to notice that she copied my clothes and the particular combinations in which I wore them.

"You can have it back now," she said, starting to pull the T-shirt off. "And you can have your silk blouse back, too, when it's been cleaned."

"I didn't mean that, Martha, you know I didn't. Now don't pick a fight! Keep the T-shirt. I just meant that I'd forgotten about it and thought I'd lost it somewhere. Likewise the silk shirt."

"You're always telling me not to get dirt and crud on my good clothes, so I kept the T-shirt at school to wear during drama class when we're painting scenery and stuff. And I got some . . . some paint on the silk blouse. Here!" She hurled the T-shirt at me. "Now let's stop this *boring* conversation. Like something out of a fifties sitcom."

I caught the T-shirt, noticing that Martha's ribs under her bra resembled an old-fashioned scrubbing board.

"And just how would you know about a fifties sitcom? You weren't even born."

"I've seen reruns. Happy, happy suburban family, with know-everything father, mother baking cookies and happy, happy, *boring* kids." Yanking a bureau drawer open, she pulled out a sweatshirt and put it on.

I recognized this trap, too. She was trying to make me angry enough to bite back at her. Then she would retreat into a sweet, compliant victim—a compliant, non-eating victim, I mentally corrected myself.

"Dinner's as soon as I can fix it," I said, turning to leave the room.

"How's the perfect child?" Martha asked. Her game was not proceeding according to custom. Since I hadn't risen to the previous bait, she sharpened it a little. Calling Jamie "the perfect child" had once or twice produced exactly what she wanted: a flaming row.

"The perfect child is taking his perfect dog for a walk," I said pleasantly, and got myself down the hall as rapidly as possible. "Dear Lord," I prayed silently. "Don't let us have a row tonight." I also knew that (theoretically) it took two to create a fight and had once or twice managed to refuse Martha's many gambits when she was determined to make me lose my temper. But it was wearing. It was also basically dishonest. No child should be able to get away with gratuitous insults: it was not fair to me, to Jamie or to herself. Who, in her future life, would put up with it? On the other hand, she carried a powerful weapon: my fear of what her illness would do to her.

Jamie came in about half an hour later, preceded by Motley, who started going into his starved-waif act: paws on the kitchen table, nose in the air, melting look in the eye, soft whimper in the throat.

"When did you feed him?" I asked Jamie.

"He had one or two munchies when I got home from school."

"One or two? Or six?"

Jamie grinned. "He said he was hungry."

Jamie was so exactly like me that at times it made me want to laugh: the same thick hair, though redder than mine, green eyes, freckles and big mouth (in the literal as well as metaphorical sense). But he had his father's more equitable disposition and stocky build.

"What's the state of your room like?" I asked.

"I'll go clean it," he said, an alarmed look in his eyes.

"No, don't. Stay and talk to me. We'll take it as read that your room is a mess. Right?"

He grinned. "Right."

"How was school?"

"Okay. But I didn't get on the first ball team."

I glanced at him. "Does that bother you a lot?"

"Maybe I'll grow next year."

"Maybe. Are you that enthusiastic an athlete?"

"No. I just don't like to be not chosen."

I identified with that immediately. "Nor do I. Was it just size?"

"No. The coach doesn't think I'm a born athlete. Not like Martha."

It was a sore point. Jamie and Martha went to a private coeducational school. Jamie followed her trail of excellent marks and outstanding athletic achievement. "What do you want to be when you grow up?" I asked. I hadn't asked it for at least a year, so I thought it was time I could try it again.

"I dunno. Like I said last time." And then, out of the blue. "I like math."

"You must get that from your father's side of the family. I can't even add."

And math was the one subject where Martha got mediocre grades. I sighed. Nothing was easy. On the other hand, who said it was supposed to be?

Dinner was a strained meal, as, unfortunately, it frequently was. Jamie was, as usual, voraciously hungry. He polished off his hamburgers, rice and vegetable with unbecoming speed, and even deigned to eat his salad—never a favorite. When he reached for his second muffin I debated telling him he'd had enough. Jamie was on the border of being overweight—and if heredity was as powerful as many seemed to think, then he, like his father, would struggle with the problem his entire life. On the other hand, boys were notoriously bottomless pits. Once they reached puberty, said those in the know, they'd lengthen out and get enough height to balance their width. All those calories would go into lean muscle (proving, as feminists frequently point out, how unfair nature is; those same calories in a girl of the same age would go into a much higher percentage of fat).

"It's not fair," I said aloud, and reached for some more salad for myself.

"What isn't?" Jamie asked, already on the second half of his second muffin.

"Nature. It favors the male in all sorts of subversive ways."

"Yeah? Well you don't have to shave, the way I do—will," he amended hastily.

"And you can hardly wait," I said.

He grinned, and I saw his hand, holding a piece of muffin, go quickly under the table. Three seconds later Motley's tail flapped against me as he gobbled his treat.

"And if there's any food on the floor when we finish dinner," I said, "guess who's going to clean it up?"

"Motley never leaves anything. He's better than a vacuum."

"True. Motley," I said, "maybe I should pay you a weekly wage."

"That'd be neat," Jamie said. "I could open up one of those accounts for him."

"Using his paw print, I suppose."

There was a sudden noise under the table, then a yelp.

"Get away," Martha said.

Jamie's face flamed red. "You kicked him. You lousy rotten sadist!"

"Hold it, Jamie!" I said quickly. "What was that for, Martha? He wasn't doing you any harm?"

"When Jamie or his pet gets anything on the floor, it's a big joke. When I do, I get threatened."

"Motley and I aren't *sick!*" Jamie said. He'd left his seat and was busy stroking Motley, who didn't seem overly wounded. Still, I noticed often that he gave Martha a wide berth.

"I'm *not* sick! I just don't want to grow up looking like some kind of a pig—"

"Be quiet! Both of you."

There was a sudden silence. I knew they were looking at me. I let the silence go on for a moment while I did the rapid sorting out that I was so often called on to do: Was there ever such a thing as absolute justice? I doubted it. In all my groping I had never found it as between a fairly well-balanced child who was my own and a profoundly disturbed one who was not.

"Jamie, I don't think Motley is actually hurt, although he certainly was doing no harm. I brought home some ice cream. I'll fix some in a dish for you. Take it into the living room with Motley."

Quickly I spooned some of the chocolaty stuff into a dish, pulled a cookie out of a box and handed it to my son. "Run along, honey. I'll talk to you later. If you've finished your homework . . . *if* . . . you can watch a show for half an hour."

When they'd gone I turned to Martha. "I'm sorry if I seemed unfair to you, but I think you'll have to admit that there's a difference between a dog getting food on the floor and a bright fifteen-year-old girl. One goes with being an animal. The other—I don't have to talk to you about that. The rest of the time you're so tidy you make me feel like the Compleat Slob. My closet can't compare with yours."

She didn't say anything. Martha, I decided, like her mother's photographs, could look either plain, in an angular, elegant sort of way, or astonishingly beautiful. At the moment, with her thinness and her aggrieved expression, she looked plain. Her long, silky, dark hair clung to her face and, I thought, could use a washing.

"I think I'll go to my room," she said.

"How about some dessert?"

"No, thanks. I'm getting fat."

"You know, objectively, that that is not true. All you have to do is look in the mirror."

"It *is* true. I saw myself in the mirror in the gym at school. Ugh! I'm practically ready for the circus."

"How much was that the result of the binge—the pizza binge? Or do I have it the wrong way around? By the way, where were you this afternoon? You were late coming home."

"I was at my therapy group." She got up. "I'm going to my room now."

As she retreated I said, "I'm sorry to say I don't believe you. You left that group eight months ago, saying you never wanted to be in group therapy again." As she continued across the dining room I said, more loudly, "You must know, Martha, that I will check with the therapist."

She turned around then. "You spy on me all the time. You don't trust me. It's like living in a prison. You don't spy on Jamie this way. I suppose it's because he's your own child. Being a stepdaughter, I don't rate the same degree of trust."

"It has nothing to do with being step or not step. You know how often you have lied to me. We've talked about it, so I'm not making any new accusation. When you're well, of course I trust you. In all the years your father was alive—I trusted you then. You must remember that."

I was startled at her sudden reaction. "Don't talk to me about my father. He shouldn't ever have married you!" And with that she left the room, slamming the door behind her.

I stood for a moment, feeling almost too depressed to go on. Idly, I picked up the coffee pot and poured out about two tablespoons into my cup. Then I swallowed some and made a face. It was tepid and bitter. Making some more would be easy, involving only boiling some more water. All I had to do was to go into the kitchen and put the kettle back on. But for some reason I was unable to make myself move. From the living room I could hear sounds that meant the television was on. From Martha's room down the hall there was only silence. Despite occasional backsliding, the progress of her illness had, over the past two years, been up. I was sure of it, or at least I had been. There were occasional regressions, but they had become fewer and less intense. Until now.

But, my mind argued with itself, what she had done for the past few days was no worse than what she did in some of her periodic backslides. So why did I feel it was more serious?

The answer was, I didn't know why I felt a greater sense of alarm now than on previous, more or less similar occasions. But I did. Perhaps it was that last comment she made. Whatever she had said before, she had never by word or act appeared to quarrel with the marriage between her father and me. In fact, during those years, she seemed a happy and affectionate child, glad to have a mother figure in a household that for so long had lacked one. She was almost as demonstrative with me as she was with her father, although it was true that her devotion to him had an element of near-worship. She adored him. He could do no wrong. But she and I were fond of one another and the relationship was a good one, and remained that way until a while after his death.

Following that, nothing was the same. At first, she seemed to withdraw. She became neat, meticulous and compliant. She started rummaging around old drawers and in albums to search out as many photographs of her father as she could. These she would rotate on her walls and on top of her bureau and desk. All of which, in view of her loss, seemed natural. Her marks went up and stayed at the top.

On the other hand, she put, increasingly, some kind of distance between us that I could never overcome, and over which I felt a large share of guilt. Because those early years of my widowhood were the ones I spent at the seminary. Soon after Patrick's death I received my doctorate in clinical psychology and decided to enter the seminary in New York. We were due to move out of the rectory anyway, so I bought the apartment in New York, registered at the theological school and spent at least part of my days there—like any other working widowed mother. But I did not have the excuse that I needed to earn a living. I had never had any doubt that I should study for ordination, and the fact that the original suggestion came from Patrick seemed to make it doubly right—and doubly necessary to make up for everything I'd lost. If, of course, I had known what shoals Martha was headed for, I might have delayed my entry . . . If, if if. But I didn't know. She was happy and excited about the new school in New York. And the nice Scotswoman I had found as housekeeper and nanny for Jamie seemed sent from heaven . . . I was busy studying, learning new subjects, enjoying Jamie, who was a wonderful and satisfying child, pleased at the grades Martha was bringing home, at the neatness of her room, at her docility . . . And I wasn't really paying attention. There are jokes about the doctor's children going without medicine, the cobbler's children without shoes. I, a psychologist, should have been alerted by a dozen signs of oncoming trouble. But I wasn't. And then, shortly after I had been ordained, I looked across the dinner table one night and saw a near-skeleton. . . .

The months after that were a nightmare. Eventually, I put Martha in the hospital, where she remained, hating every day, for three months. The struggle continued after she returned home, but the direction of her health had been upwards. I had been quite convinced of that—until now.

Wearily I took the plates and used silver out to the kitchen, rinsed them off and placed them in the dishwasher. When the dining room was finally cleared, I decided to go down to Martha's room and remind her that I would, if she didn't improve rapidly, send her back to the hospital. I had done this only once before, and it had been immediately effective. The food droppings disappeared, Martha made obvious efforts to eat three more or less balanced meals a day and her behavior stayed nearer to the middle of the pendulum swing, the extremes of which were total compliance at one end and passive rebelliousness at the other.

Going down the hall, I knocked on her door. There was the sound of some scuffling, a drawer opened and closed and then her voice, studied and aloof, drifted out. "Come in."

She was sitting on her bed, reading a book, and looked up with all the languor in the world, as though I had pulled her away from material that was absorbing her. "Yes?"

Even though I was morally certain that that quick scuffle just before she told me to come in meant that she had hidden something (probably food) that she didn't want me to see, I decided to ignore the matter and go straight for the heavy artillery.

"Martha, in case you have any doubt, I love you very much. You're not my daughter, and we've never fooled each other about that. As you well know, love doesn't come only in the conventional packages. So please try to remember that as I tell you also that unless you get your act more together you're going back to the hospital."

I saw her face, already pale, go even paler, becoming almost gray. It was pinched beyond her years, giving her the appearance, sometimes, of an aging woman.

"I don't want to do this—" I started.

"You wouldn't do that to Jamie!"

"On the contrary, Martha. As it has been pointed out to me by somebody else, if it were Jamie, I'd probably be much stricter. And if by some horrible chance he had this disease—or any other psychological problem—I believe I'd be less liable to let him cop out. I agree with you that you may very well get different treatment from Jamie—but not the way you think. I let you get away with more because you're my stepdaughter, not less. But I mean what I said about sending you back to the hospital. If you're so ill that you're going to put yourself back into the ranks of the starving, then I cannot help you here."

"You hate me."

"No, I don't hate you. I love you." Sometimes I felt as though I were saying those three crucial words in a language she'd never heard of.

"I don't want to get fat."

"You're not, and you won't."

She'd been talking with her profile turned to me. Now she turned. "I'm nearly sixteen. I don't have to do what I don't want to do. You can't commit me to a hospital if I don't want to go."

"I don't know whether that is—legally speaking—true or not. If it is, then if you're adult enough to make that decision, then you're also adult enough to pay your own way and to support yourself. You can't have it both ways, Martha. If you're my responsibility, then if I send you to the hospital you have to go. If I can't, then you're your own responsibility, which means you're responsible for your food, your shelter and your school fees. Besides," I said, "you're not sixteen—not yet."

"I soon will be. Carey said . . . ." Carey Strong was her best friend at school and, I considered, a bad influence.

"I'm not surprised that this declaration of legal adulthood comes from Carey. But just remember, it cuts both ways. Do you want to live alone?"

At that point Martha burst into tears. "You hate me," she repeated.

I sighed, considered briefly taking a tougher stance and then abandoned it. Going over to the bed, I sat down, put my arms around her and let her cry against my shoulder for a while, well aware that to some degree I was being successfully manipulated.

"So," I said, after a few minutes, "you're going to try and get better, eat right and not give me too hard a time, okay?"

Martha blew her nose. "All right," she said.

I kissed the top of her head. "Good night. Sweet dreams."

When I got back to the living room Jamie had switched to one of the cable news channels.

"I saw you on TV," he said excitedly. "It's terrific, a murder at the church and everything. You didn't even say anything about it. Why didn't you tell me?"

"I guess I just didn't think to. Also maybe I wanted to forget it for a while. What did the news say? What was I doing on camera?"

"You were standing beside Mr. Shearer. Did you ever notice he always looks over people's heads, like he was looking for somebody?"

"No, I didn't." I thought about it for a moment. It was true, Norbert did have a funny habit of sticking his profile up in the air and talking sort of at an angle. He did it more some times than others. Lately, I decided, he'd been doing it a lot.

"I guess it's a nervous habit, Jamie. Some people scratch their heads and some people nibble at their hangnails . . ." I put my hand out and removed Jamie's finger from his mouth, where he was, indeed, chewing at a bit of loose cuticle.

"Come into my room later and I'll snip that off for you," I said.

"Who do you think did it?"

"I don't know, Jamie. I suppose it could be anybody. We have a lot of people wandering in and out of the parish house, and because he, Dick Grism, was business manager, people—strangers—may have thought he had money on him."

"You think it was an outside job?" Jamie was plainly trying to sound professional.

"Yes," I said after a miunute. "I do. I can't think of anyone in the church—I mean on the staff or any church member—who'd have any reason to do that."

"Maybe he took all the money in the church and gambled it on slot machines. Wouldn't people in the church be mad at him then?"

"They sure would. But I don't think . . . well, I don't think that'd be possible."

"Why not?" Jamie put out a hand and rubbed Motley's stomach. Motley, a picture of profound relaxation, was lying on his back, his four paws facing up, snoring slightly. "What happens to the collection on Sunday morning? I see all those dollar bills piled up. I bet you a lot of people would think about what they could do with all that money."

"Come on, you go to Sunday school, not church. You don't see vast piles of dollar bills."

"I've been to church sometimes. And anyway, we can see the men all coming back with the collection plates to where they count the money—it's near where we have Sunday-morning storytelling. What do they do with all that money?"

"Put it in the bank, I guess. So that they can write checks for things like the heating bill and the staff salaries."

"But maybe they hadn't put it in the bank yet. After all, it's only Monday. Banks aren't open Sunday, are they? Maybe the robber knew that the money was going to be put in the bank and came in to get it from Mr. Grism's office. Only Mr. Grism tried to stop him and got hit on the head. I mean, after all, Jack Plunket at school says St. Anselm's is the richest church in New York."

"How does he know?" I asked. For some reason Jamie's rapid rundown of what sounded like any good TV plot was probably the assumption that most people, including the police, were going on. In which case, why did I feel dismayed?

"He says that's what his father says. Besides, people at school say so when I tell them you're a clergyperson."

"I see."

"Well, you are, aren't you?"

"Yes."

"Then why're you mad?"

"I'm not mad."

"Well, you're something. You have that funny look on your face, like you tasted something bad."

"Maybe it's because I'd like St. Anselm's to be known for something besides being the richest church in the city."

"Like what?"

"Like preaching the Gospel, or being good to the poor, or, most obviously, keeping the great commandments.'"

"What are those?"

"What do you mean, what are those? What are they teaching you in Sunday school these days?"

"Urban and environmental enlightenment."

I looked at my son across Motley's stomach. "You just made that up."

He grinned. "Well, not exactly. I heard somebody say it in the parish hall the other morning."

"Who?"

"Mr. Cunningham. He was walking down the hall in front of us with Mr. Swade, who was asking him if he'd like to teach a class this semester."

"Brett Cunningham? Teach a class? On what? The actuarial tables?"

"What kind of tables?"

"Never mind. It was just a joke. But what would Brett teach in Sunday school?"

"I dunno. He just gave a funny laugh and said he wasn't up on urban and environmental enlightenment."

"And? Don't stop."

"And Mr. Swade said that was why he thought Brett would do a good job on something basic like the Bible."

"Did he say he'd do it?"

"He said he'd think about it. He's pretty good, you know. He came and taught our class one time."

This was an entirely new light on Brett. "What did he teach?"

"Well, he read parts of the Sermon on the Mount and then got us talking about how it applies today. It was pretty neat. Why don't you like him, Ma?"

"I guess because he's always seemed to me to represent the most reactionary elements in the congregation. When he was business manager he specialized in telling the rector that any really original project the rector dreamed up would cost too much—whether it would or not. And he's shot down plenty of my projects—or at least he's persuaded Norbert to shoot them down." After a few minutes of silence I glanced towards Jamie, who was staring dreamily into the empty fireplace. "What are you thinking about?" I was all set for a mother-son exchange that could plumb the depths and be remembered for decades.

"I was wondering who committed the murder."

Everyone else was wondering that, too.

After the police had declared themselves finished with it, Dick's office had been put back in order. Drawn by some impulse I couldn't define, I stopped by the following morning. A variety of men from the New York Police Department were there. Dick's blood was still on the beige carpet, and there was some splattered on the white wall behind.

"What . . . what actually killed him?" I asked Detective O'Neill.

"You don't know? It's been in all the papers and on television."

"Well, I didn't look at television, and I didn't read the papers. I guess I wanted not to think about it for a while."

"We think it was the companion to this."

O'Neill was pointing to a heavy bronze object that I recognized as one of two bookends that had held up a variety of volumes on a shelf over Dick's chair. At the moment, in place of one of the bookends, was a large ashtray.

"That was used?"

"It looks that way. The shape of the wound fits exactly the lower edge, here—" He pointed out the bottom part of the bookend. Expensive and very modern, the pair had been presented to Dick on the occasion of his becoming business manager and resembled nothing so much as a roundish blob resting on a squarish blob. Poor Dick's skull had been bashed in by the squarish end.

"I suppose the police have it," I said. "I mean the one that was used."

"No. We're looking for it. That's why we can only say that we suppose it was used. It fits. The companion to the other bookend is missing, and it seems an obvious choice. I was coming around to talk to you later. You're . . ." He flipped the pages of a notebook. "The Reverend Mrs. Claire Aldington. Is that right?"

"Yes. That's right."

"We can talk here if you like, or we can go to your office."

I gave a sudden shiver. "Let's go to my office."

I ensconced the detective in a chair in front of the desk and then said, "Okay, what is it you want to talk to me about? Dick's . . . Dick's death?"

"Yes," he said. "Grism's murder."

I stared at the fairish middle-aged man as the word "murder" seemed to spread through the room. I realized then that Dick's death, awful as it had been, had, in my mind, been some kind of tragic occurrence, the sad result of a compassionate policy on the part of the church that tried to give some of New York's homeless a place in which to sit down, to eat twice a week, to talk occasionally if they could find a staff member not too busy to listen for a few moments.

But the word "murder" somehow changed it. Someone came in and picked up a heavy bookend and brought it down on Dick's skull, breaking the bones, penetrating the brain perhaps. Extinguishing life.

As though reading my mind, Detective O'Neill said, "You found the body. You saw what had been done to him."

Yes, I thought, remembering. I had seen: the glaring eyes, the blood over half the face, the slumped body. I did not have to go across the room to make sure Dick was dead. It was obvious. So, after a frozen moment, I walked in cowardly fashion down to the next office, picked up the phone and told Josie to call the police immediately: somebody had killed Dick Grism. I repeated this now to Detective O'Neill.

"You didn't want to use the phone in the same room as the body?" Dick had now become "the body."

"No. I'm a coward. Dick was so plainly dead. I didn't want to come nearer."

And suddenly Dick was there, alive, with his eyes that looked straight at you, almost hypnotically, yet never seemed to connect. It was as though someone had told him that sincere and trustworthy people always looked you straight in the eye and he was making sure he qualified.

"Did you like him?"

"Not very much," I said finally.

"Why not?"

Now that he'd nailed me down, I wasn't entirely sure how to explain my lack of enthusiasm for Dick Grism. As far as unbuttoning the church pocket was concerned, he was certainly a big improvement over Brett Cunningham—or so I had thought, until this minute. But when I considered the matter, I realized he had been no more forthcoming on one or two of my pet projects and schemes than Brett had been. Brett had a way of ruffling my feathers by saying flat-footedly, "We can't afford it." While Dick would give every sign of listening sympathetically, then murmuring, "Let me see what I can work out, Claire. I'm sure I can manage something." And when he said that, I was so convinced of his power to manage anything that it never occurred to me to doubt that the money was in the bag. But the fact of the matter was, my department was as underfinanced as it had ever been . . .

I became aware that the detective was still waiting patiently for me to answer.

"I'm not sure why I didn't like him," I said finally. And then I surprised myself. "At least with Brett you knew where you were."

"Brett?"

"Brett Cunningham, our previous business manager. He's really chairman of the board of a bank, but he served as part-time treasurer and business manager for a year. To tell you the truth, I don't know what I thought about Dick. It seemed so remarkable that he could do all he did, considering his disability."

"Would you have liked him if he hadn't had a disability?"

For a moment the answer seemed absolutely clear: no. Then I made a gesture. "It's not a valid question. If he hadn't had this disability, if he hadn't had to put up that struggle—and only he knew what a struggle it must have been—then he would have been a different person."

The detective smiled. "Fair enough. By the way, what kind of projects are you involved with? Don't you do priest work here?"

With a name like O'Neill he almost had to be a Roman Catholic, I thought. But the Catholics had priest counselors as well. "I'm a pastoral counselor. That is, I work in the chancel on Sunday—read the liturgy, consecrate, conduct the service or assist—like any of the other priests. But during the week I conduct private and group therapy."

"Just for members of the church?"

"No. We're part of a neighborhood help organization, which also funds some of our work. So some of my clients are not members of the church. But many are."

"Do you have any you think could commit violence?"

That question would be, to any therapist or psychiatrist, like a red flag being slowly waved in front of the eyes.

"Detective O'Neill," I finally said. "That's a loaded question, as I'm sure you know."

He gave a small smile. "Yes, I've asked it before."

"So I'll give you what I'm sure you'll think is an evasive answer, though it isn't. Anybody, including you or me, could, under certain circumstances, be violent. Do you have children?"

He looked up a bit startled. "Yes. All right, I get your point. If somebody threatened one of my children, I, too, would go to any lengths to stop them. But I wasn't asking that, as I'm sure you know."

"No. Well, in answer to what I think you were asking. No, I do not at the moment have any patients wandering around having paranoid hallucinations. In other words: no."

"What would you say most of your patients suffer from?"

"The human condition." I got a swift, straight look from the detective. "All right, mild and less mild depression, fear, anxiety about job, boyfriend, husband, a sense of failure, loneliness, despair, an all-around worry about not being able to cope."

He wrote for a few minutes. "I wonder what they did before the advent of shrinks and therapists."

"Went to the church, had it out in the family, leaned on the community. Most people lived in smaller groups fifty years ago, their social structures, meaning the church, the community, the family, were stronger, or they went quietly—or noisily—mad and were locked up. As we all know, many of the homeless today would have been institutionalized a couple of decades ago. In fact, many of them were."

"Now we just turn them out on the streets. Do you think that's better?"

"No. There should be some kind of interim supervisory housing for them. They weren't getting any better warehoused in the old psychiatric institutions. On the other hand, most of them are too confused, to put it at its mildest, to be able to cope with the welfare and disability systems. So they just wander around."

"There seems to be a general feeling among those I've talked to in the church here that Mr. Grism was killed by one of the street people who wandered into the business manager's office to get a handout, was refused, went into a rage, then picked up the bookend and hit Grism on the head. Is that your view, too?" He stopped writing and gave me one of his straight looks.

"I'll admit I'd like to think that."

"Yes, it lets everybody out, doesn't it?"

"Can you blame us?"

"No."

"But you don't think that?"

"Right at the moment I'm still collecting information. Part of which is: What time did you get here yesterday morning?"

"A little before eight. We have an eight-fifteen service of Morning Prayer every weekday, and I like to go to that."

"Did you see any street people—looking maybe for a handout—wandering around?"

I frowned, trying to remember everything that had happened when I came in the front door. "I came in the front door, picked up my telephone messages . . . I did see one or two of the people who had been sleeping on cots coming upstairs, carrying coffee cups and/or buns."

"So you give them breakfast as well."

"Just coffee and buns."

"What happened then?"

"I went upstairs to my office."

"Did you have any telephone messages at that early hour?"

"Yes."

"Who from?"

I hesitated. Then: "One from a client who wanted to cancel an appointment, another from somebody who wanted to make one, and one from the assistant headmistress of the school my daughter—my stepdaughter—goes to."

"What school is that?"

"Is this essential information?"

He looked up again. "At this point, Reverend"—he seemed almost to parody the title—"all information is essential, and will be until we can begin to sort out what is relevant from what isn't."

"Why don't you just call me Mrs. Aldington. The title Reverend, used by itself, is not a custom in this Church."

"Sorry. We're not as well informed about such things as we probably ought to be."

He had managed, very neatly, I thought, to make me feel petty.

"Anything else?" I asked.

"Is your husband a member of the clergy, too?"

"My late husband, Patrick Aldington, was rector of St. Thomas' Parish in Upper Hills, New Jersey. He died five years ago. I am now a widow."

"I see. You live with this stepdaughter? Any other children?"

"I live with my stepdaughter, Martha Aldington, and my son, James Aldington. My home address is 28 East Eighty-second Street. I'm sure you'll have no trouble getting my telephone number if you want it."

"Do you resent my asking these questions?"

Until he asked them, I hadn't realized, or acknowledged to myself, how resentful I was. The reason fairly leapt to the mind: Like Larry Swade, I, too, loved St. Anselm's and was terrified of what these ferreting cops would find, of what was going to happen.

Instead of answering his question, I asked, almost for reassurance, "Don't you think it's at least possible that somebody from outside came in and killed Dick? After all, he was the business manager or treasurer, or both. And we are reputed to be a rich church. I'd think that for anyone desperate for cash for the next meal or shelter, it'd be an obvious place to go."

The detective got up and put his notebook in his pocket. "The trouble with that is that there was some four hundred and fifty-three dollars plus change lying around very loose in Grism's cashbox in his desk drawer. Whoever did it wasn't after the cash."

4

THE REALIZATION that a fairly sizable sum of cash readily available in Dick's office had been left untouched seeped slowly through the parish house, and people's reaction to the fact of the murder changed: Dick being killed by a desperate street person was one thing; by somebody other than a street person was totally different.

"At least when we thought it was one of the poor," Johnny McKnight said, "it wasn't so bad." We were all going into the conference room for a hastily summoned late-afternoon staff meeting.

Jennifer Riddle, the seminarian, who was also working part-time as general parish dogsbody, added, "At least with those street people it would be understandable. One could hardly blame them."

From the nods around the room it would seem she expressed a commonly held attitude. I felt the same sudden prick of irritability that I had when Norbert had said more or less the same thing.

"Sorry to sound a note of law and order, but even with street people murder is a crime."

"Yes, but when one thinks about the violence society has done to them," Jennifer went on, her kind, earnest face tense with feeling, "one sees how violence is forced on them as a way of life."

"You mean," I said, "that if it turns out to be some middle-class Wasp or working-class ethnic who did it, then you'll feel differently about it?"

"Of course. Wouldn't you? I mean, when we've had so much privilege for so long."

"Speak for yourself," I said. "I doubt whether a working-class Polish or Russian American would feel that privileged. My father was a small-town district attorney. I grew up thinking a crime is a crime is a crime, no matter who commits it. And I also do not feel overprivileged—at least I didn't until I inherited some of Patrick's money. My upbringing was definitely not gilded."

"Even so," Norbert said, coming in and walking to the head of the table, "you can hardly compare your circumstances with any of these people's out there." We all sat down as he pulled out his chair. "I can't tell you," he said, "how much this has brought home to me the shame of our cities and our society. It is not the poor, wretched street person who committed that crime—oh, he may have actually held the weapon—but it is we who are guilty for allowing such conditions to exist . . ."

His well-bred voice went on. Many of the things he was saying had been said by Patrick. Yet something was different. Perhaps it was because Patrick was younger, or maybe because I was. Whatever the reason, I was not moved or convinced by Norbert as I had been by Patrick. The same phrases in Norbert's mouth had, emotionally, almost no impact on me.

When Norbert finished, Jennifer suddenly said, "Or she."

Norbert tilted his senatorial head. "Or she what, Jennifer?"

"He or *she* may actually have held the weapon," Jennifer announced punctiliously.

"No sexism even in crime," I said.

There was a sudden snort from Larry, who had spent the minutes in the room involved in one of his elaborate doodles.

"Since I insist on adding the feminine pronoun on all other occasions," Jennifer soldiered on, "then justice demands the same when it's a crime."

"Quite right," Norbert said.

There was a short silence. I came out of a slight daze. "But, Norbert," I said, "since there was plenty of cash in Dick's cashbox, untouched, it seems very unlikely that some wandering street person, desperate for money, committed the crime for cash."

"My dear Claire, it simply means that whoever it was was frightened away before he—or she"—Norbert glanced at Jennifer and then back to the rest of us—"could get the money."

"But then wouldn't somebody, somewhere in the building, have seen whoever it was running out?"

"If so, we can only hope the police will be able to discover it. Not that I have that much faith in them."

"Oh, I dunno," Larry said, admiring his doodle. "I mean, given their cuts in personnel, they do a pretty good job."

"They didn't do that much good even before they had cuts in their personnel. They're very ready to push the poor around. Somehow the white-collar crime seems to flourish on."

Suddenly, and surprisingly, I missed Brett Cunningham. During the three years he had taken leave from his bank to be the church's treasurer-cum-business manager, he would never have let Norbert get away with a statement like that unchallenged. Norbert, like Patrick, had brought with him from the sixties a view of the police as the Enemy. This was an attitude that had been far more prevalent in the seventies. Since then most of the clerical firebrands and marchers had outgrown their romanticized vision of society as perpetually on the barricades. The fact that Norbert hadn't was always a surprise. With all his activism, he seemed so much the urbane, moderate, civilized member of a civilized Church. But occasionally—such as now in his comment about the police—there was a reminder. And Brett, if he was here, would have picked him up immediately on it, as he had done before. But Brett and his deflating tongue were no longer part of the staff. Surely I couldn't be missing him? I thought. It would be a little like missing a sore tooth.

"I've called this meeting," Norbert said, "because it's obvious by now that we're going to be falling over both police and press every time we walk down the hall. Since the whole furor over the possible sale of St. Cuthbert's, the press has hardly let an issue of the newspaper or television news come out without a mention of St. Anselm's. It's an honor I could bring myself to do without. But, there it is. In a free society, et cetera, et cetera . . . that is, free for the likes of us. But the fact that the press is here doesn't mean we have to talk to them all the time, or answer their persistent questions, or let ourselves be trapped into statements we didn't want to make or didn't know we were going to make. I think the best thing for all of you to do is refer any news people to Brett Cunningham."

"But he's not here," I said.

"He will be. I've persuaded him to come back, on a part-time basis, at least until we can find a permanent replacement for poor Dick. And I think he's a good person to deal with the press. As we all know, Brett has no trouble about saying no to people"—a wintry smile lit up Norbert's face—"it's one of his major talents. So, if you're confronted by a newshawk with a Pulitzer prize—or even the evening news—on his mind, just refer him—or her—to Brett.

"As for the police, well, you can refer them to me. As rector of this parish I probably should carry the burden of having to deal the investigations that are going on, and I have the authority to tell them when I think they're going too far—as they nearly always do."

I still had the curious feeling that Dick, the dead Dick slumped in his wheelchair with the blood pouring down his head, was lost in all this.

"I think we ought to give the police all the help we can, Norbert. And I'm sure Brett would agree with me," I said.

Norbert gave his famous aloof smile and rose, a tall, impressive man. "This is a red-letter day, Claire, if you're going to actually come out and say you agree with Brett about *anything.* I think that's all for now," he said, dismissingly, to those who had scraped to their feet.

"Yes, but—" Larry struggled up, his round face troubled. "Are you telling us not to cooperate with the police?"

"No, of course I'm not, Larry. It's our obvious duty to help them. But that's not the same thing as feeding them a great number of red herrings. I've had experience with the police. If they can't get something out of you that they want, they'll get something out of you that you definitely don't want." He stopped, then added abruptly, "I don't want the poor, who come in here to get help of one kind or another, to be badgered or have their privacy taken away. It's as valuable to them as yours is to you. All right?"

He swept out, his shoulders bunched, a rather formidable look on his face.

"Well," Larry said, "I think he knows who did it."

"And is moving heaven and earth to protect him. Poor Norbert. That can't be easy."

Norbert was right about the omnipresence of the police and the press. There was a uniformed cop posted on a more or less permanent basis outside Dick's door, and as I went out to grab a sandwich and pick up some shoes I'd left at a shoe repair shop, I was approached by an attractive young woman hovering outside and backed up by a TV camera and a cameraman. A van with the name of one of New York's television news stations was parked around the corner.

"May I ask you a couple of questions?" the young woman said. From the corner of my eye I saw the man bearing a camera on his shoulder moving nearer.

"I really have no information," I said. "And I am in a hurry."

"One of your parishioners has been quoted as saying that a murder for money was only to be expected in view of the kinds of people who fill your parish house these days. Do you agree with this?"

I'd been irritated by Norbert's high-handed instructions about handling the press. But as I became aware that this charming young woman was deliberately baiting me, my sympathy swung erratically over.

"I'm afraid any information or interview should be arranged through our business manager, Mr. Cunningham."

"But Richard Grism was your business manager, the man who was murdered. Was he fired before he died? Was there some kind of trouble?"

I took a breath. "Brett Cunningham was business manager of St. Anselm's long before Dick Grism. He has kindly offered to fill the post until we elect a new one."

"But sources inside the church say that Brett Cunningham was ousted in a coup instigated by the more progressive element in the church."

"Oh," I said, astonished. "Who said that?"

"I don't reveal my sources."

"Then you probably made it up," I said, "simply as good baiting material."

"May we quote you as saying it's not true?" She was a pretty and charming young woman, but her shining eyes reminded me of a predator closing in for the kill. Also, belatedly, I was aware of Norbert's wisdom in telling us to refer all press questions to Brett.

"No, you may not quote me as saying anything," I started, when to my unspeakable relief I saw Brett's tall figure coming up the steps. "Better still, here Brett is. You can talk to him now."

"We heard that you were ousted from the business manager's job by the liberal element in the church, Mr. Cunningham."

"Did you now? Well, you're absolutely right. I wanted to put the women back in long dresses and have the men and the women sit on opposite sides of the church. I was astonished at how much opposition there was, led by my friend here, the Reverend Claire Aldington." He came up and slipped an arm through mine.

"Seriously, Mr. Cunningham—" Ms. Reporter began.

"I'm almost never serious before lunch. I'm too hungry."

I saw the reporter's slender jaw stiffen. "And what does the Chadbourne Guaranty Trust say about your becoming business manager here? Can you do both jobs? Isn't the job of business manager full-time?"

"Yes, and yes, in answer to your questions. And as to Chadbourne, they're generously giving me a part-time leave of absence. I told them to look upon it as tithing. Claire, I'm sorry to be late for our lunch date, I don't blame you for starting without me. But here I am, coming along now."

"I'm a passionate believer in the First Amendment," I said as I was borne off by Brett, with Ms. Reporter's voice still audible behind us as she talked into her microphone.

"But there are moments when you long for a benevolent despotism," Brett said.

"Or a monarchy," I added. "Although the British press are as nosy and pushy as ours, at least when it comes to scandal."

"They're only doing their job," Brett said. "Have you eaten, by the way?"

"No. I have to do an errand and I don't have long—"

"Good, neither do I. Let's go into the coffee shop here."

And suddenly, and before I could think of a decent reason to refuse, I was sitting at a small table for two in the corner of a crowded coffee shop.

"Why am I here?" I said as a waiter, who obviously knew Brett, put some coffee down in front of him. A cup was placed in front of me.

"Coffee?" the waiter said.

"Yes, please."

Brett put down his cup. "Because you were ambushed."

"Exactly. Why?"

"Because there are a couple of things I wanted to talk to you about." He paused as the waiter came back with the coffee pot and refilled his cup.

"You seem to be known here."

"I come here fairly often. What'll you have to eat?"

"A grilled-cheese sandwich," I finally said.

"Make it two."

"I always think of you lunching in places like the Knickerbocker Club or the Union or the Colony."

Brett winced. "In case you haven't noticed, I'm male. The Colony Club is for women."

"You know what I mean—the ladies you would have lunch with would be members."

"Only old Mrs. Chadbourne. I have an annual lunch with her there. I don't know why you have me among the heriditary blue bloods. I'm from Seattle and from a very modest family. My father owned a drugstore, and I worked behind the soda fountain, in the days when they had soda fountains."

"But you have risen far and exude corporate power."

"What's wrong with that? Where do you suppose that money you're living on—that you inherited from your late husband—came from? Blue-chip stocks purchased by trust officers from the filthy lucre of all the robber barons Patrick was descended from. And don't tell me you'd rather be living in a fifth-floor walk-up in Queens, because I wouldn't believe it." He watched while our cheese sandwiches were placed in front of us. "You know," he said when the waiter had gone, "I don't think that socio-babble that you mouth to me from time to time sits naturally on you. You have too much midwestern common sense for that. In fact, I strongly suspect that you only take it out and dust it off for my benefit."

"That's because of your cheeseparing ways when it comes to helping out pastoral therapy with funds."

He took a huge bite of his sandwich and chewed for a few minutes. "Does it ever occur to you that it might be because we—the church—

are going broke, and unless we take in our sails to some extent there won't be funds for anybody? And if we didn't have the church, then a lot of poor people would not be fed, or helped with medical expenses, or given therapy, or half a dozen other things I could mention, including, one hopes, hearing the Gospel."

"That's nonsense," I said sharply. "Between pledges and gifts and endowment we have millions—quite literally."

"You're missing the point. If you take in five million, I'll grant you it sounds like a lot. But if you give out seven million, or even six million, you're still in the red. The same principle applies whether it is millions or thousands or tens. To keep going, the income has to exceed the outgo. Quite obvious, my dear Watson."

"Are you trying to tell me that we're spending that much in our various charities? I don't believe it."

"They certainly contribute to the outgo. But no. Scrooge that I know you think I am, I can't blame our current parlous condition entirely on that."

"Then what?"

He hesitated. "I'm not quite sure. Of course, like any other institution, all our regular expenses—labor, heating, staff salaries and so on—have gone up. And it's also true," he said pointedly, "that before we go into more outreach that can cost millions, we ought to know where we stand."

"And we don't? I thought Dick Grism was a whiz at this."

"So did I."

"Are you trying to tell me that you've found out in some way that he wasn't?"

"I'm not trying to tell you anything in particular. At least not about that. Good grief, you're beginning to sound like our winsome friend with the mike out there."

"Thanks a lot. Then if that isn't what you want to talk about, why are we having lunch?"

"Couldn't it just be because I found the thought attractive?"

"Not really. It sounds unlike you."

"Tut! How little you know me!"

"Come on, Brett, what's all this about?"

He sighed, pushed aside his sandwich plate and drank some coffee.

"I had my annual lunch at the Colony Club with Mrs. Chadbourne and I thought I ought to tell you that she's getting in a royal fuss about her granddaughter, Martha."

I groaned. Patrick's first wife, Priscilla Chadbourne, was the daughter of the doughty old dame, now head of the Chadbourne clan, whose grandfather had founded the great Chadbourne bank. She was not, I felt, a good influence on Martha. "I suppose she thinks I am not doing my job."

"Something like that. Only she put it more delicately, or at least more diplomatically. She feels that Martha's eating problems—whatever they are, she didn't exactly go into it—are easily accounted for by Martha's grief over losing her father."

I drank some more coffee. "In a way, she's right. Martha idolized her father. She liked me all right—at least I thought she did. But she liked me as an adjunct of her father. When Patrick died, she started going downhill immediately, although I didn't notice it until she was almost a skeleton. I blame myself for that."

"Why?" He looked at me shrewdly. "Because you were probably busy at the seminary at that time?"

"Yes. How did you guess—or know?" When he didn't answer immediately, I said, "I suppose Mrs. Chadbourne allowed as how if I'd been home minding the store and the kitchen, which is what she thinks women ought to do, Martha wouldn't have become an anorexic."

"She didn't use that term, anorexic, but I gathered it was that. I haven't seen Martha recently, in fact not since the last time she came to church. But I didn't think that overweight was the trouble."

"Martha is five foot five. The last time I knew what she weighed, it was one hundred and seven pounds. Since then she's lost at least ten pounds. I don't have time over a short lunch to explain anorexia—"

"You don't have to. My daughter had that problem."

I stopped short. Along with everybody else in the church, and with, probably, half the Upper East Side, I knew that Pamela Cunningham, Brett's wife, had walked out on him. Vaguely I'd heard something about a daughter. But I couldn't remember now what it was.

"How long did it take for her to get over it?"

"She didn't. She died. After a while the effects of starvation became irreversible."

The clatter from Lexington Avenue, which I hadn't noticed before, seemed loud. An ambulance, its siren going full blast, sped by. Underneath there was the dull roar of the Lexington Avenue subway. As my mind occupied itself with these things, I knew I was avoiding all the implications of what Brett had just said. "I'm sorry," I finally said. "I didn't know."

"It's all right. It happened long before you came to St. Anselm's."

I stared at him, stirring another cup of coffee. "Wasn't there any way to get her to eat?"

"Not that we could find, or that worked for Sheila."

"Was that before, or after, Pam . . . left?"

"Before. About two years before. I often wondered how much that failure to keep Sheila alive contributed to Pam's departure. It wouldn't have been obvious or conscious, because Pam would have had no hesitation in giving it as a reason. She was very free and open about the reasons she gave. But I think it might well have been grinding away down there in her unconscious."

Why is it, I thought, that we almost never ascribe personal tragedy to the people we dislike? Registering the fact that Brett not only had a wife who left him but a daughter who died on him from a self-inflicted disease was going to force me to regard him as a human being who had suffered his share of tragedy. And once I did that, I would find it much harder to give him the villain's role in almost everything that went wrong with the church. I was being robbed of my pet enemy, my scapegoat, I thought, and felt a spasm of self-dislike.

"Do you have other children?" I asked.

"Yes, a son."

"What's he doing?"

"Playing the guitar and trying to find himself." There was more than a touch of sarcasm in Brett's voice.

"How old is he?"

"Twenty-one. At his age I had two jobs and was sending money home to help out my family."

"Well, you don't have to sound so virtuous about it."

Brett made a gesture with his hand. "Touché. You'll be heartened to know that that's what Adam says when he and I have words. Which is just about every time we meet." He glanced up at me. "You're a therapist—I wish you'd help me to understand kids like Adam, who were given everything, resent it all and consider themselves ripped off."

I had no wish to stay in a dim coffee shop explaining the younger generation to an establishment-type father who still lived mentally in the fifties. "That'd take longer than I have," I said.

He pushed back his chair. "Okay." Then he looked at me with a certain cold humor in his eyes. "I wonder if that's the kind of comment you make to a parent in distress who comes to you for advice about a child he or she doesn't understand."

Even if he had not said that, before I finished speaking I knew I had behaved churlishly, that I had let my prejudice against Brett dominate ordinary kindness. "I'm sorry—" I started.

"Don't let it worry you. *I'm* sorry. I suppose you think I was trying to get cheap service by buying you a coffee-shop lunch."

Since that ugly thought had sifted through my mind, I could feel myself blushing. "Of course not—"

"Don't bother to lie, Claire. It's probably to your credit, but you don't do it very well." And he strode off to the front of the shop after leaving two dollars in tips at the table.

I waited for him outside the coffee shop. "Brett—"

"I'm afraid I have to run. An appointment. I'm overdue. Thanks for the company." He raised his hat and was gone.

I went back to the church, stopping at the shoe repair place on the way to pick up my shoes. Ms. Reporter was still outside by the steps.

"No comment," I said as she approached.

"I thought you might be interested to know that two pieces of evidence have come up you might not have heard." She paused.

I longed for the strength of mind to say I wasn't interested. But, of course, I was. "Well," I said. "What are they?"

"Do you know someone called Rafael?" she asked.

"Yes, of course I know Rafael." Everybody in the church knew Rafael. He was one of the younger members of the homeless and turned up regularly for our meals. A Hispanic of about thirty, he always claimed that he couldn't find a job, although there were times when I felt that could be interpreted to mean that he couldn't find a job he considered worthy of himself. "What about Rafael?" I asked, hating myself for taking the bait.

"He was seen early yesterday morning at about the time the police figure Grism was killed. He says he came in to get warm, but he's down at the precinct now explaining it all."

"Oh." Rafael was a liar and a braggart. One always had to bear in mind that whatever adventure he was recounting could be the truth, the approximate truth, fiction with a small kernel of truth or absolute fiction. I personally wouldn't leave anything female and vulnerable around him for very long. Yet I found it hard to visualize him committing the brutality of clubbing a crippled man on the head.

"Is that your only comment?" the reporter asked. " 'Oh'?"

"What else could there be, until the police make some sort of announcement?"

"The rector said he's sure there's some mistake, that the poor and the homeless and the minorities are always the first target for any police suspicion."

Norbert was right. I should have referred all comment to him. If he was going to take that line, and it was predictable that he would, then as a member of his staff I should at least keep my different comments to myself.

"What other piece of news do you have?" I asked instead, trying hard to sound as though I didn't care. "You did mention another, didn't you?"

"Somebody thought that somebody else reported seeing a woman around early yesterday morning."

"Just a woman? Or a specific woman?"

"Just a woman. You were here early yesterday morning, weren't you, Reverend?"

I debated putting her right about the customs of address pertaining in the Episcopal Church, but decided that that would do nothing but produce more insinuations of one kind or another.

"I'm here early every morning, because I like to attend Morning Prayer, which is celebrated at eight-fifteen every morning Monday through Friday, as I'm sure you know. Why don't you come sometime?"

She looked a little startled, as I hoped she would. Then she said, "Maybe sometime I will. When this case is cleared up."

I managed to get inside the building without further questions.

I was starting to go upstairs to my office when, on impulse, I veered off and went to Norbert's office. His secretary, Sally Hepburn, was sitting outside.

"Is he busy?" I asked Sally.

"When isn't he! But he's alone, so go on in."

Norbert was standing beside his desk looking out his front window. His was the biggest office in the parish house, and sunlight poured in from windows on two sides. Books lined the walls, and a fine beige carpet covered the floor. On the parts of wall not covered by bookcases were taped paintings made by some of the Sunday-school children—wild splashes of color with vaguely marked symbols, a cross, a crown that might be thorns or might be something else, stick figures and animals. Norbert loved the Sunday school and taught there whenever he could find the time.

"Is this a new batch?" I asked, going from one picture to another.

"Yes. Johnny brought them up last week. They're pretty good, I think. Don't you?"

To be truthful, I didn't think they were particularly. I didn't have that kind of sentimentality. Jamie's early efforts at art were dear to me, and were tucked away among treasures in various boxes. But I never thought they were particularly good. What made them valuable was that they were Jamie's.

"Well," I said, "I'm not much of a connoisseur of youthful artworks."

"Surely you don't have to be," Norbert said. "What I like about them is their freshness. Nothing stale, nothing taught, is there?"

I decided to leave the subject. "Norbert, I heard from our girl reporter outside that the police are questioning Rafael. Is that true?"

"Unfortunately, yes. As I predicted, they pounced on someone who manages to combine in his person being poor, homeless and a minority member. Perfect for them."

He spoke with such bitterness that I hesitated. "Yes . . . but what made them choose him?"

"I just told you."

"But granting your suspicions are true, even the police have to have something they can point to as incriminating evidence."

"They say he had some of the loose cash on him from Dick's slush fund."

"But I thought that was all intact."

"Well, they've dreamed up a witness—one of the girls from the bank—who said she'd given Dick six hundred in bills only the Friday before he died, so that, short of finding where Dick might have used it, there's a . . . a deficit in the sum left. Naturally, they assumed one of our homeless had taken it and made Rafael turn out his pockets. He had—quite innocently, I'm sure—a couple of fives, a ten, two twenties and some ones. The bank teller is almost certain the ten and the two twenties are part of the lot she gave Dick. Rafael should have had a lawyer present, of course. But the police wouldn't tell him that, you can bet. They had no legal right whatsoever to make him turn out his pockets . . ."

"But there's a chance he might have killed Dick. I mean, since he did have the money."

"You can be damn sure that if they thought a son of some of our wealthier parishioners—Adam Cunningham, for example—had some of those bills, they wouldn't have asked him to empty his pockets."

I pondered the matter. At first it seemed to me he might be right. Then I remembered Detective O'Neill. There was something about that officer that made me say, "You can't know that, Norbert."

I saw the finely arched brows frown.

"But speaking of Adam," I said, hurrying on. "Do you know him at all?"

"Of course. He went to school with some of my nephews. Why?"

"I was talking to Brett about him at lunch. Brett seems to feel he's a typical sixties dropout, except that it's now the eighties."

"Brett Cunningham is probably an excellent banker, and he did a good job as business manager and treasurer of the church, in the sense that he kept the books and the church portfolio well. Naturally, since I was one of those who wanted him out, I wasn't enthusiastic about his policies regarding church expenditures. And his understanding of a sensitive boy like Adam, a boy who saw through the postures of our society and found them materialistic and worthless, is probably not very high. He's the kind of citizen we all know who tells you that when he was young he put himself through college, held down a job and also helped his dear old mother."

"You've been talking to him, I see."

Norbert turned and a wintry smile broke over his face. "Did I hit the bull's-eye? No, I haven't talked to him. But I know his type. They can't understand the disgust that today's youth feels at the rich, overindulged world their parents and grandparents created."

The trouble with talking to Norbert was that he often handed me the lines I was inclined to give to people like Brett. When they came from Norbert, they aroused in me both contrariness and skepticism. "You know that isn't all bad, working and helping your family. We're always trying to talk about community commitment and stirring up what little there seems to be. Well, the family is the smallest and earliest kind of community. And you know perfectly well, Norbert, that if Rafael, or one of his brothers, was holding down two jobs and trying to help his family, you'd be singing his praises to the skies."

"You sound like you've been taking coaching from Brett." There was that curious note in Norbert's voice that I'd been hearing more of late: not quite hostility, but not friendly either. It was as though he were speaking from a distance, remote, removed. I felt I had trespassed. But suddenly, as I was defining this to myself, I saw a hole in something he'd said.

"Why did they make Rafael turn out his pockets? No—" I waved my hand as Norbert was about to speak. "I mean, of all the poor and minority members of the homeless that are in and out of the church, why did they pick on Rafael?"

The evasive look was more marked. "How should I know, Claire? They have their methods. Perhaps you should question them."

There was a silence. "Norbert," I said finally. "Why are we quarreling?"

He had turned back to the window and was still staring out. When he didn't answer I went on.

"I'm not the enemy. I'm not Brett Cunningham or the people in the congregation who think like him. It was I who started the counseling fund for those who couldn't afford therapy but desperately needed it. *I* began the group meetings that are taking place now in various people's houses—including those who were on the streets and on drugs. It's *my* project to extend the amount of free therapy we give to include some summer camp courses, a project that Dick had done nothing about . . ."

He turned and smiled then, and relief washed over me. His smile had all the affection and warmth that in the past had so often had the power to move me and others. It was one of the reasons why, at a fairly early age and after a late start in the priesthood, he had become rector of such a large and important metropolitan church.

"Sorry, Claire, of course you're not the enemy. I didn't mean for one second to imply that I thought you were. Without you a great number of our parishioners would be a lot worse off. Forgive me. It's just the appalling events of yesterday and today that are troubling me. Was there something else?"

"No. I'm sorry, too. I shouldn't have bothered you at a time like this. Let me know if I can be of any help." And I left rather hurriedly.

For the rest of the afternoon I found that my four afternoon clients were responding, like tuning forks, to Dick's murder and Rafael's interrogation down at the precinct. Curiously, however, I found that they divided along unexpected lines: The two who came from poor and/or minority homes were preoccupied with the horror of someone on the church's staff being the victim of murder on the church's premises. The two who were well-to-do—one the daughter of a rich parishioner, the other an editor in a leading publishing house—echoed Norbert's fury at Rafael's arrest and for approximately the same reasons. I finished the day having profound thoughts about symbols and how much effect they had on our lives and judgments.

Just before I was due to go home, the telephone rang and an unmistakable voice said, "This is Emily Chadbourne . . ."

I knew, of course, that she was going to ask me to drop by, or have lunch, or make an appointment for her to come by the church. She wished to talk about Martha, and I would not enjoy one moment of it. I was right on all counts. Of all the alternatives, I decided to drop by her apartment. It would save having to spend a whole day—or more—dreading it. And Jamie would be involved with one of his various clubs at the school until just before dinner, when I was due to pick him up.

As I left I passed Josie Beardsley at the reception desk. "Any news?"

I asked idly, knowing that she would be up to date on whatever was going on.

"Yes." She glanced at the distant figure of the officer guarding Dick's room down the hall and at the reporters still thronging around the steps outside and visible through her window. "They've formally charged Rafael. I *do* think it's a shame," she broke out. "He's a flake, but he wouldn't do that."

I stood there for a moment. "Has Norbert gone to see him?"

"No, he's got some kind of meeting going on in his office. He said he was going later this evening. Are you going to go?"

I thought about Emily Chadbourne, sitting behind her regal teapot on upper Fifth Avenue, awaiting the arrival of her granddaughter's unworthy guardian. "Yes, I am going to see him. Where is he?"

"Down at the jail near Foley Square. Give him my best."

"Josie, would you call Mrs. Emily Chadbourne at this number"—I was scribbling as I talked—"say who you are and tell her I'll be an hour late. Okay?"

Thrusting the piece of paper at Josie, I pushed open the door and fled down the steps past the mikes reaching out to me and into a handy cab cruising by.

5

"I DIDN'T DO IT," Rafael said. "I told the cops, yes, I took the money from Mr. Grism's drawer—the day before. Sunday. Sometimes he gave me odd jobs. Take this here, take that there. You know. Like a messenger. And he'd pay me from the money in the drawer. So I took it. I had a right to. I know it's wrong. Mama would say it's wrong. But I can't get work. It's not my fault. It's their fault."

"Who's 'they,' Rafael?"

"The system. Everybody. It was like what I learned at college . . ."

As I listened and watched, I reflected that I knew very well Rafael had never been to college. He had not even finished high school, but had, like so many of the young people of his community, El Barrio, simply dropped out at fifteen. Which did not mean he was either stupid or ill informed. In his crazy way, he had accumulated a fair amount of knowledge of one kind or another.

" 'From everyone according to his ability,' " he went on, quoting Marx's famous dictum, " 'to everyone according to his need . . .' That's the way it should be. I have read it." His dark eyes were fixed on me, as though daring me not to believe him.

"Yes. I know, Rafael. Couldn't you get any alibi for when Mr. Grism was killed? I mean, weren't you with anyone who could verify that you were with them on Monday morning?"

He blinked, then said, "They are out of town." And then, as I started to speak, "But they will be back."

We were sitting in a room to which the policeman had led me and to which Rafael had been brought. Fortunately, I was wearing my clerical collar, so I didn't have much trouble persuading the authorities to let me talk to him, saying that I worked at the church where he was (occasionally) employed, where he was definitely fed two or three times a week, and that the Reverend Norbert Shearer would be by later. I also said I was the church therapist and let them draw the conclusion that Rafael was one of my patients.

"Well, I think you ought to persuade whoever you were with to come forward and confirm that you were with him—or her."

"Yes. I will do that." He stared at me. "It is good of you to come and see me. Women, they are full of compassion. It is the reason they can't do men's work."

I recognized this as a line Rafael handed out from time to time. As much as he was passionately anything, he was passionately a male chauvinist.

"Let me know if there's anything—anything at all—that you'd like one of us at the church to do, won't you, Rafael?"

"Yes. You can—" He paused.

"What?"

"You can tell Mama that I am innocent."

"I'm sure she knows that."

"Sometimes she knows it and sometimes she doesn't." At which point he let loose a flood of Spanish. He went on, finally, in English, "And tell her . . ." He paused. "No, that is enough. *Bastante!* Good night." And he rose to go, making a graceful bow as he did. The policeman in the corner rose with him.

"By the way," I said belatedly, "Josie sent her love."

"She is truly a woman." He spoke with conviction and more than a touch of melodrama. "I return my love to her." He bowed once more and then was led away by the policeman.

I was stopped by my friend Detective O'Neill, who asked me to come into his office.

"Rafael didn't do it," I said as I sat in the chair he indicated. "I'm sure of it."

"What makes you so sure?"

"I think Rafael is many things, including a grade-A con man, but I don't think he's violent."

"Are you his therapist?"

"No."

"From your professional knowledge, would you say he was incapable of violence?"

"We talked about this before," I said. "And we agreed that under some circumstances nearly everybody is capable of violence. I just don't think he killed Dick for a few bucks, and I *do* think it's a tragic mistake to charge him with it."

"A few bucks may seem pretty large to somebody like Rafael, and by the way, we haven't charged him—yet. We're holding him for questioning."

"I heard he *was* charged."

"I can't help the exaggerations of the rumor circuit."

"I'm glad he hasn't been. But I was told that you had discovered that Rafael had money from Dick's cashbox, some of the same money given Dick by a bank teller the previous Friday."

"That's true. Furthermore, Rafael has admitted to taking some money from Grism's cashbox when he was hanging around the church on Sunday. Apparently, according to him, the door was open, and so were both the desk drawer and the cashbox. Isn't that a little strange?"

I thought it was very strange, except that Grism could be careless about a variety of things. "Yes, and no. Dick wasn't always careful. And there may be other keys to the door. I know that the rector has one, and so does somebody else—Johnny McKnight, I think, in case there are sudden emergency calls for cash. But if Rafael admits to taking the money the day before the murder, doesn't that let him out for killing Dick Monday morning? Why should he kill Dick when he could—and would—easily help himself?"

"Because he may have gone into Grism's office thinking since the first theft was so easy, he might as well get some more, and been caught red-handed rifling the box when Grism came wheeling in."

"I just don't see him picking up some heavy object and crushing Dick's head with it. He would have flown into a rage and made a speech about his rights, about social injustice and about the lot of the oppressed. But I don't think he'd have committed such a brutal act."

"You say that as though you were sure. You say he's not your patient? Yet I got the impression from the officer who let you see him that you might be."

"No. I—er—misled the officer. I wanted to see Rafael, so I said I was the church therapist and let the officer put the rest together. But you don't need to be a therapist to know that Rafael is off the wall more often than not. That's why his mother doesn't want him to live at home, even though they have an extra cot."

"She's afraid he'll lead the younger children astray, I gather," the detective surprised me by saying.

I glanced at him. "So you've been talking to her."

"Of course."

"I think he has an alibi."

"That's what he says. It remains to be seen whether his alibi will come forward and give him a cover story for the crucial hour."

"What is the crucial hour, by the way? The same as you told us?"

"You don't know? You haven't been reading the papers or watching the news shows?"

"No. They depress me."

"I see. Well, the medical examiner has more or less confirmed our own guess—that the murder occurred between six-thirty and eight A.M. By the way, do you know anything about a woman who seems to have come into the parish house early in the morning sometime—we're not sure when—but was seen leaving around seven-thirty, twenty to eight?"

"No—nothing at all. Who was she?"

"That's what we'd like to find out."

"How did you know she was there?"

"Because two people, your receptionist, Josie Beardsley, and one of the custodians, Matthew Pearson, said they saw a woman they thought was you leaving the parish house around that time."

Suddenly I remembered Josie's surprised look when I came in, and my comment, "I still work here."

Detective O'Neill was watching me. "Remember something?"

"Only that when I came in, just before eight, Josie looked surprised and said to me, 'Oh, it's you,' or something like that. I thought she was being funny or making some Monday-morning type of joke, and replied in kind."

"And she never referred to it again?"

"No—but, of course, it wasn't too long after that that I . . . I discovered Dick's body, and I guess everything went out of her mind."

I didn't say anything for a moment, then: "Did you say that Matthew thought he'd seen me earlier?"

"Yes, he was buffing the floor somewhere down one of the side halls and saw this woman leave. He just assumed it was you."

"It's funny," I said, "that they both thought it was me."

"That's what I thought, too."

"After all, other women work here. And come in early."

"I know."

"Why would I go in and go out—except maybe to pick up some coffee?"

There was something in his silence that made me look at him sharply. "Are you trying to tell me that makes me . . . makes me some kind of a suspect?"

He said carefully, "Theoretically, it is possible for you to have come into the building earlier than you said, had some kind of unpleasant encounter with Grism, killed him, gone out by another door and then back in again."

"But why would I? I had nothing against Dick."

"I only said theoretically. What makes it odd—as you point out—is that both the receptionist and the custodian thought it was you. There are plenty of women—young women—who work in the parish house. But both of them mistook this strange woman for you. Not you and/or somebody else. Just you."

There was another silence. "You said yesterday you didn't like Grism but didn't really tell me why. Can you tell me now?"

"Technically speaking," I said slowly, "I suppose I should have a lawyer with me before I answer what I'm sure are loaded questions. But I cannot take seriously the fact that you might suspect me. I frequently have arguments with a lot of people, but—to go back to our old discussion—unless somebody were attacking somebody I loved—my son, my daughter—or me, I can't imagine trying to hurt them, let alone kill them. And Dick was, after all, for God's sake, a paraplegic."

"So—why don't you answer my question? And by the way, I repeat, I didn't say I suspected you. I told you what was theoretically possible. And it's part of my job, when something's possible, either to move it towards being probable or certain or to remove it altogether. So—did you like Grism? What kind of guy was he?"

I tried to picture Grism, but all of a sudden I couldn't. Something had expunged him from my mind. But I certainly knew what I had thought of him—or so I supposed. I took a breath.

"One shouldn't speak ill of the dead and all that. Especially when the dead was crippled. One thing I'll say on Dick's behalf, he managed his disability so well that I—and other people—always felt perfectly free to dislike him. I think that's something of an achievement. He didn't have a touch of self-pity. Nor was he so obviously full of set teeth and true grit that you wanted to kick him. If he was tired, he said so. On the other hand, he didn't use his disability. Having said that . . . well, as I said, I didn't much like him. But now that you're pinning me down as to why, I'm having a hard time giving a reason. I think he was something of a climber . . . I think he used people, especially people in high business or social circles or both. He also wanted to please everybody. Brett Cunningham, his predecessor, took fiendish pleasure, when I had some expensive new project on my mind, in saying flatly, 'It's too expensive. We can't afford it.' And I knew Brett didn't give a damn what I or anybody else thought of him. But Dick—I'd propose a scheme, which admittedly would cost money, they all do, and he'd say, 'Well, I don't see how I can get that out of the budget, but leave it to me and I'll see what I can do.' And then I wouldn't hear for the longest time, until, in fact, I'd ask him how he was doing, and I'd learn that the scheme had been turned down."

"Did he have the power to do that? I mean, was he the final word?"

"Strictly speaking, Norbert, the rector, had the final yes or no. But Norbert almost never interfered. He used to overrule Brett from time to time, which he disapproved of doing. He thought it interfered with the proper functions of the various staff members. But when one of his pet schemes was involved, he'd suddenly swoop down and take over. I think that's one reason he was so anxious to get rid of Brett—it made him—Norbert—look authoritarian, which went against all his principles."

"But with Grism it was different?"

"Yes. I think so. I think Grism was much more liable to do as Norbert wanted, although he made all kinds of thrifty noises. But Norbert was the man to please, and so he pleased him."

"And that's why you didn't like him? You felt he kowtowed to the boss?"

"Yes, and was fairly two-faced about doing it. But I certainly didn't kill him over it."

"Well, I'll take your word for it—for the time being." He gave me a sharp look out of his dark eyes. "But I'd prefer that you didn't go anywhere—like out of town."

Strange, I thought. I'd watched enough police dramas on television to have heard this phrase many times. It always sounded *pro forma.* Now, when said to me, it no longer sounded *pro forma.* It sounded as though the detective, speaking for the police department, really meant that they didn't want me to go anywhere, that they'd keep an eye on me, in case I decided to disobey them.

I got up. "I hadn't intended to. I devoutly hope you'll concentrate on finding out who killed Dick Grism."

The detective rose slowly. "You can depend on it that we intend to."

When I got outside I glanced at my watch. I was going to be more than the hour late at Mrs. Chadbourne's that I had planned. It was now five-fifteen. Jamie would be at his school until six, at least. Still, I would have to check. And if it were later than six, then I would pick him up, much as I knew he would protest. It would still be light at six, and Jamie always felt that his entire manhood was undermined if I came to get him while it was still light. However, undermined or no, I was going to pick him up. I glanced around. There were two phone booths visible, both of them being used. I was considering going back into the police station—a prospect that did not attract me at all—and finding out if they had a pay phone, when Detective O'Neill came out.

"Still here?" he asked.

"Do you happen to know," I asked him, "if there's a pay phone inside the precinct?"

"There is. I take it you want one."

"It doesn't look like either of those characters over there has any intention of winding up his conversation, and I have to call Jamie's school to find out how soon he'll be finished with his club."

"Better still, use my phone. Come on," he said, one foot on the step above him, while I hesitated. "Even if you think it's bugged what are you going to say that's incriminating?"

Despite myself, I laughed. "Why should it be bugged in a police station and with you standing there?" I turned and went with him back into the station.

I dialed the school and waited for somebody to find Jamie.

"Ma, what's the matter?" he asked when he came on.

"Nothing. What time are you going to be through?"

"In about . . . what time is it now?"

"Nearly five-thirty."

"Okay, we'll be through around six."

"All right. I'm going to see Mrs. Chadbourne. The school is only half a block from her house, as you know. I want you to go over there as soon as you're through."

"Ma—I don't like going there. I feel like if I breathe something's going to fall down. Anyway, she doesn't like me."

"That's not true, Jamie."

"Well, she talks to me like I was a bad smell."

Instantly I knew what he meant. I also knew that Emily was probably totally unaware of this. "Maybe so, Jamie, but I don't think she knows she comes over that way, and even if you don't like her, I still want you to pick me up. Okay?"

"Can't I go home and walk Motley?"

"Yes, with me. Not before."

"Well, don't blame me if he has an accident. And anyway, it's bad for him to have to wait that long. He hasn't been out since eight this morning."

I paused. Jamie was right. Motley, who was as good as gold in the house, would probably strain his bladder before he'd break training. Less and less did I like this situation. I weighed Motley's physical welfare against Emily's getting more and more regally angry behind her Georgian teapot, mixed in with my dislike of Jamie's being alone after six.

"All right, Jamie. You win. Go straight home and walk Motley. I'll be home as soon as I can."

"Now if Martha would just help—"

"Motley's not her dog. He's yours. Do you want to share him? His affection?"

"No."

"Then don't complain that she doesn't share the responsibility."

"Well, okay. See you later."

I hung up and looked at Detective O'Neill standing in the doorway. "Can I make one more?"

"Be our guest!"

I dialed Emily's phone.

"Hello," she said.

My heart sank a little. She was sounding depressingly polite and formal, which meant she was angry.

"Emily, this is Claire. I'm sorry to be late—or rather, still later than I'd planned. I've been visiting one of our parishioners who's been arrested, and I was here longer than I thought. It will take me at least half an hour or forty-five minutes to get to you. Do you still want me to come, or shall we make another appointment?"

"You don't have to talk to me as though I were the dentist. Of course come along. I want to talk to you."

"All right. I'll see you in a while."

The detective followed me out the precinct door. "Now where are you going?"

"To the nearest subway stop. Where is it? We seem to be equidistant between two."

"We are. If you'll tell me where you're going I'll take you there—if it's not in outer Brooklyn, that is. I have my car and I have to go uptown."

I looked at him, sorely tempted. This was still the rush hour, and I did not look forward to working my way up to Ninety-second and Fifth by either east or west express. "Ninety-second and Fifth."

"My car's over here."

When we got in he said, as he started the car, "Who lives there?"

"Is this polite or police interest?"

"Both. There's hardly any difference anyway, in my case."

"You mean you live your job?"

"Something like that."

"What about wife and family?"

I had a moment's impression that he didn't relish the question, and was pleased that he would then feel what it was like when the tables were turned.

"They're not living with me," he finally said.

"I'm sorry."

"No, you're not. You're just pleased that you're asking the awkward questions this time, aren't you?"

"Yes, as a matter of fact."

"Okay. I answered yours. Why don't you answer mine?"

"I'm going to call on Emily Chadbourne, Mrs. Winfield Chadbourne, my stepdaughter's redoubtable grandmother. Her daughter, Priscilla, was my late husband's first wife."

"The same family as the Chadbourne Guaranty Trust?"

"Exactly the same."

"I didn't realize you were connected with that."

"Why should you?"

We negotiated traffic for a while. Then O'Neill said, "And how old is your son?"

"Eight."

"I take it Motley's his dog."

"You take it right."

"How old is your stepdaughter?"

"Martha's fifteen."

"So's my daughter."

"What's her name?"

"Bridget. Bridget Mary."

I couldn't help smiling. "You can't get much more Irish than that, can you?"

"Not much. I'm not that big on the romance of the old country, but my wife—I guess I should say my former wife—is." He negotiated the car onto the East River Drive. "My mother was German, maybe that influenced me. When the O'Neills and the O'Byrnes—those were the cousins—got together she was inclined to snort."

"What's your daughter like?"

"A pain in the ass—if you'll forgive my candor. She thinks she's a Valley Girl, that is, when she isn't thinking how desperately unlucky she is to be surrounded by middle-class values and rules. She got herself expelled from her Catholic school, so now she goes to a public school, and is flunking out." He stopped for a red light. "Her mother says it's all my fault."

A small portion of me was well aware that the highly intelligent cop sitting beside me was offering these personal glimpses in an attempt to soothe and lull me into thinking I was off the suspect list. Nevertheless, I found myself responding.

"Well, Martha, my stepdaughter, is an anorexic. Her grandmother thinks that's my fault. She hasn't actually come out and said so, but she's made it clear that in her belief if I had stayed home instead of venturing into fields better left to men, then none of Martha's self-starvation would have happened."

"Do you agree with her?"

It was like a knife under the ribs. "Yes," I said, not able to believe that I was saying it. "I do."

"That must be a pretty heavy load to carry."

"You should know."

We were making our way up the Drive, past the Animal Medical Center, when some sense of self-support came to my rescue. "But I have met parents—and I'm sure you have—who as far as anyone can tell are perfect—mother home baking cookies, father playing ball on the weekend—and not all their kids turn out like dream kids."

"Would you be happy staying at home playing housemother?"

"No. I wouldn't."

"Then the chances are they—your kids—wouldn't either. As long as you have the training and the option is there, you'd be mad as hell sitting at home and trying to cater to a resentful teen-ager. How does your son seem to feel about it?"

"Jamie's a joy. I know that's probably horrible prejudice because he's mine, but he is. He's easygoing and doesn't seem to have any alarming repressions. What he thinks, he says. He gets on pretty well with other kids, gets medium grades in practically everything except math, which he's fairly good at. Likes sports. Adores his dog. Thinks his stepsister is a pain in the behind, which she is."

"How does she feel about him?"

"She calls him 'the perfect child' in a sarcastic voice."

"You have my sympathy. Is she pretty?"

"Very. That is, when she isn't looking like something out of Buchenwald."

"Do they look at all alike?"

"No. Jamie's got my hair, only a lot redder, and he's square, like his father. Martha looks like her mother. Medium height, slender, of course, dark brown hair. Good bones. If she left herself alone she'd be a beauty."

"Ummm." We turned off the Drive at Ninety-sixth Street, leaving the shimmering East River, orange and mauve where the late-afternoon sun hit it. Even the grim fortress on its island in the river, Manhattan State Hospital for the insane, looked softer, less threatening.

Ten minutes later we drew up at the impressive awning of 1103 Fifth Avenue. The doorman hurried up.

"Thanks for the ride," I said as I got out.

"De nada," O'Neill replied. He smiled. He had, I decided, a nice smile.

Emily's maid met me at the door, and was obviously expecting me, because she stood back before I could say anything.

"Mrs. Chadbourne's in the drawing room, Mrs. Aldington," she said.

Emily was no longer behind a Georgian teapot. She was sitting in an armchair, reading.

"Good evening, my dear," she said, getting up. "I think it's a little past tea. I'm sure you'd like a cocktail or some sherry."

"I'll have a scotch on the rocks," I said.

"Splendid. So will I. Only I think mine will be Bourbon." She reached over and rang a bell. "Do sit down. It's early for a fire, but I thought it would be reassuring."

It was a warm early October, but there was no doubt about it, the small fire that blazed in the big hearth was reassuring. A faint smell of wood smoke added to the general air of coziness. The maid appeared in the doorway.

"A scotch on the rocks and a Bourbon on the rocks, Trudi. And bring the tray in case we should want a refill."

My heart sank a little. Emily was settling in for a long talk. I glanced at my watch. Nearly six. Jamie would be going home in a few minutes. It was still light, and we had not yet had the change back to standard time, so it would remain so for at least another hour. Nevertheless, I did not like to leave him at home by himself past seven, and I could not be absolutely sure that Martha would be home with him.

"Yes, my dear," Emily said, sitting down again. "I know it's late. But that's hardly my fault, is it?"

"No, it isn't. I was glancing at my watch because . . ."

". . . because you don't like to leave your son by himself at this hour. Quite right. You should have told him to come here. He could have waited in the study and looked at some of Ralph's pictures of horses."

"Emily," I said. "He doesn't know anything about horses. He's not horse mad. Anyway—" Suddenly I decided to be a little more honest with her than I was accustomed to being. Perhaps it was the thought of the scotch. "He thinks you don't like him."

She paused in the act of rearranging the cushion behind her back. "Why on earth does he think that?"

"His actual words were," I said, going for broke, " 'She talks to me like I was a bad smell.' "

Emily sat there totally still. According to her portrait, the one over the mantelpiece in the dining room, she had been a stunningly beautiful young woman. Beautiful, not in the even-featured, photographer's-model sort of way, but because of her magnificent bones, which she had passed on to her daughter, and her eyes, with their impressive Italian lids, seeming half closed when actually wide open.

Instantly I regretted my abrasive frankness. There must have been some other, gentler way I could have told her. But was she gentle with me?

"I see," she said. "I'm very sorry. I had no idea. How uncomfortable he must have been when with me."

I remembered then, of course too late, the times she had taken great trouble to give him pleasure: the afternoons at the circus, the day at the Horse Show, the long drive in the country in her big car with the chauffeur when he was recuperating from a bout with flu and was going almost crazy with being locked in our apartment.

I opened my mouth, but at that moment Trudi came in with the drinks tray, which she put on the oak table across the drawing room. I got up to retrieve both drinks, though I knew that Trudi would bring them to us.

"I'll get them, Trudi," I said, and took them from the tray. I stood there, looking through the windows onto the reservoir in Central Park ten floors below, watching the runners trot around the cinder path surrounding it. Some of the trees were tawny and there was a pale touch of red here and there. I heard Trudi leave, then I went over to Emily's chair carrying her drink.

"You know, when a small boy says that, it doesn't mean what it would if I said it, or you, although I can't imagine your saying such a thing. I should have thought of that, Emily. And of course he doesn't always think that when you're together." I heard the words and knew they couldn't make up for the harm done. "I'm sorry," I said finally. "I suppose I am defensive because I know you're going to give me a rough time about Martha and I feel guilty enough already about her, without your adding to it." I took a big swallow of my drink. "Take a big swallow of your Bourbon. It won't make what I said any more palatable, but it might make you care less."

"I already have. But why should you feel guilty?"

"Because there are times when I think—and I'm sure you think it all the time—that when Patrick died I should have stayed home and minded the store and not gone to the seminary and got ordained."

"Well, I did. But I talked about it to our rector here, and he said he thought that it might have been worse if you had. That as long as the opportunity was there for you to do that, you would have resented not being able to go ahead. After all, if you were willing to give Jamie over to somebody else's care—"

"Jamie had very little of somebody else's care. I took him to a day-care school for part of the mornings, but I managed to arrange my classes so that I did not have to spend that much time away from him, and by the time I had a job, he was at school. As long as he was only there part of the day, I had only a part-time job. As for Martha, she's eight years older and has been in school full-time since her father died. So the problem with her didn't arise."

"You *are* defensive, aren't you? That's probably my fault, too."

"Partly," I said. "But there are my own inner voices, too, which swell the crowd of critics. I didn't have to work. I could have stayed home a few more years. I just didn't want to." Suddenly I noticed that her drink was almost finished. I glanced down then and noticed that mine was almost as empty. "Now that we're both more relaxed," I said, "why don't we start all over again. What, specifically, did you want to talk to me about concerning Martha?"

She held out her glass. "Please fix me and yourself another and then I'll tell you."

When I had the drinks poured and was back in my seat, she said, "I have the feeling that there's something wrong with Martha, something more than her silly eating problem. I don't know what it is. But it's there. And I think we ought to find out."

"Emily, I'd be happy to find out. But how? If there is indeed something there, then a good therapist would find it, I'm pretty sure. But as you know, she's gone to three and left all of them. Either she's totally docile or she's in full rebellion. She doesn't like Jamie, she picks on him or on his dog, she's sarcastic with me when she's not withdrawn, she has her anorexic attacks from time to time when she leaves food around all over her room. Miss Webster from the school called me yesterday morning. She had not turned up for her drama rehearsal or her editorial meeting for the school paper, which she was due for at seven-thirty, and when she finally did show up very late, she admitted being out on some eating binge with a fellow student. After which, of course, she went to the bathroom and was busy throwing it all up when the headmistress tracked her down there at my suggestion. I confronted her with this yesterday evening, and finally used my biggest weapon on her: threatened to send her back to the hospital. She's had these regressions before, and come out of them. This time . . ." I stopped as I remembered my uncomfortable feeling that this time there was something more.

"This time you think there's something more?"

"I don't know, Emily. God knows, I don't want to think so. And it isn't as though anything terribly different has happened . . . I guess she just seems sharper, more hostile, flakier, generally."

"Yes. I agree. She was here yesterday afternoon, you know."

"No, I didn't know. She said she was at a drama rehearsal or something."

"No. That was earlier—or so she told me." Then Emily said slowly, "I don't want to have to say this to you, because things between us are not as pleasant as they might be, already. But one of the things Martha said yesterday, when she was here, was that she was convinced that her father made a mistake in marrying you. That it wasn't the same as when he was married to Priscilla."

Suddenly I remembered her yelling at me, "He should never have married you!" And my own conviction that this was something new with her.

"Yes. She said something of the same to me." And I repeated to Emily what Martha had said. "Was there anything else?" I asked.

"Only that he loved her mother completely and exclusively. It seemed extremely important to her."

We both sat there a moment, silent, listening to the faint crackle of the flames. Then Emily asked, as I knew she would, "Do you have any idea what she meant?"

"None. Patrick and I had our spats—what married couple doesn't? I'm sure that he and Priscilla had, too. The only difference was that Martha wasn't really old enough to know. By the time I came along she heard any disagreement that was going around. But there weren't that many, and they weren't that serious."

"Was Patrick faithful to you?"

"Patrick? Good heavens, yes." I paused. "Theoretically, I suppose, any married person who isn't in the presence of his . . . or her spouse one hundred percent of the time could be unfaithful . . . but Patrick was such a . . . a teddy bear. So much *not* the Don Juan type. I mean, he just wasn't." I looked at Emily. "You knew him. What do you think?"

"I think any man is capable of straying and any woman who doesn't know that is"—she glanced at me out of her hooded blue eyes—"is deceiving herself. However, I agree that with some men it is more likely than others."

"Do you think it has something to do with that? I mean, Martha's present state of mind?"

"I have no more idea than you have, Claire. I am *convinced* that there's *something* there, and this is the first time she's brought that up. That's all. I do know she's more disturbed than she was. I am her grandmother, and even if it offends you and you resent it, I want to find out what it is."

"It does not offend me."

"Doesn't it? Every time I ask you to come here for a talk about

Martha I have the strong feeling that you're turning up in the spirit of the schoolgirl summoned by the Head. And now that you've told me how Jamie feels . . ." She was staring at the bottom of her glass, empty once again. Sometime in the previous five minutes she had refilled both our glasses.

I got up, went over, put my arm around her and kissed her cheek. "I'm sorry," I said, fully aware that if I hadn't had the liquor inside me I would not have had the courage to do it.

"Yes," she said, "that's all very well. I'm fond of you, too. And I'm fond of Jamie. But I've only had daughters, and I'm not sure of myself around boys. But there's something wrong with Martha. She's very like Priscilla. Idealistic, and furious when her ideals don't prove to be correct. With Martha, it's not eating. With her mother, it was dropping out and going off after communes and living in the ghetto and trying to pass herself off as a very light black."

"Good heavens, I didn't know she did that. That could have got her into a lot of trouble."

"Indeed it could. Thanks to an extremely nice black schoolteacher she stopped that after a few days. He told her that if she didn't get her . . . herself back downtown, she'd be in more trouble than she could imagine. That what she was doing could be interpreted as condescending and she'd be made to pay for it as soon as she was found out, and she'd be found out in very short order . . ."

"So she came home?"

"No. She went out and joined a civil-rights group that seemed to specialize in marching . . . that's where she met Patrick, of course."

Suddenly I remembered the picture of them together on Martha's bureau. "They were very alike, Patrick and Priscilla."

"Yes. They both thought the world ought to be perfect and were deeply enraged if it wasn't. Which was why I was so surprised when he married you. Not that I wasn't happy for him," Emily hurried on.

"But I'm not the idealistic type," I said drily.

"Not in the way they were. You're basically rather pragmatic. There's a difference," she said slowly, "between wanting to reform and wanting to help. You're more inclined to help people where they are. Patrick and Priscilla wanted to change the world and its systems. Probably Patrick found you a relief after Priscilla's wild sorrows for all the people and institutions that weren't the way they should be. Still," she said, staring down at her glass, "I wish so much that I had Priscilla to bring up over again."

Or Martha, I thought silently.

I stood there for a moment, my hand on Emily's shoulder. "Are you trying to tell me that Martha's problem is related to that—to disappointed idealism?"

"I am trying to suggest that you might think about it."

"But I don't know where to begin. I don't know what . . . what great ideal—if that's what it is—has been lost."

"I've read some of the literature about anorexia. Aren't the girls who suffer from it—and it seems to be nearly always girls—aren't they supposed to be perfectionists, of one kind or another? And isn't that a form of adhering to an ideal?"

"Yes." I sighed. The task seemed to be even more monumental than I thought—monumental because it was so befogged.

As I went home on the Fifth Avenue bus, Emily's suggestions whirled around in my head. The trouble was, I couldn't get enough of a grip on any of them to know where to start. "Martha—is there something going on in your life—in our lives—that strikes you as desperately unideal . . . ?" My mind played with some dialogue beginning there. But, like Emily's suggestions, it didn't go anywhere. And it also didn't make Martha's snide comments and uncooperative attitudes easier to take either. Why didn't idealism ever seem to express itself on a one-to-one level? And suddenly I thought of Norbert, idealist par excellence. It was well known throughout the church that, however much Norbert yearned over the unfed and the unhoused, when certain not very appealing middle-class people with personal problems wanted to see him to discuss them, he was nearly always out on an appointment. . . . Well, I thought loyally, he's got more important things to do.

I let myself into my apartment. "Jamie, Martha?"

Motley came roaring out and flung himself on me.

"Yeah?" yelled Jamie.

I went back to the living room. There, on his stomach on the floor, was Jamie, watching a television show. I didn't know which one, but cops, cars and chases seemed to be all mixed up. Going over, I turned it off.

Jamie slowly sat up. "Yes, Motley's been for his walk. We were out half an hour and I almost ran. And I've almost done my homework."

"What do you mean by 'almost done'? Almost finished?"

"Well . . . not exactly. I mean, I've almost started."

"We're going to have dinner as soon as I can get it on the table. And while I'm doing it, you're going to start your homework. Honestly, Jamie, I ought to be able to trust you to do that before you watch that garbage."

"Well, you didn't *say* that I was to do it. I just said I'd walk Motley, and I did."

"It's an ongoing rule and you know it. When you get home you walk Motley and then you do homework."

Jamie's face got visibly squarer, redder and more mulish.

"Okay?" I said.

"All right. Come on, Motley."

"Is Martha in?"

"I haven't seen her."

I sighed, went back to her room and knocked on her door. No answer. I knocked again. Then I opened the door.

The bits of food were everywhere—on the floor, on the bureau, on the desk. And a large roach scuttled away as I walked on the carpet over to a pile of crumbled cake. Bending, I picked up the pieces, but knew that nothing short of a thorough vacuuming would do any good. I straightened, only to see another roach over the baseboard.

I have a great fondness for all life and sometimes feel that if I lived up to my principles I'd be a vegetarian, because to me all that lives is in some way linked. Except for cockroaches. Not all the mystic sense of my relationship to the whole can make me do anything but loathe them.

I moved over quickly, knowing as I did so that the wretched roach would simply disappear behind the bureau. Which, of course, it did. I stared behind the back of the furniture, trying to figure out whether I would have to move it, or would one of the narrow fittings to the vacuum be able to slide there?

It was then I saw something white and red crumpled up and stuffed behind the back of the bureau.

Feeling full of despair and rage about my stepdaughter, I leaned over and pulled it out. It was the silk blouse I had lent her, the one she had referred to and on which she had said she had dropped some paint. As I opened it up, I could see the red smears on the front. And then I stared at the stains and tentatively scraped my finger against the dried liquid. As I had known immediately, it was not paint. I put the blouse up to my nose and smelled. Unbelieving, I finally realized it was blood.

6

I SAT ON MARTHA'S BED staring at the blouse. The questions in my mind rang like an alarm that could not be turned off: Where did Martha get this blood? Was it hers? If not, whose was it? Above all else, why did she say it was paint?

Finally, I went across the hall and knocked on Jamie's door.

"Come in," he yelled.

"Do you know anything about this?" I asked, holding the blouse out.

"That's not mine," Jamie said, as I should have known he would if I had not been so traumatized. If anyone attempted to push him around, Jamie was not averse to using his fists, which, of course, meant that at times he ended up with a bloody nose.

"I know it's not yours," I said patiently. "It's Martha's. That is to say, it's mine actually, but she borrowed it. Did she say anything about it to you? She told me she'd spilled paint on it at school, but it's not paint, it's blood."

"You know she never talks to me, or practically never. What's the matter? Somebody punch her in the nose? She probably deserved it."

The thought of Martha having a bloody nose had not occurred to me. I looked back at the stain. With a feeling of relief that I didn't stop to identify I realized that a nosebleed was almost certainly what had produced the stain. "That's what it probably is," I said.

"You'd be mad as anything if it was mine."

"No, I wouldn't. Come on, Jamie, when have I really been mad at you because of a nosebleed?"

"You don't think much of fighting. You're always saying that reason should be used. But I don't see what good reason is when some tough comes and pushes you around."

"You have a point. And furthermore, I've said that before. I don't suppose it's any use asking you if you have any idea where Martha is."

"Nope. It's no use asking me."

I decided not to wait dinner, and we were in the middle of eating when Martha came in.

I got up. "I'll get your dinner," I said.

"I've eaten."

"Where?"

"With some friends at a burger place."

"Why didn't you tell me you were going to?"

"It was a last-minute thing."

"Why didn't you telephone me, then?"

"None of us had a dime."

"Martha—that's just not good enough. You know I can't let that go on. Who did you have dinner with?"

"I told you—just some friends from school."

"Okay—give me their names."

"I'm not going to give you their names so that you can get them into trouble."

"I'm not trying to get them into trouble, Martha."

"You think I'm lying, don't you, Claire?"

"I think it's a possibility."

"You see, you always think the worst of me. And then you wonder why I have problems."

"Martha—I've told you. If . . . if this kind of thing gets worse I'm going to send you back to the hospital."

"What for? Not telling you that I was having dinner out?"

She started to walk back to her room, her hips slouching in a familiar way. She always walked that way when she had just pulled something off. This time it was like gasoline on my anger. Leaving the table, I snatched the blouse up from its roost in the kitchen a few feet away, then marched in pursuit.

"How do you account for this?" I said, pushing the bloodstained blouse under her nose.

She stared at it. "I had a nosebleed yesterday. I bent down to pick something up and hit my nose on the desk. When I felt something wet come out of my nose, I put my hands up, and then brushed them against my blouse before I knew what I was doing. Then the blood fell on it. Sorry. I know it's your blouse."

"That's not important. But why did you tell me it was paint?"

Martha shrugged. "I didn't want another boring fuss."

"Why did you push it behind the bureau?"

"Because, knowing how much you like to snoop in my room, I thought you might find it before I could get it to the cleaner's and then your feelings would be hurt. Since you've found it, then maybe you'd put it with the next batch to go to the cleaner's." And she swayed down the rest of the long hall and into her room.

I stood there watching her. I didn't believe she'd been out with friends for dinner. I was pretty sure she had eaten nothing, and then come in late claiming to have eaten, so that she wouldn't have to have dinner. I didn't know what to believe about the blouse. What she said made more sense than anything else. I also felt like an inadequate fool.

"You can't win, Ma," Jamie said as I sat down again in the L off our living room. "Not with her."

"It looks that way," I said.

Jamie, I noticed, had polished off his hamburger, his entire baked potato, skin and all, and was finishing his salad. His broccoli was untouched.

"Why didn't you eat your broccoli?"

"I don't like broccoli."

I pondered the experience of a friend of mine who went to an English boarding school. She didn't like fish and one day left it. The fish —the same fish—was presented to her the following meal, instead of the meat that was provided to the others. When she didn't eat the fish then, it came back the meal after that, and the meal after that. Eventually, she ate it. There was no other way to get rid of it.

"You should be glad you're not in an English boarding school," I said.

"Why?"

I told him about the fish.

"That's cruel and unusual punishment," Jamie said. "What's for dessert?"

While he was eating his fruit, I said suddenly, "If somebody asked you what was wrong with Martha, what would you say? And I don't want a smart-ass answer, either."

Jamie put almost a quarter of an apple in his mouth and chewed.

"She's always been queer. But I think something else's going on."

"What makes you think so?"

"Well, she and I've never been buddies. But she was getting to the point where every week or so we'd actually have a conversation without her being sarcastic about my weight or Motley or something. But it's back to the sarcasm now. I don't know. Something's bugging her. But she's not going to tell you what it is."

"Why not?"

"Because then you'd go back to not paying so much attention to her. To paying more to me."

"All right, Dr. Freud." I stared at my eight-year-old son. I couldn't believe that he'd thought that out by himself. He was no student of psychology or anything else. On the other hand, he had more than once come up with some sharp perceptions. From the standpoint of grades, he wasn't the brightest thing around, but he was wise.

"Did you think that up all by yourself?"

"Not exactly. Jack's sister was walking home with us one day, and she said she thought Martha did her things to get attention. And that she was jealous of me."

"I thought you were supposed to be jealous of her—her grades, her great brain, et cetera."

"Laura said she thought Martha envied me because people liked me."

"Well, it's nothing to be smug about," I said.

"I'm not smug. You asked me. Can I have a chocolate-chip cookie?"

"No. You can help me clear up."

After he had helped me, grudgingly, to clear the table, I gave him a chocolate-chip cookie.

It was several days later that Norbert came into my office and said, "Rafael's girlfriend has just stated that Rafael was with her Monday morning—that he didn't leave her apartment until nearly eight o'clock."

I turned from my desk. "Terrific! I hope the police released him immediately."

"You know better than that, Claire. It's going to take more than the unsupported word of a Hispanic girl who's already had her share of trouble with the cops to get them to let Rafael go."

"What kind of trouble?"

"Oh, the usual—minor drugs and a little hustling. What do you expect of a girl hampered by language and race and unaided by an inadequate educational system?"

"Well, she might do as Susan Bailey's done," I said.

Susan Bailey was the parish secretary. She came from a black home in the heart of the ghetto. Her father had died when she was twelve, and her mother, working as a cleaning woman, put her four children through parochial school, from which three of them won scholarships to colleges. In addition to having a B.A., Susan was a crackerjack stenographer, a skill she picked up in her spare time while at college. She was now saving her money and going to night school to get her master's in clinical psychology.

"I'm surprised at you, Claire," Norbert said agreeably. "Falling into that trap."

"What trap?"

"It's one of the reactionary's favorites: 'Since the Susan Baileys of the ghetto have made it, it just proves that it's up to the individual and there's nothing wrong with the system.' "

"Look—stop sounding like an editorial from the *Times* or the Washington *Post!* I'm not saying anything about the system. I'm just saying that a girl from the ghetto doesn't have to go on the streets or get into drug dealing. There are other options—even on One Hundred Fortieth Street!"

"Sorry—I guess I've heard Susan dragged up as an example too often, so I fill in the rest of the blanks. But you've got to admit, she's unusual for a product of the ghetto."

"She'd be unusual if she were black, white or candy-striped. But what's that got to do with it?"

Norbert's wonderful smile suddenly appeared. "Let's not fight. We both agree she's marvelous. Now if the cops will just take Tessa's word about Rafael, we'll all be much happier." He took his hands out of his pockets and started moving towards the door.

"What's very interesting indeed," I said, rolling some fresh paper in the typewriter, "is that if Rafael is innocent, then who killed Dick?"

Norbert turned at the door. "As I said, I don't think they're going to get their clutches off Rafael that easily."

"Yes, but it looks as though they may have to, which leaves the question of the year: who's the murderer?"

"Good heavens, Claire, you sound like something out of Agatha Christie. It's surely more serious than that! This isn't a whodunit. It's real. Dick is really dead. His sister and brother-in-law are really coming for the funeral service tomorrow. Rafael, a young man with his whole life in front of him, is really in jail."

"I didn't say it wasn't serious, Norbert. What on earth's the matter with you? So, far from treating it as though it were a paperback mystery, I'm profoundly aware that if Rafael is not the culprit, then someone else is. As you just pointed out, Dick is dead, and somebody is responsible. If not Rafael, then who?"

Norbert was a brilliant man—an Oxford degree on top of one from Yale certainly attested to that. So did packed churches, silent and mesmerized under his considerable powers as a preacher. Yet trying to get him to cooperate in a line of conversational logic was like trying to catch fog in a sieve. It was impossible.

"Well," Norbert said, standing in the doorway, "there's talk about some woman they said had gone out the parish house door at around the crucial time. Only nobody seems to know who it is."

"I know. That charming man, Detective O'Neill, did more than just hint that two people—Josie and Matthew Pearson—thought it was me. He even told me not to leave town."

"Were you planning to?"

"No, of course not. Still, it's unnerving."

Norbert frowned a little, looking at me as though seeing something he hadn't seen before, and then, with a wave of his hand, walked away. And he left me with an uncomfortable and unfocused feeling that I couldn't quite identify.

Dick Grism's funeral service the next day had a respectable number of people in attendance. Three strangers sitting in the front pew turned out to be his sister, his brother-in-law and another sister. The rest were members of the congregation who showed up more out of loyalty to the church, and as a gesture of showing the flag, than out of affection for Dick. It was ten o'clock in the morning of a workday, so, of necessity, the congregation was more made up of housewives and the retired element than of those who were out in the marketplace. Ironically, because of that fact, those present were drawn from the heart of the stalwart conservatives. Ironic, because of Norbert's homily.

It was not long, but it was to the point. "This will, of course," he said in his beautiful voice, "be an opportunity for those of the community—here and elsewhere in the city—who have opposed the Church's help to the poor, the outcast and the ill to beef up their cries against opening up our gates to allow in those less fortunate than ourselves."

The deliberate slang, "beef up," added color and bite to Norbert's measured words delivered in his Anglican and Anglo-American cadences.

"But I prefer to think," he went on, "that even more will see it as a sign for greater effort. This terrible death rises above its police categorization as an individual crime. It is the inevitable result of an unequal and unjust society . . ."

From where I sat in the chancel, vested to assist in the service, I could see Brett's face. He was sitting in a side pew, his eyes on Norbert's face, a quizzical look on his own. This sermon is for you and those like you, Brett, I thought, so take off the quizzical look and put on one more suited to accompany the penitent's *mea culpa*. The words were no more formed in my mental processes than Brett's eyes abruptly switched to meet mine. Ever so slightly, one eye winked.

It was so apt, so outrageous that I frowned immediately and then lowered my own gaze in mortal fear that I would giggle. This is terrible, I thought, my eyes glued to my pumps, my lips almost soldered together to prevent an ill-bred, ill-timed and totally unwanted laugh to escape. It was not funny, I raged at myself, to be struck on the head and killed as Dick was. To keep a sense of where I was and why, I looked at the coffin on its stand, a huge spray of roses nearby in a vase.

Dick Grism was a big man. Because he was always in a wheelchair one forgot that and thought only of the withered legs in a perpetual sitting position. But his torso was large, even fat. The huge muscles that had once carried Dick across a football field became fleshy rolls bulging against his shirt. His belly was soft and protruded almost to his knees. The humiliation of it to a onetime athlete must have been one of the greater galls to his pride. And I knew from personal and uncomfortable experience that he was sensitive.

Martha would sometimes drop by my office for lunch during school holidays, most often when we'd arranged it, but occasionally to surprise me. This usually only occurred when her illness was more or less in regression. One unhappy time when, although I didn't know it, she was about to embark on another period of aberrant behavior, she came to my office a little early and was told I was downstairs at a staff meeting. Restless and unwilling to sit and wait, she came back down the stairs again and saw the meeting going on through the open conference room door. I saw her and, since my part of the meeting was over, came out. As we left the area of the conference room, Martha said in her clear, carrying voice, "Who's that terribly fat man who was sitting beside you? He's truly gross."

I didn't answer her until we were upstairs in my office with the door closed, at which point I lit into her. "You wanted him to hear that, didn't you?"

She shrugged. "Can I help the acoustics? I just talked in my normal voice."

"No, you did not. You were being deliberately loud. How can you do such a thing? Dick's a paraplegic. My God—couldn't you see he was in a wheelchair?"

"No, I couldn't. And anyway, all the more reason why he shouldn't let himself get that obese. It makes me feel sick . . ."

We never had the lunch. Instead, we had a fight. Martha, enraged and in tears, fled down the stairs and out. I stood by my window for a while, debating whether I should go down and make some kind of apology—Dick could not have failed to hear—or just ignore the whole thing. Finally, picking up some paper representing projects I was going to have to talk to Dick about, I went down. His door was closed. Knocking, I went in. As I did so, he looked up.

His eyes had a curious shine to them. For an appalled moment I wondered if what I was seeing was tears. Then I knew it wasn't.

"What can I do for you, Claire?" He spoke in a hearty voice.

I hesitated.

"More projects?" he said, holding out his hand. "Let me see."

I wanted so much to undo the harm that was done. But in unspoken yet powerful ways Dick was conveying an unmistakable message: don't bring up the subject.

Later I debated writing a note and tried to bully Martha into sending one, with no apparent effect. In the end, I did nothing.

"How did Dick become a paraplegic?" I finally asked Sally Hepburn. As the rector's secretary, she often knew more about the staff than anyone else.

"A hunting accident. It was pretty awful. He was headed for a partnership in a big accounting firm, married and so on. Then he had the accident. About a year or so later, when he was learning more or less how to go out into the world again, he found his wife had been having an affair. They were living in the suburbs. He divorced her and moved into the city. He got the job here at about that time."

I told her what had happened.

"No, don't try and make it up to him. It's the one subject that he can't bear to talk about. He was a star football player. Haven't you seen that team photograph behind his desk?"

"Yes, but I didn't put it together with him."

"Well, there he is, slap in the middle. Looking large and lean and tough. Heaven knows, he had the football player's build. But it was all muscle. What on earth made your stepdaughter say something like that meaning to be overheard? It's so cruel."

"It's because she has an obsession about fat. She's an anorexic."

"Oh—yes. I know. I heard somebody on the radio one morning interviewing somebody who'd written a book about it. That must be a worry for you."

"That's an almost British understatement."

Then, a few days later, I discovered some food hoarded in Martha's room, and I knew we were in for another siege.

I thought about it now as the professional pallbearers struggled under what was obviously a heavy load. Poor Dick, I thought. And almost as an act of prayer tried to think of something about him that I liked. And I came back to my statement to Detective O'Neill: I liked the fact that I felt free to dislike him. But as a valediction it lacked warmth.

I found myself walking beside Brett on our way back to the parish house.

"I wish I'd liked him better," I said.

"Dick?"

"Yes."

"Why? Because of the nature of his death?"

"Yes."

"Claire, you're a sentimentalist. Even bastards die. And some of them die violently because they're bastards."

I looked quickly at him. "Are you telling me that—"

"I'm not telling you anything. I'm just making an obvious statement."

"You picked him as your successor," I said, as I had said before.

"He was a good business manager. And he wanted mightily to please, so he'd be more inclined to be lenient about budgetary matters than I would."

"If you believed you were right in your constant nay-saying, then I'm astonished you'd recommend somebody you knew would run things differently. It sounds almost as though . . ."

"As though it were unprincipled?"

"Yes. As though you were saying to yourself, 'Well, I'm not going to have anything to do with sending the church into debt, but I'll bring in somebody who will.' "

"What a downbeat view you have of people." Brett put his hand under my elbow as we mounted the parish house steps. We could have come into the parish house through the church but had chosen to come the long way around. "As long as I was running the church business and treasury, then I had to do it according to my own priorities. I couldn't do a good job if I did them according to somebody else's. Dick had a different set. So I thought he might do better following Norbert's lead."

"Do you really disapprove of all this?" I pointed to the line, two and three deep, of men and women queuing up inside the parish house and outside on the street for one of the twice-a-week free meals.

"No, I don't. That's one of the activities of the Church and the church—both capital and lowercase *C*—that I approve of. We're supposed to feed the hungry, help the sick, visit those in prison, support those in travail, et cetera. But I don't think that includes, for example, free therapy. Nor do I think it includes some of the younger people queuing up here who could get a job if they wanted one—not a nice job, not a well-paid job, not a job with a great deal of dignity, but a job. If you will look carefully, some of those are quite young, and they're not that badly off. Some of them could work. But they have chosen not to—as a lifestyle. They are also, sometimes, violent. As I said before, ask some of the older people in this line. I think we're making it easy for them to prey on others. That's why some of the older ones won't go to a shelter . . . you know that. I don't have to tell you. And old-fashioned as it may sound, I think we need to give a little *more* money to the missions."

"Missions are not fashionable."

"How well I know. Yet without the schools, clinics and hospitals in Third World countries, the people there would be even worse off than they are now . . ."

I glanced at him as we went through the door. "You just don't like Norbert," I said. "That's your trouble. You two may be old Yalies together, but you still don't like him."

We paused just inside the lobby, at the foot of the short flight of steps going into the central hallway. Past us on the right stood the homeless, the vagrant, the hungry and, I supposed, according to Brett, the younger dropouts lining up for a free meal. I watched them for a minute and then, as I saw them looking back at me, tried to smile.

"Hi, lady," one of them said. He was old, or at least looked old, probably because he didn't have many teeth.

"Hi," I said. And then because I felt I ought to say something more: "It shouldn't be too long now." The words were no more out of my mouth than I felt even more stupid. I knew that the lines started forming around one o'clock and that the food was in the cafeteria ready to be served by two-thirty or three—after the regular lunch people had cleared out. Except for the cook, everyone concerned was a volunteer, with one shift serving on Tuesday and one on Friday. As I stood there with Brett, Janet MacHeath, who ran the Friday shift, came down the line counting.

"Hello, Janet," one or two of them called out.

"Hello, everybody. Ready for lunch?"

"Ready and waiting," several yelled, led mostly by two women standing together halfway up the steps. Somehow I expected them to be old. But neither of these seemed to be, although one, also toothless, could have been any age. The woman who was toothless had stringy yellow hair coming out from under a knitted cap. On her feet were sneakers, reinforced with rags of various kinds. In the immemorial fashion of the New York bag lady, she carried two shopping bags. The woman next to her was light black. She had her teeth, but she was emaciated-looking, and there were sores around her hairline. Something told me those women were in their forties, although they could have been taken for fifty or sixty.

"How're you doing?" I asked Janet.

"Fine, though we're short two helpers today. Molly is still in the country, and Ann is on a business trip."

I opened my mouth to offer my services, impelled by an overwhelming sense of obligation and responsibility.

"If you need help—" I started, and then realized that I had four clients coming this afternoon. Their needs, though different, were also great.

"Yes?" Janet said, turning.

"Nothing." I felt silly and angry at myself.

Janet glanced at me curiously. "If you hear of anybody doing nothing and willing to pitch in, for heaven's sake let me know."

"I will."

As Brett and I went up the short flights, we passed three more men and two women. One of the men was young. He was bearded and looked angry and reminded me of Rafael. The man standing beside him twitched constantly, rubbing his body, shaking his head. There were more along the hall, some talking, most silent. A strong odor of unwashed bodies pervaded their side of the corridor.

"Do you think they have lice?" I asked Brett.

"Many are very clean, but some of them, almost certainly, do."

"I wonder what's done about that."

"I think the helpers and the staff take enormous pains to sterilize and fumigate anything that could spread the—er—wildlife. I know, because some of the bills I get are for various fumigating and sterilizing paraphernalia." As we got up into the hall near Brett's office, he said to me, "You were about to volunteer your services, weren't you?"

"Yes. How did you know?"

"Because if ever I saw a living illustration of the text 'Here, Lord, take me,' it was your face. What stopped you? The thought of other things you might be having to do?"

"Yes." Brett's customary dry tone irritated me. "I don't expect you to understand."

"Of course not. My name is Ebenezer Scrooge. The milk of human kindness is unknown to me."

"Well—did you have an impulse to help out? Or rather to clear them all out and save the money?"

"The latter, of course." He raised his hat an inch and went into his office, hanging the hat on an old-fashioned hat rack in the corner.

I stood there at his door, feeling foolish and also a little mean. Then I went in. "I'm sorry I said that. I shouldn't have."

"That's all right. Norbert would be the first to sympathize with your feelings."

I was reminded of my statement concerning his dislike of the rector. "I was right, wasn't I? You two don't much like each other."

"Not a lot."

"Just because of your difference in viewpoint?"

"It's more than that."

"How do you mean?"

"It's a large subject, Claire, but to begin at the end, I don't like Norbert's deliberate manipulation of the all too easily manipulatable guilt button. Did you feel guilty out there, looking at those living representatives of the poor?"

"Yes."

"All right. Why don't you liquidate the money your husband left you and, leaving just enough for you and your two children to live on, give the rest to any fund you think would manage it well on behalf of the poor and the homeless? There's nothing to stop you. You could move to

Brooklyn or Queens, pay far less rent and send the two children to public school. If you feel that strongly, why don't you do it?"

"Because—because it's money left to them as well. For their education."

"Is that the only reason?"

I thought of my spacious apartment, with its three bathrooms and view of the Museum and Central Park, with the pleasant and well-mannered doormen, guarding my security and taking in packages for me . . . all of the delightful things that money meant. "No, it isn't. I like having money."

"Good for you. At least you're honest. Somebody I once heard on television said guilt is the price we pay willingly for doing what we are going to do anyway. You have the money to live the way you do, and you like it. But to make yourself feel better about yourself, you offer up so many units of guilt. And that is what Norbert plays on. You heard his homily less than an hour ago. The people he's really addressing are not those like himself—the ones in the congregation. He's talking over their heads to what he considers the enemy—the great American middle class, the bourgeoisie, which has always been anathema to the elite, whether it's the intellectual or aristocratic elite. And Norbert qualified under both. People like him have gallons of guilt and are constantly shoring up the underclass—whoever the underclass is at the moment. With Tolstoy, it was the peasant. With Norbert, it's the homeless and the minorities. The Norberts of our society sit on boards and dispense funds for worthy objects and build up merit points either for heaven or for their own self-esteem—more likely the latter. If they didn't have the poor they'd be lost. There would be nobody to vent their virtue on. And the people they most loathe are those in the middle who are still operating on a touching belief in the work ethic and expect others to. Talk to Norbert someday about the middle-American work ethic—he'll explode. Try it and see."

"I would like to think," I said slowly, "that you are a bigoted, biased, narrow-minded, judgmental pain in the derrière. But I shall ponder what you said. Just tell me one thing—did you feel nothing but scorn when you saw all those poor people?"

His dark brows went up. "Who said anything about scorn? There, but for the grace of God, is my feeling. What I said was, I didn't feel guilt. Nor did I feel the need to find a scapegoat to flog. Why should I? What I felt was compassion. And I prefer to act on that."

"Do you?"

"Yes. I do."

"How?"

"I don't think that's any of your business. Come to think of it, how do you express your guilt?"

I went out and slammed the door.

One of my clients canceled out around three-thirty, so I wandered downstairs, ostensibly to pick up any mail that may have come in with the late delivery, but more out of restlessness and a need for company. The thought of doing paper work that was beginning to pile up was more than I could face.

"What's the matter?" Josie asked as I pulled a couple of letters from my box.

"Do I look like something's the matter?"

"Yes. You look like you're expecting the worst."

"I feel like Chicken Little," I said. And was surprised to realize that that was exactly the way I did feel.

"Is your sky about to fall in?"

"It feels that way, but don't ask me which part."

Josie laughed. "Heard the latest about Rafael?"

"No. What about him?"

"The cops are letting him go. They've confirmed what his girlfriend said. He was languishing in bed with her when Dick was killed. Apparently her landlord chose that moment to go in and scream for some rent. I guess he thought maybe Rafael had some that he could get his hands on. Anyway, Rafael's sprung."

"So now where does that leave us?"

Josie shrugged and picked up the receiver as her switchboard buzzed.

"St. Anselm's Church," she said.

Then she looked at me. "It's for you."

"Who's calling?"

Josie repeated the question into the receiver. Then she looked at me. "Detective O'Neill."

My Chicken Little feeling took a giant leap in size.

"Tell him you can't find me."

"I can't. He knows we're talking. What's the matter, Claire?"

What the matter was, was panic. Nevertheless, I was ashamed of myself for behaving in such a cowardly fashion. I might feel like Chicken Little, but there was no excuse for behaving that way.

"All right. Give me a chance to get back up to my phone."

"You can take it in there, if you want." Josie indicated an empty office behind her. "There's nobody there today."

"Thanks a lot," I said drily. "Okay. Put it in there." I went into the office, usually occupied by Norbert's assistant, Robert Hardcastle, now on vacation, and closed the door.

"Hello," I said into the phone.

"Mrs. Aldington?"

"Yes."

"I'd like to come and see you this afternoon. Will you be in your office?"

"What time?"

"Oh, in about half an hour." He paused. "Unless, of course, you could come down here, which would be even better."

"Why would it be better?"

"Because it would save me a journey."

"With all due respect, Detective O'Neill, this comes under the heading of your job more than mine, so why don't you come here."

"All right. See you in half an hour."

"No. I can't do it in half an hour. I will be with a client. The earliest I can see you is four-thirty."

"How come you're not with a client now, Mrs. Aldington?"

"Because my client for this hour canceled out due to a bout with the flu or a virus, or maybe just a desire not to hassle with her therapist. No matter what the excuse, you always wonder."

"All right. Four-thirty."

I replaced the receiver and sat there looking at it. I had not, until that moment, seriously considered myself in the role of suspect. And it seemed to me now ludicrous that anyone else would. Nevertheless, a hand squeezed something in my chest and I felt out of breath. Slowly I walked out of the room.

"What did he want?" Josie asked.

There was a short silence. Josie's a nice girl, if somewhat uninhibited about intrusive questions. But as we looked at one another I could see that she, as well as I, could put together the two facts: Rafael was no longer a suspect. Ergo, they (the police) were turning their attention to someone else, and Detective O'Neill was coming to see me.

I wanted to say something light, such as "I hope you'll come and see me when I'm in jail." But I couldn't. This was murder, and the person who was murdered was someone we both knew. Instead I said, "He's coming at four-thirty. So when he arrives, send him upstairs." And walked down the hall.

A therapist, like a doctor, has to develop a facility of turning off personal concerns while listening to clients and patients. Up to a point I was able to do this, but behind the words coming at me from the woman and the boy who, successively, sat across from me, and behind my own words going back to them, lay both fear and pain.

The boy, my last client of the day, left at four-fifteen, and I was able to confront my own problems. It did not once occur to me simply to leave, although I'd been aware while talking to O'Neill that he had to take into consideration the fact that I might. When finally Josie buzzed me and told me O'Neill was on the way up, it was almost a relief.

He came in, shrugged off his raincoat and put it on a chair by the wall.

"Sit down, Mr. O'Neill," I said, indicating the armchair across from me.

"Is that where your patients sit?"

"Yes, but since I'm not a psychiatrist—an M.D.—I call them clients." I paused. "I heard you let Rafael go."

"Yes. His alibi stood up."

"And you're now here to find out if I'm that woman that two people claimed to see."

"Are you?"

"No. I had not been in the parish house before the time Josie looked up and saw me and identified me as me—the time when I picked up my messages."

"Then who do you think it is?"

"Mr. O'Neill—how would I know? Some other woman."

"Some other woman who looks enough like you, at least at that distance, to have two people mistake you for her."

"I'm medium height, medium build. That could cover a lot of people."

"You're medium height but I would say on the slender side, at least by my standards you are. And you have unusual-colored hair. Does anyone else you know have that color of hair?"

"Only my son, and he's an eight-year-old boy. I don't think that the wildest leap could have mistaken him for me."

"Where were you between the hours of seven and seven-thirty?"

"At home."

"What time did you leave your apartment?"

"Around seven-thirty, seven-forty."

"Is there anyone who could verify that?"

"No. Both my son and my stepdaughter left early for pre-school meetings."

"Well, like I said, you have unusual-colored hair—a dark red-brown."

I knew then why I was so afraid. I was afraid because, as clearly as though it were in front of me, I could see the shelf in the hall closet where there was a reddish-brown beret that both Martha and I often wore. And at the cleaner's was the silk shirt on which, she said, her nose had bled.

7

"THANK YOU," I said, as lightly as I could. "If it's meant as a compliment—about my hair, I mean."

The detective was looking at me steadily. "You sound nervous. Are you?"

"Isn't it a little nervous-making to be considered the lead suspect in a murder case?"

"I haven't said you were the lead suspect."

"Maybe not. But I sure feel like it."

"Then that's probably because of something you know rather than any treatment of mine."

He was so on target that I was badly shaken.

"What is it?" he asked suddenly.

"Nothing. If you don't think being questioned again and again as to whether I was the woman that those two people saw isn't enough to make you feel like a leading suspect, then you don't know as much about people's feelings, Detective O'Neill, as I thought you did."

Suddenly he shifted gears. "How well did you know Dick Grism?"

"Haven't we talked about this before?"

"No, I asked if you liked him. I didn't ask how well you knew him."

"I didn't know him well. I knew him in relation to his job at the church—would he give me money for causes that I thought were worthwhile?—that kind of thing. As we have discussed, he wasn't my favorite person—which means that he wasn't somebody I'd drop in on in an idle moment to chew the fat with. We had perfectly amiable relations, but I didn't see him *à deux*, so to speak, unless there was a reason, which usually turned out to be me asking for money."

"Then I take it you don't know that there are large sums of money missing from the church's capital holdings."

I stared. "No, I didn't. Who—why—?"

"If we knew who or why, then other things would probably come clear."

After a minute I said, "Who told you?"

"The rector, Mr. Shearer. But he got the information from the present business manager, Mr. Brett Cunningham of the Chadbourne Guaranty Trust." Detective O'Neill's voice was so dry when he said that that in spite of my horror and growing anxiety I smiled.

"One doesn't go around questioning chairmen of the board in the same way one does someone like Rafael, does one?"

The detective said woodenly, "We don't play favorites in homicides, Mrs. Aldington."

"Come on now, Detective O'Neill. Don't give me that. With the Rafaels of the world you haul them downtown, question them and, if you're not satisfied, throw them in the clink."

"And if we have disregarded one single item of the various rules governing questioning, your Rafael will go free, and live to rob, rape or kill somebody else, because some cop left a word out of the Miranda statement when he was reading him his rights. You know that as well as I do. A young teacher who was alive last week is dead now because a creep that everybody knows is guilty as hell of raping and killing was free to walk into a school classroom after everybody but the teacher'd gone home. You read the papers."

"So—are you taking Brett downtown for questioning? The way you did Rafael?"

"Rafael had stolen money in his pocket—money which had come from the victim's cash drawer—and was suspected of being involved in Grism's murder. Brett Cunningham, who discovered the financial discrepancy, is not suspected—as yet—of having anything to do with his predecessor's murder. How much clearer can I make it?"

"All right. What do you want from me?"

"I want you to tell me about the woman who came into the parish house early, went into Grism's study, had a fight with him about something, killed him and then left and was seen going out the parish door by two people who know you quite well and thought it was you."

"Are you charging me with killing Dick Grism?"

"No, I'm not. But I know you're hiding something, and I want to know what it is. Furthermore, sooner or later I'll find out."

"In the meantime, unless you intend to charge me, I'm going to ask you to leave. And the next time you want to talk to me, I'm going to have a lawyer present."

The officer got up. "You're sounding more and more like a leading suspect."

"Good afternoon, Detective O'Neill," I said, and turned my attention to a blank sheet of paper stuck in my typewriter, to which I kept my eyes glued while I heard O'Neill leaving the room. At the top of the page I had typed, in all caps: SUNDAY'S SERMON. Only this morning had I realized, with a sinking heart, that it was my turn to deliver the homily at Sunday's eleven o'clock service. Of all my various duties, this was the one I liked least. Participating in the liturgy, leading the prayers, reading the lessons from the Old and New Testaments—all these gave me the sense of sharing immense and ancient riches; they brought peace, assurance, even exaltation. But composing a ten-minute homily was a duty that I avoided as often as possible.

"I don't know why you feel that way," Norbert had said once. "It's not as though you weren't good."

"No, I'm not, Norbert," I had replied, driven to honesty. "At my best, I'm adequate. But whatever inspiration I have comes when I am helping people on a one-to-one basis. Getting up and telling them how to live and what to do makes me feel such a phony."

"Who said you had to tell them what to do?"

"Isn't that one of the functions of a homily? It was described in at least one dictionary as a 'tedious, moralizing discourse.'"

"Is that what you think I give?"

I looked quickly at him. Norbert was a man of many moods and reactions. His face could freeze faster than anyone else's. But with a spurt of relief, I saw he was smiling. "You know I don't, Norbert. Your sermons are nationally known—look at all the invitations you get from other churches. But who can compete with that?"

"Come on now, Claire, we're not in competition. You know better than that . . ." And he had changed the subject.

I stared now at the totally blank page under the optimistic headline.

What I wanted to talk about was life as a thirty-five-year-old woman with an anorexic stepdaughter whom it was my job to protect and help at whatever cost and however much she resisted being helped.

"Oh God," I said, pulled the paper from my typewriter and threw it in the wastebasket under my desk.

I was sometimes vain about my capacity for self-discipline but to write a sermon today was beyond my powers. What else needed doing? I glanced at the papers on my desk. On top was an application filled in by one of my clients who had just lost his job. He wanted a church grant for his therapy that would extend at least six weeks until he had been able to collect some unemployment compensation and look for another job. That meant, of course, going to see either Brett or Norbert. I hesitated, knowing that, of the two, I would have a far better chance with Norbert. On the other hand, the protocol of the church was such that I should at least try Brett first. If he turned me down, then I could go to Norbert.

I glanced at my watch. It was ten after five and I had every excuse in the world to go home. On the other hand, I preferred to avoid the worst of the rush hour if I could, and in another twenty-five minutes the buses might be a shade less crammed. Or did I just want to have another talk with Brett? When it occurred to me that the answer might be yes, I paused, application in hand, astonished at myself. Why on earth would I want to see that disagreeable, reactionary, hidebound banker-cum-business manager with whom I disagreed on almost every subject?

Because, the answer finally came to me, although he was just as disagreeable, hidebound, reactionary, et cetera, as I thought he was, he had a way of supplying hard, pragmatic comments that were often helpful. Which was the reason why I was thinking of confiding my state of mind to him rather than to Norbert, who was my rector and technically my spiritual director. Also he had a nice smile.

I ran down the stairs and saw Josie packing up her tote bag before going home. "Listen," I said, on the spur of the moment, "can I ask you something?"

"Sure. But make it quick. I have to get across town and down to the Village before six."

I took a breath. "Did you really think it was me you saw early on the morning that Dick was murdered?"

Josie didn't answer for a moment, but went on stuffing her bag with various packages she seemed to have acquired. Finally she looked up.

"You know I'm sorry I told that cop that I thought it was you, but he caught me when I wasn't thinking. And I did think it was you." She seemed defensive. "But I don't want you to think that I was trying to get you into trouble. I wasn't. And I can't believe you'd have anything to do with Dick's death."

It was a very nice statement and a testament of faith. Yet it left me feeling far more uneasy than I had been. The fact that she felt impelled to say she couldn't see how I could be mixed up in anything like the murder, meant to me that, shocking though it might be, she was, now, making that connection.

"It's okay," I said, as evenly as I knew how. "In a sense it makes my job a lot easier than yours. I *know* I didn't pop in here early on Monday morning and whack Dick on the head, whereas you have to hang on to the belief for dear life . . ." It was an unfortunate metaphor, I decided.

"Yeah," Josie said, picking up her tote bag. "Well, keep the faith and all that." And she walked from behind her desk into the hall and, with a slight wave of her hand, out the parish house door.

I had not, until that moment, come across anybody who believed I might be responsible for Dick's death . . . that it was I who had rammed that heavy bookend against his skull, crushing parts of it, cutting open the skin so that the blood vessels would break and pour blood down the face and over the dead eyes . . . But now I had. For Josie Beardsley, the not very efficient receptionist whom I had taken for granted and occasionally made jokes about, it was not outside the realm of possibility that I could be a murderer. My sense of shock appalled me. Worse still, I had an odd feeling of disorientation, as though an essential part of my personality that everyone knew as me had been called into question. It was far worse, somehow, that Josie should consider it possible that I had killed Dick than that Detective O'Neill did. To a degree I felt that it was part of his job to feel that way about everybody, and that it just happened to be my turn and would undoubtedly, in the course of time, become someone else's.

"What's the matter?"

I turned. Brett, in his shirt sleeves and with his collar open, was coming out of one of the cupboards where we kept stationery supplies. Under his arm was a package of typing paper and in his hand some envelopes.

"Josie would get those for you if you wanted," I said, and to my astonishment and horror burst into tears.

"Hey—what's the matter?"

I shook my head, unable to speak and humiliated by the tears. In a minute they stopped and I mopped up my eyes with a tissue dug out of my pocket. "Sorry about that," I said, and completed my shame by hiccoughing.

"Come into my office," Brett said. "Now come on, don't argue."

Since I had come down to see him anyway, I didn't attempt to, but walked meekly beside him into the office that had once been Dick's.

I looked around. "Does it spook you to be in here?" I asked him.

"No. It's been cleaned and various articles, including the carpet, are at the cleaner's now. There are those who believe that violent emotions impregnate walls. But even if that's right I don't intend to be here long enough to let them bother me."

I was standing beside an armchair next to the desk. He came towards me and with his hand on my shoulder pushed me down into it. "Now what's bothering you?"

"It's nothing really, I was just being stupid for a moment—"

"You mean that at"—he glanced at his watch—"exactly five-twenty in the afternoon you burst into tears as a matter of habit?"

"No, of course not—idiot!" I said, half amused, half angry.

"Then what is it?"

His blue eyes, very steady under the level dark brows, were watching me with—I suddenly recognized—great kindness.

"Josie thinks I murdered Dick," I said.

"Even Josie, limited as she is, couldn't be that stupid."

I felt some of my identity that had seemed lost or misplaced restored. "Thanks for the vote of faith. But she does. And so does Detective O'Neill."

"Why?"

I took a breath. "Both Josie and Matthew Pearson—one of the

custodians—saw a woman leaving the parish house at around seven-thirty, twenty to eight, Monday morning, and both thought it was me. So when I really came in a few minutes before eight, and Josie came in, she was startled—and said so."

"Was it you?"

"No."

"Then is it just the shock of thinking those two lame-brains might feel suspicious that has upset you?"

I looked at him. "You believe me."

"Of course."

There was a silence while we looked at one another. Finally I said, "Thanks." And then: "Brett, you're really going to think I'm flaky, but although I was unstrung for a minute when I thought that Josie seemed to accept my guilt that easily, it's not me I'm really worried about. It's Martha."

He frowned. "What's she got to do with this?"

"Because I think she was here early that morning. As Detective O'Neill didn't fail to point out, my hair is rather—er—conspicuous. In other words, it's easy to spot. According to him, both Josie and Matthew mentioned it. The trouble is, Martha has a beret she often uses that is almost the same color. As a matter of fact, to cloud the issue, we both use it. And there's blood on the silk blouse she wore that day which she says was from a nosebleed . . ." My voice trailed off.

"You think it's Martha."

"No, I don't. I can't see how it could be. But I'm worried."

"Why would she want to kill Dick?"

"I don't know. But I've told you about her. An awful lot that she does doesn't make sense. She's an anorexic, which means that in one phase she's obedient and compliant. Will do anything anybody asks. She was like that for a while after Patrick died. And then about a year afterwards, she started acting up—not eating, being hostile and rebellious in a sort of passive way, hateful towards Jamie—a thoroughly unpleasant person. Even Emily dragged me in to talk about it—well, you know how Emily feels. She said she was sure something was bothering Martha, but she didn't know what. We started talking about Priscilla then—Martha's mother—and by various steps that led her to ask me if Patrick was faithful to me, which struck me as really off the wall."

"Was he?"

"Yes, he was. He was simply not the womanizing type—honorable to the nth degree, and filled with views about the equality of the sexes and the old double standard, which he considered an obscenity. I can't imagine him two-timing anyone."

"I wonder, then, why Emily brought it up."

"I don't know. I wonder, too."

"To be hostile, unpleasant and anorexic is one thing. But do you think that means she'd kill? I don't see the connection."

"I don't either."

"Have you talked to her about this?"

"No. It hadn't been remotely necessary to do so until today, and I haven't seen her today at all. She was gone long before I left this morning."

"What does she do on these early-morning jaunts?"

"Various school activities. When she's well and functioning properly, she's engaged in half a dozen things. She's editor of the school paper and is involved in the school play. Plus she's something of a gymnast and likes to practice early when the teacher's there."

Brett was walking slowly around the room, his hands in his pockets. "Have you heard about the shortfall on the money?"

"Yes—I'd forgotten that. O'Neill told me. How much is missing?"

"A lot. A couple of hundred thousand, if I'm right."

"Did Dick embezzle it?"

"It looks that way, although there's no solid proof as yet."

"How was it done?"

"Well, as you know, the church has to live on far more than is taken in in collections or pledges. A rich church, like a rich college, has bequests, gifts, endowments and so on given to it by wealthy parishioners. These are invested, and the income put into a checking account from which money is drawn for various uses. What Dick—or somebody—was doing, was selling the capital holdings, but always leaving enough money in the checking account, so that if anybody looked at it, the balance would, at least on a casual inspection, seem to be okay. But there's no income coming in from those holdings, or at least from some of them, because they'd been sold."

"And nobody noticed?"

"No, because the checking account would look more or less as it should. Sooner or later, of course, the whole thing would come apart, and then the church would notice with a vengeance. But for a while, at least, it could be covered up."

"That's terrible," I said inadequately.

"It is indeed."

I tried to picture Dick, his eagerness to please, his ingratiating ways, slowly draining the church of its funds, to do—what?

"What on earth did he want the money for? I mean, I suppose that's a stupid question. People want money because of what it can buy. I guess what I meant was, I wonder what he did with it."

"We don't know yet. To be fair to him, we're not yet sure that he did it, or if he did, that he acted alone. And we certainly don't know where it went."

I sat and stared out the window. Park Avenue on a late autumn afternoon is a sight I'd measure against any comparable scene in the world—the Champs-Elysées, Piccadilly Circus or the huge arch at Hyde Park Corner. Opposite the parish house was the Colony Club, where Emily Chadbourne had Brett for lunch. Further down, the great glass skyscrapers were lit up, and the trees down the center island were bearing the last leaves of the year. The western sky, what could be seen of it between buildings, was beginning to get a pre-sunset pink.

"New York," I said out of the blue, "is really much more beautiful than it gets credit for being."

"Yes."

"How did Norbert take the news?"

"With commendable calm. He simply said that it made the selling of St. Cuthbert's all the more urgent, if the church is to continue its outreach." Brett stopped by the window and stared out for a moment, his hands in his pockets. In the back of his shirt, I noticed, was a tear with a few clumsy stitches holding it together. A wife would have done something about that long since, I thought. And then wondered if I was old-fashioned in my views. During my marriage to Patrick, it was I who snatched various garments out of his hands and mended them. He was supremely indifferent to what he wore, and once left the house with an unseemly hole in his trousers, an inch or so from his fly. I didn't discover it until he came home. When I told him I felt mortified for him to be seen that way, he accused me—only half joking—of middle-class values and puritanism.

"You don't believe that Martha hit Dick on the head, or do you?" Brett asked now.

"I'm not entirely sure. I just can't imagine why she'd do such a thing. It's true that she can be . . . well, if not violent, at least rough. She once lowered a broom handle on poor Motley's back. Luckily he got out of the way in time, but it could have hurt him."

"Would you say she's cruel—as a regular thing, by nature?"

"No. Not at all. She had a rabbit once that she adored . . ." My voice faded away.

"What happened to it?"

"I'd forgotten this. Patrick, my husband, her father, who could be very . . . well, dumb about some things, once said that he couldn't understand people who spent time and money—especially money—on animals when they could give it to people in need. When Martha heard that, before I could stop her, she took the rabbit to the vet and had it destroyed."

"Umm. Well, in a grim way, it follows. Sheila, my daughter, would pretend that she'd love presents we gave her when, as I discovered later, she hadn't the faintest interest in them. An awful lot of things came to light when she got sick, and the passion to please was one of them." He sighed and sat down in his chair on the other side of his desk. Slightly rumpled, his hair showed more dark than gray, which made him look younger. Also, it seemed to me that his face, lately, was thinner.

Suddenly he said, "Let's try and think the way a detective would. With your stepdaughter, Martha, in the frame of mind you describe, I can't imagine anything worse than going off half cocked to accuse her of being in the building. Is there any connection you can think of between Dick Grism and Martha? For there to be a motive for killing —and for a high school girl it would have to be a powerful one, or seem that way to her—there has to be a connection. Is there one?"

"A connection?" I said blankly.

"Yes, a connection. If he did steal this money, what would it have to do with her, if anything? Was there any place where their lives, or anything about them, met?"

"The only thing I can think of was that awful time that Martha—with her obsession about weight—made a rude remark about Dick's being fat and gross well within his hearing. She didn't know he was a paraplegic," I said quickly. "Although I'm bound to say when I told her that she simply said it was all the more reason why he should watch his weight."

"Did he hear it?"

"He couldn't have helped but hear it. I went down to his office later to see if I could explain that she had an obsession on the subject and kind of smooth it over, make him feel better, but in some way it's hard to describe, I knew, beyond any doubt, that I must *not* bring it up. He was heartier than ever. But he held me at arm's length and drowned me out. Sally Hepburn explained that it was sort of an obsession with *him,* because he'd been a star football player and athlete and it was the one subject he couldn't bear to discuss. I felt awful."

"Yes," Brett said, "he fought the good fight against getting fat, but in the last couple of years it gained on him. A lot of the thickness of his chest, of course, was muscular, hauling himself around in and out of the chair. But below that it was pure fat. And what the hell else did he have in life—no wife, no sports. Because of having to watch his intake of liquid like a hawk—for obvious reasons—he couldn't drink. When he went home about all he could do was eat and watch television and/or read."

"And collect power," I said, without thinking.

Brett looked at me sharply. "What makes you say that?"

"The way he liked to make people grateful to him. You never cared whose feelings you trampled on in your efforts to save money. But he'd lead you on to believe that he was going to find a way of fitting in your own particular pet expense. Of course, a lot of the time you found out he didn't. But by then you'd been feeling warm and cozy for some time."

"You're speaking of yourself, I take it."

I sighed. "Yes."

"Let's get back to the connection between Martha and Dick. To your knowledge, that's the only time there'd been any meeting between the two."

"Yes."

"Did she come here much?"

"No. In fact, that was the last time. Before that, before she got so ill, she used to come here, but I was with her the whole time. She'd come to my office and then we'd go out to have lunch. As far as I know, she'd never even seen him before that fatal time she came down and saw us all there around the conference table. In fact, if she had seen him before, then she wouldn't have made that comment in exactly that way."

Brett had turned his swivel chair and was sitting staring out the window, with his feet on the radiator. "Then if there is a connection, that meeting—when she was being offensive—must have something to do with it. But why?"

I got up. "The only way to find out is to go and ask her."

"Will she tell you? You can't force the information from her. If she's as sick as you tell me, she'll be able to withhold whatever she wants, as long as she wants—unless, of course, you hand her over to the police."

He had turned and was watching me.

"No," I said. "I'm not going to do that."

"I'm quite sure you wouldn't. But you have a revealing face, and I wouldn't lay bets on how long it would take Detective O'Neill or any other experienced cop to worm enough out of you to turn their attention to Martha." Idly, with one hand, he rapped a ruler against the top of his desk.

We sat there for a while. Finally I glanced at my watch. "I have to go. It's more than late enough for me to go home." I got up, and Brett rose slowly to his feet. "See if you can go at it obliquely," he said.

"You don't think she's going to tell me anything?"

"She may say a lot of words. Whether she's going to tell you what connection—if any—there is, or was, with Dick Grism is something else. If that blood is his, she has a lot to hide. She'll have read the papers and listened to television along with everybody else."

He pulled his jacket from the back of his chair, put it on and tightened his collar, pushing up the knot of his tie. "I'll drive you home," he said.

"Do you have a car here?"

"Sometimes I bring it down. There's a garage under the bank, and I can use that."

We walked the five blocks to the bank and then waited while one of the attendants brought his car up.

"I ride in a car so seldom," I said, "I almost don't know how to act. I thought cars in the city were mostly white elephants."

"I suppose, as usual, you're accusing me of being some kind of a conspicuous consumer snob. I don't normally come to work in a car, but I thought I might have to use it this evening to go out into the wilds of New Jersey."

We got into the car and Brett eased towards Park Avenue and the line of cars waiting for the light to change.

"What were you going to do there?" I asked.

"Talk to some of Grism's former neighbors and employers, some of the people who used to work with him."

"Where did he come from?"

"Originally from a small town near Buffalo. But he lived for quite a while in Fairacre. That was before his accident, while he was still with that firm of accountants."

"Fairacre's near Upper Hills, where we used to live. Patrick was rector of St. Michael's there."

"That's right. It's the next town on the suburban line. You didn't know Dick then, did you?"

"No. How long ago was that?"

"About five or six years ago."

"Well, Patrick died five years ago, and we moved out of the rectory a few weeks after that and into New York a month or so following that. So I guess we weren't in New Jersey at the same time. Are you going out there to see if something in his past will provide enlightenment?"

Brett changed gear and turned the corner onto Park. "More or less. The firm he worked for is downtown, near Wall Street, but it also had a branch near Fairacre, and that's where Dick worked."

"His wife took off after he had that accident, didn't she?"

"Yes. It was a rough time for him."

"Did he have any children?"

"I don't think so. He hadn't really been married that long."

"I know I've asked you this before, but do you think he stole that church money?"

"You did ask me before. I told you the evidence looked that way but I had no proof."

"You trained him, didn't you?"

"I only trained him on handling the church finances. I hardly knew him before that."

"But you liked him well enough to push him for the job."

"What are you trying to do, pin this on me? I had no particular feeling for him one way or another. It was Norbert who wanted him to take the job of business manager, and was pushing him. I saw that he'd give Norbert a lot more of what he—Norbert—wanted, so I went along, as I explained to you a day or so ago."

We drove for a while in silence. Then I said, "You know, Norbert must have felt he could get what he wanted out of him, because on the face of it, Dick was about the last person he'd like—in fact, he represented what Norbert most disliked—the upwardly mobile middle class."

"Norbert, like most people, even clergy, are willing to forgo their pet prejudices when it is to their own interests."

We stopped at a red light at Seventy-ninth Street. "Did Norbert go into the Church right after Yale—no, I remember now—it was a late vocation, to use our Roman brethren's language. What did he do?"

"He went to England. That's when he got his Oxford degree, but he was over there for quite some time, doing what, I'm not quite sure. Traveling, I think. Since he has a handsome private income, he was always more or less free to do what he wanted."

"Weren't you on the Search Committee when they went looking for a rector?"

"I was."

"And you approved of Norbert? Given your views, that surprises me."

"I was one of those who voted against him. But he had a stunning record of activism in his previous church, and I—and my side—lost."

We pulled up outside my apartment. I had been wrestling with something all during our drive up Park Avenue. Graciousness would indicate that I should invite Brett to dinner. And anyway, since he had to go to New Jersey, he would surely refuse. I decided to be gracious.

"If you don't have to be in outer New Jersey immediately, why don't you come in and have dinner. It'll be chicken casserole and a salad. But you're welcome."

"I'm not going to New Jersey till tomorrow. The people I was going to see couldn't see me tonight. So I accept your invitation with pleasure."

I didn't know whether to be glad or sorry. "Well," I said, opening the door, "as you have probably gathered by now, I'm not sure of what you'll encounter."

"Lead on. I'm not unacquainted with family life."

As usual, Motley hurled himself against us as I opened the door. Then, seeing a stranger, belatedly barked.

"A fine watchdog you are," I said.

"I can see where the name Motley comes from," Brett said, winning Motley over by scratching him in particularly pleasurable places. Motley stood there, as Brett's hand rubbed him up and down the spine just in front of the tail, with a look of rapture on his canine face.

"You've made a friend for life, obviously," I said. "Come into the living room." I could hear the television set going from down the hall and, as I entered the room, saw my son, stomach flat on the floor, chest resting on a cushion, absorbed in the sports report.

"This is my scholarly and studious son, James," I said with heavy irony. "And, Jamie, this is Mr. Cunningham."

Jamie looked over and then slowly got to his feet.

"Our side didn't do too well in that game, did it?" Brett said, holding out his hand.

"Well, if they'd just . . ."

They're off, I thought, watching the two males embark on a conversation whose language I couldn't even understand. "Before you're lost to all rational thought, Jamie, is Martha in?"

"No."

"Has she been in?"

"Not unless she came in before me and been in her room since."

It was the answer I expected. Even so, a small hope I'd been nourishing that, despite all evidence, Martha was getting better died quietly.

I went down to her room and knocked. When there was no answer, I pushed open the door and, caught off guard, gave a cry of horror and astonishment. The place was a wreck. Drawers were open, clothes spilled out on the bed, bureau, desk and floor. Pieces of bread, fruit, chocolate and even pats of butter were littered around. Without thinking, I walked over and looked at them individually. Then I poked a piece of cake. It was so stale it fell into crumbs, and as I moved, I saw the roach scuttle away towards the closet.

The pats of butter were almost completely melted and, where they rested on the carpet, had left a dark oily stain. More roaches slid away, also to the closet. With a fearful dread I went over and opened the closet door.

It was easy to see where they had their nest—somewhere on the top shelf over my head. Individual roaches were scrambling around up there. Dragging a chair over, I climbed on it and put my face on a level with the shelf. There were mothers and fathers and uncles and aunts and lots and lots of half-grown children—a whole extended family of the species, the Great American Cockroach. I stared at it for a long time. They seemed to be centered on a half-closed round tin box, the kind that English "biscuits" or cookies used to come in.

Lifting the box, I then dropped it with a screech as some of the roaches skittered over my hand and along my arm. And I stood there, on the chair, frozen with horror, like something out of a Victorian cartoon, as the stale cookies spread all over the floor, along with the roaches that seemed to nest among them.

"My God!" Brett said from the door. Then as I tried to summon up some energy or resolve: "Do you have any spray exterminator—not that I think anything but a professional job would do."

"Yes. In the kitchen. In the cupboard under the sink."

Brett left and then came back, followed by Jamie, who took one look and said, "Yikes! And you yell at me for not keeping my room clean!"

"All right, Jamie," I said, getting off the chair, "but you're not sick. Why don't you go out and finish watching whatever you were watching." When he left, I glanced at Brett and said, "I suppose this is very middle-class of me, but I am mortified beyond words that you should be here and see all this."

"Don't be. As I told you, I lived through it, too."

"She always made such a thing about people respecting her privacy—that her closets and her drawers should be completely sacrosanct."

"I told you," Brett said, turning the spray of the can in pursuit of the roaches, "I've been through this."

I stared as the roaches seemed to come out of nowhere and race across the floor.

"They flee like the hosts of the Midianites," I said plaintively.

"No need to be depressed and biblical," Brett replied amiably.

I got back up on the chair. "Give me the can. But first, take these and put them on the floor."

I handed him a couple of handbags, a pile of books and some three-ringed loose-leaf binders. Two boxes were left on the shelf. "I suppose I ought to open these," I muttered. "Probably more roaches will be inside."

"Not unless there's food there," Brett said.

I took the first box and pulled off the lid. It seemed to contain some letters, news articles, poems and old photographs. I put on the lid and handed it down to Brett. The second, larger box held books that, after a glance, I could see were diaries. Replacing the cover, I handed it to Brett and stared at the now empty shelf with the vague feeling that at some time or other I had noticed something else up there. But the shelf was now bare, except for the scurrying forms of the cockroaches. "Can I have the spray, please?"

I turned the acrid-smelling fluid backwards and forwards and in the corners. "Pew!" I said.

"Better not inhale that too long."

Getting down off the chair, I went over to the corner windows and opened both, grateful for the cross draft.

Then I turned to Brett. "I invited you to dinner and you're welcome to stay, although I certainly wouldn't blame you if you didn't want to. But before we eat I'm going to have to empty out these drawers, spray the insides and get all the food out of here." What a hell of a time for me to succumb to graciousness, I thought grimly, and wished Brett, banker, chairman of the board and leading vestryman, were anywhere but here, witnessing my humiliation.

"Do you want me to leave?" he asked.

I almost jumped. It was as though he were responding to my unspoken wish.

"I will go if you want me to," he went on, and added slowly, "although I'd like to stay and be of help."

"That's kind of you, Brett. But other than getting the wildlife out and cleaning up the place a little, I don't know what else is to be done."

"All right." He paused. "Is anything missing?"

"Missing?" I repeated blankly. "You mean you think there's been a robbery?"

"No." He hesitated. "Are there any clothes missing?"

As I stared at him, it finally dawned on me what he meant. "You think she's run away."

"Has the room ever looked like this before?"

"Not this bad, no."

"It's a possibility."

I turned and looked at the closet. "Her gray suit is missing. She's probably wearing it. She has so many sweaters and blouses I'd have no way of knowing if more than the one she's wearing is missing."

I went down the hall to the coat closet and looked in there. As I expected, her red beret and raincoat were not there. Which proved nothing. I went back to her room. "Her raincoat and beret aren't in the closet, but that doesn't mean anything."

"Then maybe she hasn't."

"Did your daughter run away?"

He smiled a little. "Several times. Any suitcase or overnight bag gone?"

I remembered then why her shelf looked empty. "There used to be an overnight bag—nothing much more than a large tote—on the shelf there. I wondered why it looked empty."

"When did you last see it?"

"Weeks and months ago."

"That may not mean anything either."

"Well," I said. "I guess I won't know for a while."

"Do you want me to go now?" Brett asked.

As he spoke, the evening seemed to stretch, long and frightening, and I didn't know what lay at the end.

"No," I said, surprising myself considerably. "Don't go yet."

8

THERE WAS NO MORE FOOD in the drawers. But just for good measure I took everything out, including the lining paper, and sprayed them. It gave me a certain angry satisfaction to reflect how the (usually) fastidious and perfectionist Martha would hate the strong, unmistakable odor of the exterminating fluid. In fact . . . I paused. Would she be able to sleep in here at all?

I put the can down. I could spray the rest tomorrow. In the meantime, the wind from the open windows could do its work.

Before I left the room I folded her clothes and placed them on the bed. Seeing her pillowcases—part of a set that Martha and I had picked out for her room—gave me a stab of pain and tenderness.

"They're so pretty," Martha had said when we bought them.

We had gone shopping to buy her a birthday present and talked about a dress or a suit or a small new desk for her room. This was before her illness had become noticeable and she and I were as close (I thought) as though we were truly mother and daughter. But before we could reach the dress floor, Martha had lost her heart to the beautiful blue-sprigged sheets, pillowcases and ruffle. "They're so pretty," she repeated, "so delicate." So they became her present . . .

What had happened to that girl who had loved, not frilliness, but delicacy and elegance? How could she be related to the hostile, bitter, starved creature who left spoiling and decaying food around for roaches?

The thought that she might have run away swept back. I decided to call her friends now, while they were at dinner, and also call Miss Webster at the school. As I knew, she was often there late. And, of course, I should have called her as soon as the possibility of her running away occurred . . . and yet, with Martha, there had been so many alarums and excursions that I tried not to sound too hysterical or wildly imaginative.

There was a phone in my bedroom and I used that.

Miss Webster was not there. I didn't recognize the voice of the man who answered, but he sounded as though he might be a custodian.

"There's nobody here, ma'am, I'm tellin' you. I've gone into every classroom and lab and study room and the gym, to make sure they're empty and their windows are locked. Who did you say you were looking for? Martha Aldington? Sure I know her," he said with more than a little irritation, as I tried to describe her. "Medium height, skinny, brown hair. A junior."

"Yes."

"Well, I saw her leave here early this afternoon."

"Did you see who she left with?"

"Nope. Sorry. You her mother, did you say?"

"Yes." I felt unequal to going into nice distinctions.

"Yeah, well, I wouldn't worry. You know how kids are. She'll be home soon."

"Are we going to eat now?" Jamie asked in an aggrieved voice as I went into the living room.

"Right now. I'm sorry it's been so long. Has Motley eaten?"

"Of course. I wouldn't let him go hungry."

"If that reproach is for me, save it." I was about to add that I was extremely worried about Martha and then paused. During the past year and a half that could have been said three nights out of five, and on some occasions, five out of five.

As I stood there, those smug, accurate, irritating words went through my mind: "The squeaking door gets the oil." In our family life, Martha was the squeaking door.

I went over to where Jamie and Brett were sitting side by side, watching another sports show, leaned down and hugged my son.

"It may seem to you sometimes that I don't pay as much attention to you as I do to Martha."

"You don't."

"But I love you—I love you a humongous great amount." I bent then and kissed him.

"Okay, okay," he said. It embarrassed him to be kissed in front of someone else, especially a man.

"Appreciate it, my son!" Brett said, not taking his eyes off the screen. "Strong men have fought and bled and died for just that."

"Yeah . . . well . . ." Jamie said.

I put one hand in his thick red hair and gave it a friendly pull. "Dinner coming up A.S.A.P."

The casserole and salad were ready in twenty minutes. Luckily, I had been overenthusiastic about the casserole recipe, so there was more than enough. Just after I took the first bite something else struck me. "I'm the pits as a hostess, Brett, I didn't even offer you a drink. I know I have vodka and I think I have scotch. Is it too late?"

"Much too late. And anyway, I didn't even think about it."

"What kind of day have you had, Jamie?" I asked, determined that he should get a small part of his share of my attention.

"Okay."

"How was the biology class?"

"Yucky. We had to dissect a lizard. I'd rather have a live one."

"I don't blame you. I didn't like it either when I was at school. How was history?"

"Look, Ma. I know you're worried about Martha. You don't have to ask all these questions."

"Maybe she really wants to know," Brett said.

"I got a C on the test."

"You don't like history?" Brett asked.

"It's boring."

History was one of those subjects on which Martha regularly got A.

"What do you like?" Brett asked.

"Sports—and math."

"Well, the world certainly needs mathematicians. What's your favorite sport?"

"Football."

"You on the team at school?"

Pause. "No."

"Ever tried running?"

"You mean, like jogging around the park?"

"Yes."

"That looks sort of dumb."

"You ought to try it before you pass judgment."

"Do you jog?"

"Yes."

"Every day?"

"Almost. Sometimes I miss a day."

Helping himself to his third piece of buttered French bread, Jamie stared at Brett. "I thought you had to be real skinny to be a good runner."

"Skinniness is the perfect runner's build. I don't have the perfect build. But I run."

"Do you like it?"

"Yes. I'm not that good and I don't run that fast—maybe about a mile in eight minutes. But I enjoy doing it, and I like the way it makes me feel the rest of the time."

I could see Jamie pondering this as he spooned up his ice cream. "I'd look pretty silly running. I'm not that thin."

"People of all kinds, ages and shapes run. If you want to trot around the reservoir someday to see whether you like it, you can view them all there—the fat, the thin, the short, the tall, all ages, colors and sexes. Even some dogs, although theoretically they aren't supposed to be up there."

"Do you run around the reservoir?"

"Sometimes. Usually, in the morning, I do the big loop around the park."

"How far's that?"

"Six miles."

"Wow!"

"But the reservoir is a great place to start. Run a little, walk a little, until you can run all the way around. But get the right shoes."

"Jamie," I said, rising and picking up some plates, "please help me clear up."

"What about my homework?"

"You postponed it watching the sports show, so you can postpone it a little longer helping me."

Ten minutes later the table in the dining alcove was cleared and the dishes were in the dishwasher. "Okay," I said. "You can do your homework now. But first say good night to Mr. Cunningham."

Jamie ambled to the kitchen door. "Ma . . ."

"Yes."

"What's the matter with Martha? Has she gone nuts or something?"

I was about to deny it when I decided to be honest. "I don't know, Jamie. I wish I did."

"Well, the way her room was, it looked like she freaked out."

I turned around. "Do you think she has?"

"Cripes, Ma! How would I know?"

"I'm sorry. I shouldn't have put that on you."

"It's okay." He started out again and then stopped. "I told you I think something's bugging her."

I looked at him. "Have you any idea what it is?"

"Nope. You know she'd never tell me."

"One more question. And it's not a loaded one," I added quickly. "Even though it may sound that way. Do you care?"

He shoved his hands in his pockets and stood there in profile. His thick red hair was standing up and—endearing and wonderful as he was—there was no doubt about it: He was a tub-shaped boy, reminding me of his father. I repressed the desire to go over and hug him again. He'd probably had enough unsolicited demonstrativeness for one evening.

"That's tough to answer," he said. "I like her when she lets me like her. But mostly she doesn't. And then I don't."

By eight o'clock I started calling among her friends—an action I knew she bitterly resented. "I'm not a kid, Claire, and you don't have to treat me like one," was a frequent complaint when she was in one of her regressive periods.

"If you don't show enough responsibility to let me know where you are, then you must be treated like a much younger child," was my equally frequent reply.

None of her friends seemed to have any idea where she was, and one or two seemed surprised at my call. "Martha and I haven't seen much of each other for weeks, Mrs. Aldington," one unusually frank girl said. "I think she's deep in her own space right now."

I winced at the tired jargon. "What exactly do you mean by that, Althea? That she's withdrawn, unfriendly?"

"Yeah, well, you know how she is when she stops eating. I mean, she gets really flaky then. Besides . . ." the young voice sort of petered out.

"Besides what?"

"I think she's got something on her mind."

"She's got a lot of things on her mind. You mean something special?"

"Nothing that she's talked about, but yes."

Finally, around eight-thirty, I came to the end of the friends and acquaintances.

"No boyfriend?" Brett asked, putting down his *Wall Street Journal*, when I returned to the living room to report failure.

"Not really. She's always seemed more interested in being thin than being with boys, which I think is pretty odd. Surely the whole point of being thin is to be beautiful and attractive."

"Yes, but haven't you also been told—I'm sure you must have been—that part of anorexia, which incidentally nearly always stops menstruation, is to remain a child?"

"I guess I wanted to think that she was over that."

I went and stood by the window and stared out, depressed.

"I take it you called her grandmother," Brett said, opening up his paper again.

I heard the words but I found myself distracted by the sight of Brett Cunningham comfortably reading his paper in my living room, and it occurred to me that since this was the first time I had invited this rather important and powerful man home for dinner, I had done extraordinarily little to make sure he enjoyed himself. "I'm sorry about tonight," I said. "It must be terribly boring for you."

"If it were, I would have long ago found an excuse to go home."

Suddenly, what he had said penetrated. "Emily?" I said. With a shock I realized I hadn't even thought of her. "But Martha wouldn't go there. Not when she's relapsing. Emily has no hesitation about pointing out her sins and infractions."

"But wasn't she there recently?"

"Yes. Day before yesterday. But she's never gone there when she was on the verge of running away before."

"Has she run away previously?"

"No. But she's been within inches of it. And Emily's rather formal living style is the last thing she wants to tangle with when she's like that."

"Okay. You know her better than I do."

With the seed planted, however, I could not fail to check with Emily's apartment. I went over to the living-room phone and dialed.

"No, Mrs. Aldington," Trudi said, her Scandinavian accent sounding unusually thick. "I have not seen her."

"Do you know if she phoned?"

"No. Very often Mrs. Chadbourne answers the phone."

"Please let me speak to Mrs. Chadbourne, then, Trudi."

"Mrs. Chadbourne is out."

"When did she go out?"

"Well . . . she . . . she went out around six, I think."

It was like pulling teeth. But then with Trudi it often was. I was never entirely sure whether her grumpy uncommunicativeness was due to hostility towards me (which occasionally occurred to me, but which in my better moments I considered paranoid) or to an inherent Nordic gloom.

"Well," I said. "That's that."

Brett put down his paper. "I take it she's not at Emily's."

"No."

We sat there for a moment in silence. Finally I burst out, "I keep wondering if this has to do with Dick's death. I can't help thinking about that damn blouse with the blood on it. And then I decide I'm being unfairly suspicious. Martha's illness by itself would make her behave this way—it has, or nearly so, often enough."

Brett leaned forward, clasping his hands between his knees. "At some point we're going to have to think about calling the police."

I looked at him. "We?"

He flushed a little. "Sorry," he said stiffly. "You."

"I didn't mean it that way, Brett." I paused. "Truly."

He didn't reply, but kept his eyes on his linked hands. I could, I thought, ask him to leave. And if I did, now was the time to do it. Automatically I glanced at my watch. Nine-fifteen. Considering he'd only been invited at the last minute, it was time and more than time that he should leave . . . In fact, if I did nothing at all, common good manners would ensure that he would, in a very few minutes, make his excuses and go . . .

"I'm glad you're here," I said. And I was.

The expression in his blue eyes changed subtly. He smiled and got up. "I'll stay as long as I can help."

For some reason my mind fastened on ten. If by ten I hadn't heard, then I would call the police, and would do my utmost to present my anxiety as nothing more than any mother's—or stepmother's—over an absent teen-ager who had a severe physical and emotional problem . . . But how long would it take an alert cop—Detective O'Neill, for instance—to find out that my fears embraced a lot more than that?

The phone rang. I leaped to pick up the receiver.

"Mrs. Aldington? Detective O'Neill."

For a moment I had a wild thought that investigative science had reached the point where thoughts could be monitored. Then I laughed.

"What's funny?" he asked.

"Nothing."

"You don't strike me as the kind of person who would laugh at nothing."

"Detective O'Neill, you don't know what kind of a person I am. Maybe I do laugh at nothing—like high spirits and all that!"

"Okay. Whatever you say. I'd like to see you again. There are a couple of things I want to talk over. And I want to be sure you'll be there in the morning."

The morning seemed a thousand hours away.

"I'm not sure whether I will be or not," I said.

I saw Brett, who was at the window staring down at the traffic, turn and look at me.

"Why not?" O'Neill almost snapped the question.

"I have to go to my stepdaughter's school. Something has come up and I must see someone there."

"What's come up?"

"Nothing to do with this case, Mr. O'Neill," I answered quite firmly. His call had removed my various doubts. No matter what I did there would be risk involved: If I did not tell the alert and suspicious Detective O'Neill that Martha had disappeared, I forfeited any help he could give and might also forfeit her life and safety as a result. On the other hand, if I told him and secured his aid in finding her, he would, no matter how hard I tried to hide it, learn about her blouse (now safely at the cleaner's) and she'd be in far worse danger.

"I think I'd like to be the judge of that."

"Sorry, it's private. It has to do with my stepdaughter's health."

"You said she was an anorexic."

"Yes."

"She having an attack now?"

"Yes." His questions were harmless enough. Yet he made me think of a predator circling his prey, with a bite here and a lunge there. And what would happen if he decided to call the school? But why should he? Unless I were indeed a serious suspect; unless he really believed that I had killed Dick . . .

I said to him, accusingly, "Do you think I killed Dick Grism?"

"Did you?"

"I've told you. No. But you keep hovering around as though you still thought I was . . . that I did."

"That's good. Keeps you off balance."

"And why do you want to keep me off balance?"

"Because I learn things that way." He paused. "You may or may not have killed Dick Grism. But one thing I'm sure of: there's something you're hiding. Good night, Mrs. Aldington." And he hung up.

At ten minutes to ten, later than I had intended, I went into Jamie's room to kiss him good night. He seemed to be in one of his more truculent moods.

"Is he still here?" he asked.

"Brett? Brett Cunningham? Yes." When Jamie didn't respond, I said, "Why, do you mind?"

"It's nothing to do with me."

"Jamie! Stop it! Of course it has something to do with you. This is your home as well as mine. What's eating you?"

"Nothing."

"Yes, there *is* something eating you. What is it?"

Jamie's eyes, looking extraordinarily green against his green pajamas, looked up. "Are you going to have an affair with him?"

It was like being punched in the midriff. I took a deep breath. "No. I am not. What on earth gave you the idea I would?"

"Some kids at school said all divorced women living alone have affairs. Toby Lester's mother, for instance—"

"One," I interrupted in a firm voice, "I'm widowed, not divorced. Two, I don't live alone, I live with you and Martha."

"Yeah, well, I said that. But Toby said his mother told him she felt she was entitled to a sexually active life."

I found my mind dwelling, inappropriately, on the absent Mrs. Lester. What kind of woman would hand such pseudo-liberated garbage to an eight-year-old boy?

"I mean," he said, "I was wondering if you were planning to be sexually active with Mr. Cunningham?"

My indignation evaporated as a terrible desire to giggle came over me. "No, I am not," I said rather loudly.

"Well, don't get mad. It's not fair when you ask me to tell you what's bugging me, and I do, and then you get mad."

"I'm not mad, Jamie. Truly I'm not. Just . . . just surprised. He's here because we sometimes work together and he gave me a ride home, and because he'd taken me out to lunch, on an impulse I asked him in here for dinner. Then, when we arrived, I went into Martha's room and all hell broke loose. He's just being kind and standing by. He had a daughter who was an anorexic."

"Oh."

His "oh" could almost have been read as disappointment. "Are you disappointed?"

"No. Why should I be disappointed? Are you going to marry again?"

"Do you want me to?"

"Sometimes I think it'd be kind of nice to have another man around."

"I see."

"Well, just thought I'd ask."

I leaned over and kissed him. "Go to sleep. I'll take Motley out later."

"Okay." He sounded half asleep.

I left the room awash with a variety of feelings, one of which was a desire to share with Brett the details of my conversation with Jamie, only because I was sure that whatever form his response took, it would be funny or apt or both. But of course, since Brett was the subject of the topic, I couldn't. Unfortunately.

Outside Jamie's door, I turned towards the living room, then paused and went back towards Martha's. I'd left the door there open, to benefit from as much air as possible. Even so, the powerful odor of the exterminating fluid hit me as I reached the door. Putting a hand in front of my nostrils, I went in. Cockroach corpses lay everywhere. Picking my way, one hand jammed to my face, I went over to the closet, got down the box containing the diaries and went back out again as quickly as possible.

Brett had abandoned the *Wall Street Journal* and was watching a local news show, with the sound turned low.

"You can turn that up, if you want. Jamie was half asleep when I left and is probably out cold by now."

"I don't have to, unless you want to hear it louder yourself."

"No. I decided to look at Martha's diaries, to see if I can find a clue as to what is bothering her—other than her usual obsessions. Everybody seems to think she has something on her mind. I'd like to find out what it is."

"Do you think she has something on her mind?"

"I'm ashamed to say that it hadn't particularly struck me that she had. When she's in one of these fits of regression, she's so hostile and remote that I wouldn't know whether she did or not."

I opened the lid and took out the books. They were smallish, leather-bound, and there were five of them—the five years covering the time since her father's death. I decided to begin at the beginning and picked up the earliest.

"I feel something of a voyeur doing this, but under emergency conditions, all rules are off. And this is an emergency."

I saw Brett glance at his watch.

"Brett, you must be tired. Why don't you go on home. I don't think there's a thing you can do, although it's been comforting to have you. But there's nothing I can do either—except wait."

Brett got up. "I think you ought to tell your friend Detective O'Neill about Martha's absence. It's true he'll get the details of her visit to Dick's office, but that doesn't mean he'll charge her."

"I can't take that risk," I said a little sharply.

"Claire—what are you afraid of? That Martha really did kill Dick?"

The moment he said that it seemed so wildly improbable that I almost smiled. But when I considered Martha's mental state over the past five years, the smile faded. Not answering Brett's question, I said instead, "I should have listened to Dr. Meitzner."

"Who was Dr. Meitzner?"

"The shrink—psychiatrist—who dealt with Martha when she was in the hospital. Dr. Meitzner wanted me to leave Martha there another three months. She seemed to feel that there might be something more wrong than just the anorexia—bad as it was. But Martha wanted so desperately to come home. She swore to me that her problem was on the mend, and that she'd get better. So I gave in. Maybe I shouldn't have."

Brett started walking slowly back and forth the length of the living room, his hands in his pockets, looking the way he did in his office earlier in the day. Then he sat down, crossed his legs and stared at the ceiling for a while. Finally he said, "There are various threads here that seem never to have been put together, or at least not in any way that made a sequence." He paused. "Emily Chadbourne called you in to tell you what others have said, including that shrink you mentioned, that something is bothering Martha beyond the usual ingredients of anorexia. After Emily said that, she asked you if Patrick was faithful to you, and then you both discussed Priscilla, Emily's daughter and Martha's mother, and how she suffered—as did many of the sixties warpath youngsters—from a severe case of disappointed ideals. In Priscilla, this took the form of going off to communes and on civil-rights and peace marches. You touched on the fact that anorexics are perfectionists, which could be taken as another form of idealism . . . Have I missed anything?"

"No." Brett's logic, moving from step to step, had the effect on me that crossword puzzles often did: I knew the links and the logic were there, but I could never see them.

"Is there anything you'd like to add to that—that you've forgotten to mention."

I thought for a moment. "Only that Martha seemed to underline and emphasize that her father loved her mother, Priscilla, exclusively." As I said that, the thread was beginning to show more clearly. I took in my breath. "And that therefore, by implication," I went on, "he was not exclusively devoted to me . . . But that's not true," I added. "We're back to square one, the question as before: was Patrick unfaithful to me? Short of being with him every minute of every day and night, there's no way on earth of giving an absolute answer. But with that impossible exception, the answer—I would stake everything—is: yes, he was faithful to me."

Brett continued to stare at the ceiling, and we sat there in silence for a while. Then he said, "That's a remarkable statement. I wonder if you realize how remarkable. Let's suppose, for a moment, that he wasn't. You've told me that Martha adored her father—he could do no wrong, et cetera. Suppose she discovered that he was not faithful to you. Would she blame him, or you?" He glanced at me then. "We're not dealing with rationality, you know. We're dealing with the needs of a perfectionist and an obsessive. To wit: if Martha had a need for perfection, and her father was her idol, that would extend to a need to find her father perfect. If she has some kind of evidence that he is not perfect, will she accept that? I doubt it. She will twist it around according to her own great need, so that the person to blame is the person he betrayed—you. In some way it has to be your fault."

I could hear now her voice in my mind, "He should never have married you," and Emily's more temperate "It wasn't the same as when he was married to Priscilla . . ."

For the first time I looked at the question of Patrick's fidelity, apart from Martha's accusations concerning it. Too restless and uncomfortable to remain seated, I went over to the window and stood, with my hands upon the sash, staring down at Eighty-second Street—running the past through my mind as though it were an old movie . . .

I had come from a middle-class, midwestern background where the received view of society was that, outside of their professions, men had their interests, amusements and jokes, and women had theirs, and the two were quite different. Standards were entirely double. No one ever quite put this into words, but most people, both men and women, felt that it was one thing for a man to tie one on and maybe play around a little when he was away at a convention or business meeting. It wasn't right, but it was life. Women knew that. With women, though, it was quite different. With men, the sin was venial; with women, mortal.

So when, in one of our first conversations together, Patrick expressed his scorn for this implicit double view of behavior, I was fascinated. If chastity was desirable, he said, with the passion he brought to all theories, it was equally desirable in men and women. If the ancient shibboleths had loosened to admit some sexual freedom before or outside of marriage, then it also applied equally to both sexes. I remember nodding enthusiastically. As a theory, it was wonderful. But I was more impressed, actually, by an offshoot of this attitude. In all the years I knew him, I never heard Patrick make any comment about a woman's body, build, figure, seductiveness, allure or general sexual attractiveness. Nor did I ever see flicker over his face that expression of instant alert, that quiver of male reaction to a female's swinging walk or unharnessed breasts. Once, when I commented about that, he said he was as human as any other male, but he tried not to consider women as "sex objects." With him, the two words always appeared in invisible quotation marks.

Which led back to the matter at hand. Never once had I seen him show the faintest interest of that kind in any of the women we knew. Was there anyone he ever expressed an admiration for?

No one except Elsie Shaftsbury—Elsie, with her straight hair, her flat body, her serious face, her earnest devotion to every activist cause in the parish . . .

"She's so humorless," I'd said once to Patrick.

"Maybe she doesn't consider social inequity and oppression, to say nothing of nuclear wipe-out, wildly hilarious." There was an edge to his words.

I remember looking at him sharply. "You sound . . . defensive."

"You're not the only one to put Elsie down."

Could it have been Elsie? I thought now.

"Let me ask you another question," Brett's voice said behind me. "Were you in love with Patrick?"

"Of course."

"I didn't say, did you love him? I said, were you in love with him? There's a subtle but powerful difference."

My mind slid back. Patrick had wanted to marry me. He made that quite clear almost immediately. We had met at a trail-riding camp in the Wind River Mountains in Wyoming. He had six-year-old Martha with him, and she had developed a slight crush on me, owing simply to the fact that, having grown up around horses, I was a good rider. Patrick, it turned out, had a vague but stubborn prejudice against horses, and was only there to please his motherless daughter, who loved riding more than anything else in the world next to him.

"I'll admit my prejudice," he said one day while we were jogging along a wide field three abreast, "but it comes from associating horses with rich people, who spend sinful amounts of money on them, which could better be spent on those in need."

"Come on, now," I said. "Horses are working animals. They may be the playthings of the rich back East, but out here they work for their food and shelter, like everybody else."

"Were you ever a cowboy?" Martha had asked, and then blushed and giggled as her father and I laughed. "Well, you know what I mean."

"Yes, as a matter of fact. A friend of my father's has a cattle ranch and I worked there for two college vacations."

"I wish you'd teach me how to ride properly," the little girl said shyly.

I was thoroughly taken with her and spent many of our subsequent rides instructing her in various techniques.

"Let's keep in touch," Patrick had said before we went back to our separate homes—he and Martha to their rectory in New Jersey, I to Palo Alto and Stanford, where I was entering my last year for a degree in clinical psychology. (It had come as a rude shock to find out that Patrick was an Episcopal priest. My mental picture of such beings was both more ascetic and more effete.) We corresponded—Patrick and I, and Martha and I—during the following year and agreed to meet at the same camp after I graduated. It was there that Patrick proposed and I accepted. It had been an extremely decorous courtship, in keeping, I felt, with his role in the Church. I was later to discover that my ideas about this were naïve in the extreme. Today's young clergy did not feel called to hold by conventions they considered outmoded any more than did their contemporaries. It was probably a combination of the distance between California and New Jersey and the almost continuous presence of Patrick's daughter that rendered our relationship so atypically chaste. Why did he ask me to marry him? I came finally to believe that it was at least as much his felt need to have someone like me—practical, pragmatic and rather down-to-earth—in his life as rector and as an acting mother to Martha, as it was any romantic or erotic passion. After our marriage, he was a warm and considerate lover, but I don't believe that he felt carried away any more than I did. And why did I marry him? Because to me, the midwestern girl, he was a fascinating amalgam of a member of the northeastern elite and a Tolstoyan type of radical. At moments when he was being most eloquent on behalf of the poor and the downtrodden, he could be arrogant and condescending to some suburban girl in her polyester blouse and her talk about "spiritual experiences." To him the Gospel was the ultimate radical statement, not food for the spiritually hungry to find comfort therein. He could be wonderfully compassionate towards the Hispanic in jail for stabbing a grocer. Yet I saw him be aloof to the point of cruelty to a chattering housewife who wanted to talk to him about prayer . . . Like Norbert, I thought, and then, shocked at myself, pushed the thought away.

"No," I said now. "I don't think I was in love with him. I was attracted by who and what he was, and I was flattered because Martha seemed to choose me as her stepparent."

"Were you ever in love?" Brett asked.

"Yes," I said. "Once."

He had been an instructor at Stanford. We had a flaming love affair throughout my freshman year. He never once mentioned marriage, but I told myself that he would, and that, anyway, it didn't matter. What was important was the relationship. In actual fact, it wouldn't have mattered what he said—or didn't say. I had fallen in love totally and disastrously the first time I saw him stroll into the lecture room, a tall, graceful, fair-haired man with interesting, rather heavy-lidded eyes which to me made him look cynical, worldly and sexy all at the same time. I found an excuse to stay behind after class and, as I encountered his amused glance, knew that he knew it was just an excuse.

A week later we were lovers, and remained so throughout the year. Jealousy, something I had never before experienced, entered my life. I would see him talking to a girl on the campus, his hand under her elbow, his handsome head bent forward, smiling. And I would want to die, to kill the girl and kill my lover all at the same time. When he talked about the future, he always said "we," and I took intense comfort from that. At the end of the year we were going to meet in London a month after school closed.

When I arrived at the modest pension in London that was to be our starting place, I found a letter from him waiting for me. It went on for several self-explanatory pages, at least two of which I never read. Because by the end of the first page I knew the main points: that he was married and had been for some years, a fact that he had managed to overlook telling me. Apparently he and his wife had had a trial separation and had now decided to go back together . . .

Brett was watching me. "I take it it was not a good experience."

I shook my head. Even now, sixteen years later, the pain of that moment in the pension was sharp and twisting. "I fell flat on my face in love with an instructor in my freshman year. We had a mad, passionate, flaming love affair that I considered on a par with that of Eloise and Abelard. The following summer, when I was waiting in London for him to join me for an idyllic meandering trip through Europe, I got a letter from him saying he had been married all along, although separated, and that he and his wife were going to have another try at getting together."

"That might have something to do with the unromantic way you went about your marriage with Patrick. It didn't sound to me as though you were flinging your cap over a windmill. At least on a domestic level, you found him safe—no wandering eye."

I smiled. "Only Elsie Shaftsbury."

"Who was she?"

"An ardent follower of all Patrick's favorite causes. She was so earnest and humorless and—to be honest—plain that I never gave her a thought. But once when I made a put-down comment about her to Patrick, he snapped right back with one of his own about me."

"If you didn't find your husband wildly attractive yourself, it probably didn't occur to you that someone else would."

"Ouch!" I looked back at Brett. "That remark had teeth."

"Sorry—maybe a little of my own experience went into that. Who was Elsie Shaftsbury? Her name sounds vaguely familiar. I take it she was a member of your parish."

"No. She came from outside the parish. In fact, she didn't live in Upper Hills at all. She lived in Fairacre . . ." I looked at Brett. "Isn't that where you said you were going—to look up something about Dick Grism?"

"Yes. It is."

We stared at each other for a moment.

Then Brett said slowly, "The reason why the name Shaftsbury sounds familiar, I realize, is that somebody named Shaftsbury was Dick's brother-in-law, his sister's husband. They're some of the people I'm going to see."

9

A FUNNY, ELECTRIC TINGLE went down my spine at that moment, and I shivered.

"Cold?" Brett asked.

"No. It's . . . it's not that kind of a shiver, I guess. It's just that things seem linked in a weird way. But even though I feel that, I can't make any sense of it."

Brett got up. "Well, don't torment yourself with it. If there's a connection of some kind, then maybe when I'm out there I'll see what it is. It's time for me to go home. I don't think there's any way I can be of further help here." He looked at me sharply. "Is there?"

I shook my head. "No. But thanks, anyway."

We went to the front door, and Brett put on his raincoat. "I'll let you know what I find out," he said.

"All right."

We were standing by the door. I felt odd, breathless, glad that he was going and sorry that he was going, all at once.

"Well," he said. "Good night."

"Good night," I said.

He didn't move. Then he muttered, "I swore I wouldn't do this," and pulled me to him and kissed me.

I'd forgotten what it was like to feel that way—the quiver down the back, the watery knees, hot, cold and shivery all at the same time. I felt his body against mine and everything else went out of my head. My arms were around him and I was kissing him and kissing him. Nothing with Patrick had ever been like this. Only once had I felt even approximately the same way. The memory of that brought fear. To desire anything so much was to make a present of yourself—or so I had learned. But Brett's not like that, I thought confusedly.

"Afraid?" Brett's voice was thick and breathy.

"Yes."

"Don't be. Can I stay?"

"No—I'm afraid. And there's Jamie."

He put me gently away and stood for a moment. "All right," he said finally. "For now."

I lay awake the rest of the night, worrying about Martha, and when I was not thinking about her, trying to cope with an urgency and need within myself that I hadn't experienced in sixteen years. It was dawn before I dozed off, only to be yanked awake by the alarm an hour later.

I was drying off after my shower when the phone rang. It was Emily.

"I called to tell you, Claire, that Martha has been with me since yesterday evening. I will not permit her to be worried or questioned, but I thought you ought to know."

Anger went through me like a flame. "I ought to have known that last night, Emily. You should have told me. It would have saved me a lot of worry, and maybe allowed me some sleep. I didn't even get undressed. For about four hours I lay on the sofa, ready, in case somebody would call. How could you let her be there all night and put me through that—wondering where on earth she was and what could be happening to her?"

"I have done more by telling you now than the poor child wanted me to. She has . . . she has talked to me a great deal—more than ever before—and while I don't take everything she says seriously, I am deeply upset about the state of her affairs, and I think it is time that I assumed the role of guardian to her. After all, she is my granddaughter, and you are no relation to her at all."

"What on earth has she told you?"

There was a slight pause, then in her haughtiest tone Emily said, "There's no need to go into the details now. But it has been made plain to me that Martha is a lonely, desperate, unhappy child, and I am going to do my best to make life more endurable for her—for Priscilla's daughter. And if you try to stop me or make trouble, I shall invoke the law!"

"Emily . . ." I paused, collecting my wits, putting my anger to one side. "Emily, a man has been killed at St. Anselm's. I don't think Martha has . . . was involved in his . . . death. But I do think she was there, Monday morning. She came home with blood all over her blouse—"

"She told me about that," Emily said. "She said it was a nosebleed, and I, for one, believe her. Of course I believe her. And one of the things that makes me give credence to her assertions about her life with you is the now obvious, horrifying fact that you could even question her statement."

"I didn't say I questioned it . . ."

"You didn't have to," Emily said, her voice as cold as a knife. "It is plain that you do." And she hung up.

Slowly I finished drying, although the process was pretty much completed by the terry-cloth robe I had thrown over myself as I went to answer the phone beside my bed.

Well, I thought, I now did not have to go to see Miss Webster. I started going back over in my mind the conversation with Emily. Martha had always been a little in awe of her formidable grandmother. And though Emily may have chosen to forget about it, I had not forgotten that at the time of Patrick's death, Martha, afraid at first that her grandmother would claim custody of her, begged and pleaded with me not to allow it.

As I made breakfast for Jamie and me, I worried at the problem. Somewhere in something that Emily had said there was an important piece of information . . . only I couldn't extract it.

"You okay, Ma?" Jamie said, his mouth full.

"Finish chewing before you speak, Jamie. Yes, I'm okay. Why do you ask?"

"Well, you brought that poached egg in a couple of minutes ago and then put it into my empty cereal dish."

I stared at him, then at his empty cereal dish. Sure enough, my egg, still in its shape, was reposing at the bottom of the bowl, afloat now in milk and sugar.

"So I did," I said. "I must have been thinking about something else."

"You've been thinking about something else all morning. You haven't even said hello." I could hear the slight grievance in his voice.

"I'm sorry, Jamie. Martha didn't come home all night, and this morning her grandmother called me and told me she'd been there. I'd like to shake both of them. She could at least have called me last night so I could get some sleep."

"She must have really flaked out if she's gone to old lady Chadbourne. She always says she doesn't like her."

I knew I should reprove Jamie for his "old lady Chadbourne." But I couldn't bring myself to. At least Jamie preferred me.

"I told you something was bugging her. She wouldn't have gone there if there wasn't." Jamie got up and started to leave the table.

"Take your things out to the kitchen," I said automatically. "Has Motley had his walk?"

"Of course."

I kissed Jamie goodbye, and then stood by the window in the living room trying to make sense of what had happened and figure out what to do. It was, of course, impossible for me to attend Morning Prayer on mornings like this when Jamie did not leave early for a special class or club activity.

No revelation as to what to do came, so, at nine o'clock, I left for the church. My first client was due to arrive at nine-thirty.

It was a strange, gray, unsatisfying day. The grayness was, at least in part, external. The crisp, beautiful autumn weather had dissolved into cold, wet slush. The rain came down, not hard, but relentlessly. By the time I got to the parish house, and despite my umbrella, my shoulders and handbag and feet were soaked. I had taken one look outside the window before leaving and decided against boots. It was, I discovered, the wrong decision.

But the grayness seemed to be as much within as without. At ten-thirty there was a staff meeting, at which Norbert announced that the feeding of the homeless would be upped to three times a week.

"Three times?" Larry said. "That's wonderful! But we tried that before and our money man . . ." He paused, as he and the rest of us remembered what had happened to "our money man." Larry continued firmly, "Our money man said we could afford it only twice. I realize," he hurried on, "that 'money man' seems a bit heartless, in view of Dick's death . . . and how he died. And I don't mean that at all. But we've always called the business manager that, so it seems, well, false sentimentality not to."

"Quite right," Norbert said. "Dick would have been the first to agree. Anyway, I'm happy to report that we've received extra funds from a truly Christian and socially minded well-wisher, and that thanks to . . . that . . . we are going to be able to take care of the hungry three times a week."

"But—" Susannah's voice floated out. "But, Norbert, that's an awful load to put on the kitchen help right now. The only reason we haven't been hit for higher raises is because we're a church."

"It will be done by volunteers," Norbert said.

"Okay," Janet MacHeath said. "But we're going to have to get up a fresh squad. There aren't too many of our present volunteers who can do it more than twice at the moment. A few might. But it'll take a week or so to make sure we have enough volunteers."

"For people for whom this is the only decent meal," Norbert said, in a voice that was both angry and very cold, "even three times is grossly insufficient."

"Yes, Norbert," Janet persisted. "But it makes most sense if we stagger the feedings that people get around the city, so that at least we don't duplicate the hours, which would mean they'd miss a meal somewhere else."

"Please don't tell me what to do, Janet," Norbert said. "On this subject I think my own opinion is quite as valid as yours. There are thousands of hungry, homeless people, cast adrift in a materialistic, indifferent society, which cares nothing for anything except profit. Through no fault of their own, these wretched men and women are cut adrift—"

"Well, one or two of them at least are mentally unstable, and refuse to go to the hospital," Larry said. "I'm not trying at all to say that it's right they're without shelter, but it's not as though some of them couldn't be in a nice warm hospital if they were willing."

"I will not listen to this kind of argument," Norbert said. "Talk about priests and Levites walking on the other side of the road! I'm ashamed that this sort of justifying cruelty should be present in my own church!"

"It's our church, too," Larry said.

Norbert stared at him. "Well then, act as though it were a trust, not a soft niche for those fortunate enough to know that they'll never be on the streets."

There was a silence. Then, roused from my preoccupation with my own problems—Emily and Martha—I said, "That's a bit strong, isn't it, Norbert? You're not the only one around here who cares what happens to people."

"As the widow of one of the outstanding activists of our generation, I think that comment, Claire, is somewhat below your standard."

"Sorry, but Janet and Larry were not suggesting that the hungry eat cake, but simply questioning whether we can afford a public meal three times a week."

"I've said we could," Norbert snapped.

"Whether or not we have the staff, volunteer or professional, to do it," I ploughed straight ahead.

"Then we'll just have to collect more volunteers. What about you, Claire?"

"I have a job of my own here."

"This is more important. Food is a greater necessity than therapy."

"That's not the point. I have made commitments to people who are in the midst of an ongoing process. I can't just abandon it and say to them, 'Too bad. Try and find therapy somewhere else, because I have more important things to do.' "

"Claire's right," Larry said. "She has her own obligations—"

Norbert swung on him. "And what about you? Perhaps you could spare some of the food you most obviously relish."

There was a short gasp.

"Speaking of cruelty," I said, angrier with Norbert than I had been in some time.

"No, Claire, it's all right," Larry said. "I'm far too fat. I know that as well as anyone else. Let's not have this argument degenerate into consideration of my tender feelings. But if I stopped eating altogether, it still wouldn't solve the problem of the kitchen, the help and conflicting times for meals."

Norbert's face had that focused, withdrawn look that lately had more and more been seen on his face. It was an expression that meant that for him there was only one reality—his preoccupying obsession. Then some muscular reflex passed over his shoulders, neck and head. He smiled and wiped the corners of his mouth where saliva had collected.

"Sorry, I didn't mean to get carried away. Where, by the way, is Brett?"

"Off seeing some of Dick Grism's relatives," I said. No one else was talking, or even looking up. I wondered if Norbert knew how wild he'd sounded.

"Ah yes. Well, that's all for the moment. Janet, come see me. I'm sure we can work something out. As you know, I'm available at all times."

"Yes, your help has been invaluable," Janet murmured.

"Larry," Norbert said down the table, where Larry was collecting an untidy heap of books, pencils and papers. "Walk back with me."

"Sorry, Norbert. But I have to go and see Rafael's family. In fact, I'm late now."

Norbert went up to him, his long legs covering the length of the table in two big strides. "I couldn't be sorrier, Larry, about that stupid comment I made. We all love every pound of you."

"Well then, that's a lot of love," Larry said good-naturedly. Gently, he moved his shoulder from underneath the rector's embrace.

I caught up with Larry out in the hall. "What on earth was that all about?" I asked.

"Lord love a duck," Larry said, trotting out one of the Englishisms he'd picked up during his year at Cambridge. "Norbert did have the bit between his teeth." He spoke lightly, but he looked strained.

"You didn't pay any attention to his tactlessness, did you?" I asked, still worried about his feelings. Fat was the one subject that, I knew, could get to Jamie.

"No one believes me," Larry said, "when I tell them I really don't mind."

"Nobody cares how much you weigh," I said. "Including Wendy."

"You're wrong there," Larry said. "Wendy keeps punching my midriff and putting me on aerated marge instead of butter. She says she does not wish to be widowed early due to an overstrained heart."

By this time we were at the row of mailboxes beside Josie's desk. Larry reached in and retrieved three letters, which he proceeded to look at. "Oh, goody," he said. "One from my Cambridge friend. Assistant to the Nobel laureate himself."

I was looking through my own mail. "Your friend? A Nobel prize winner?"

"No, dear. Works for one."

"What in?"

"Some kind of chemistry of the brain. Far beyond me."

"Can I have the stamp?" Josie asked unexpectedly. "I noticed it when I was sorting the mail. I don't have that particular denomination. Mr. Shearer promised me his foreign envelope, too."

"Sure," Larry said.

"No, don't tear it off the envelope," Josie squeaked protestingly as Larry started to tear the stamp corner off the envelope. "My boyfriend —he's the collector—said you shouldn't. Just give me the envelope when you're through."

"Okay. Will do." He waved his hand holding the letter. "Ta ta." And he wandered off.

Norbert came into my office just before my last client of the morning was due. "I shouldn't have been so carried away," he said guiltily. "But there's something about those silent, uncomplaining people, lining up to eat, that absolutely drives me wild."

I was tired. I'd had almost no sleep. I was extremely angry with Emily and worried about Martha, and I wished, therefore, that Norbert would go away. I was not in the mood to discuss his pet subject or to get into an argument. So I said nothing.

"Et tu, Brute?" Norbert said.

I looked up, not taking his meaning. "What?"

"Are you also angry with me?"

"No, just distracted by my own problems."

"Compared to being hungry, there are no problems."

"Norbert, I'm sure you're right. But that doesn't mean that other problems just fold their tents and go away. They don't. I still have Jamie and Martha to worry about. And Emily Chadbourne."

"That's what I wanted to talk to you about."

"What?" I stared up at him. He was a big man, broad across the chest, and with his hands stuck in his back pockets, his coat was strained wide. I could see the armholes of the black rabat, like a waistcoat reversed.

"I wanted to talk to you about your mother-in-law, Emily Chadbourne."

"She's not my mother-in-law, Norbert. She was Patrick's mother-in-law. She was Priscilla Aldington's mother, and she is Martha Aldington's grandmother. She is no relation to me at all."

He made a gesture with his hand. "It doesn't matter. She is what my southern kin would call a connection."

"What do you want with her?"

"I want her to make a considerable donation to the church. Specifically, to the feeding program."

"You're barking up the wrong tree, Norbert. Emily's the old-fashioned kind. She gives a tremendous lot to charity, but she feels that many of these people should be either in the hospitals or working. Nothing can move her from that."

"She must be re-educated. These people are the detritus of a greedy society—"

"Spare me the rhetoric, Norbert." I spoke more sharply than I meant. But I was angry at him for the way he spoke to Larry. "Some of the people who come to eat are, indeed, victims of the recession and should be helped. But an awful lot of them are the result of the deinstitutionalization of the mentally ill, and they stay on the streets because of the so-called patient's law. No hospital or doctor can afford to be tied up in a lawsuit instigated by one of the crazies who don't want to be confined. They are the result of a few well-intended liberal enactments that have placed them on the street, where people cannot reach them without running all kinds of legal risks. And it doesn't make them less pathetic. But it does explain a lot of them. Quite a few are violent, which is why many of the older people among them prefer the streets to the shelters. It doesn't help anybody not to be realistic."

Norbert went on as though I hadn't spoken. "I know Emily Chadbourne, and I believe that she could be persuaded to donate a sum. See if you can make her see the necessity . . ."

"Norbert," I said. "Emily isn't talking to me right now."

He frowned. "What on earth have you done to alienate her?"

"I don't think I've done anything, Norbert." I paused, fighting with irritation at his immediate assumption of my guilt in the matter. *"She's* the aggressor in this, Norbert. Not I."

His lips narrowed. "I'm sorry, Claire, but this is not the time to be self-centered and defensive. Emily is an old lady who probably has her notions and megrims, but at her age she deserves a little coddling."

"Why?" I said bluntly, by now really angry. "Because she has money?"

He turned. "Do you realize what her money could do for us? For the poor? We could start a program that would spread to every church, to every denomination. For the first time since the Middle Ages we could give obedience to Christ's command—'Feed my sheep, feed my lambs.' You know what I see every Sunday as I look out of the pulpit—the comfortable middle class, with its salaries and medical benefits and apartments and niggardly giving—and I can imagine all those hands pouring the hoarded wealth, the expensive comforts, into a great fund for those who have nothing . . . nothing."

"And you want to start with Emily. Lotsa luck. Even if she wasn't angry with me for disbelieving Martha, I can't see her making over her will to you, Norbert. I really can't."

"You can't possibly know. What on earth have you quarreled with her about?"

"About my stepdaughter, her granddaughter, Martha," I said, and then hesitated. Why would I pause before telling Norbert what he probably already knew, that at least a few people thought I might have been the woman who had been seen leaving the parish house the morning of Dick's murder. Wouldn't he be, as my rector, the person I would most confide in? I made a sudden decision. "A couple of people, Josie Beardsley and one of the custodians, saw a woman leaving the parish house on the morning of the murder, at about seven-thirty. They both thought it was me. Well, it wasn't. But Martha often wears a beret that we both use and in coats we look pretty much of a size and height. Furthermore, when she came home that night, she had blood all over her blouse, which she insists came from a nosebleed. But I don't believe her. I don't mean for a moment that I think she killed Dick, but I think she came to the parish house and probably saw his body right after he had been killed, and without thinking about it got blood on herself. And the fact that she has run away to her grandmother's, instead of going home last night, makes me more convinced than ever that at least she knows something about the murder. But Emily won't let me see her, or talk to her, and talks to me as though I were the enemy. I think Martha was scared stiff because she thinks that someone'll accuse her of the murder."

"Understandable, I would think," Norbert said. "Particularly since the accuser would appear to be someone she thought she had most reason to trust."

"Norbert," I said. He was behaving in such an odd fashion, I could almost not believe I was hearing what I was hearing. "Why are you being so hostile? You act as though you thought I was the one that killed Dick."

There was a short pause, then Norbert said, "Really, Claire, don't be paranoid. But since you react so strongly to that, I'd think you'd understand how that poor godchild of yours must feel."

"Stepchild, not godchild," I corrected automatically. And then: "But I've told you that I don't think at all she had anything to do with Dick's death—"

"Nevertheless, you're willing that she should come under suspicion. In that case, I don't find it strange that she has fled to her grandmother. And I'm sure that if Emily could see this problem among the three of you resolved, she would be more than likely, out of gratitude, to fund this essential program."

It was like talking with a boomerang. Everything I said came back, twisted almost out of shape, but still recognizable.

"We all know you've been under great strain, Claire," Norbert said gently. "And that you've borne your various burdens well and with courage. You see, I have known for several days that you were in the parish house early that morning."

"Norbert, let me get over one thing absolutely clearly: I had nothing to do whatsoever with Dick's death."

"Didn't you? Since you seem to think that Martha did, and your connection with Martha is as close as it is, I would say that there's a deep and probably direct connection linking you and Martha and Dick's death." He walked to the door. "Tell Emily I'll call later today. She and I are old friends—or did you know that?"

"No," I said, stunned. "I didn't know it."

Perhaps my conversation with Norbert had made me really paranoid, or the logic of his argument was trickling through my own defenses. But it seemed to me that Josie Beardsley was unusually busy when I passed her, so that she didn't look up, and only spoke when I said, "Hello," and then only to say a faint "Hello" back to me. When I asked if there were any messages, she merely said, "Are there any in your mailbox?"

"There don't seem to be."

"Well, then I guess there aren't." Still she didn't look up.

Never before had I had my word questioned, and never before had I lived through the sensation of having people not look at me, because of suspected guilt.

But that afternoon I experienced a variety of things I had never known before: people whispering and then stopping abruptly in embarrassment as I drew near; others not looking at me, keeping their eyes to the floor as I passed; curious looks.

"Now I know what a leper feels like," I said angrily to Larry Swade when I had fled to his office.

"If it's any consolation to you," Larry said, staring broodingly at a sheet of paper stuck in his typewriter, "*I* don't think you whacked poor Dick over the head with a bookend."

"Who do you think did?"

"There's a general feeling going around that whoever was involved with Dick in his financial hanky-panky may very well have had a quarrel with Dick and decided to eliminate him."

"I thought *I* was the general feeling going around. That is, that it was me."

"You're losing your grammar in your excitement," Larry said reprovingly. "No, when I said general feeling, I mean among the powers that be, not Josie's gossip circuit."

"Who is the person involved with Dick's goings-on?"

"That piece of information is still up in the air. It appears now, when the mares are all out the barn door, that the church had, from long ago, a very sloppy system of keeping its portfolio. One hell of a lot of the church's funds were kept in bearer bonds, which, as I'm sure you know, can be cashed by anybody. And they were kept in the safe in the rector's study—have been since long before Norbert's time. Furthermore, not only did Norbert and Dick have the combination of the safe, half a dozen secretaries, stretching back for several years, did, too."

"I'm surprised Brett didn't change that."

"Apparently he tried to. But it would have been more expensive to get a proper custodian, and he was voted down. The rector felt it was a poor way to spend money better given to a worthy cause, and the vestry followed his lead."

"So anybody could have taken them."

"Precisely."

"But—it seems so insane. Surely other churches aren't like that."

"Well, there was a prominent unnamed church of an unnamed denomination here in New York whose rector had been rector for so long that everybody trusted him without question. In that situation there *was* a custodial bank. But it didn't make any difference. The dear old rector would call up and say, 'Sell so-and-so and such-and-such a security,' and they'd sell without a question. By the time the vestry woke up to what had happened, the rector had retired a rather rich man and the church had lost about half its holdings."

"And they think that's what happened here? Or was it just the bearer bonds that were cashed?"

"A bit of both. Dick did give instructions to sell to a custodial bank we had for part of our ecclesiastical piggy bank."

"But wouldn't that person, whoever it is, say who had told him or her?"

"Oh sure. The man at the bank says it was Dick Grism, who gave perfectly good reasons for selling some securities and placing the money from the sale in the checking account. Then he'd follow this up with a note of confirmation."

"Then why do they think Dick had to have an accomplice?"

"If he didn't, then who killed him?"

"I see," I said after a minute. And then: "It's nice to know that the higher-ups have exonerated me."

"Well—er—I didn't say they'd done that. It's just that their minds are very much on the mechanics of the huge hole in our capital holdings. And they think that whoever was involved in that was undoubtedly in on Dick's murder."

"I see," I said again, not as much comforted as I thought. "Well, I can tell you one higher-up who seems to think I'm the murderer—Norbert."

"I really doubt that he does," Larry said.

He paused so long that I turned from the window I had been looking out of and glanced at him. "And?" I asked.

"You've got to understand Norbert," Larry said finally. "He is, as we all know, one of the most magnetic speakers and preachers this church has ever had. He has tripled the congregation, and although I make practical noises when he talks about jumping the feeding program from two to three times a week, he is really the only rector among the regular churches who has done so much about a terrible situation. But the other side of that coin is that he has the quality of single-mindedness taken to the nth degree."

"How do you mean?"

"I mean that he isn't thinking about Dick's murder. To him it is past and done and not very important. The only thing in his mind now is some kind of huge church revolution, in which all doctrine, all disputes, all searching for ultimate truth and inner peace, would be forgotten in behalf of the only cause he thinks today makes any difference—feeding people."

"Well, several churches are involved in feeding the poor. But they don't seem to have forgotten everything else."

"To Norbert, there is no other message. If all people can be fed, then all problems will be solved. He has a Rousseau-like belief that if you get all your environmental ducks in a row, then the perfect society will follow: that all crime and all sin comes from a society which does not feed its poor. Eliminate hunger, and you eliminate everything that's bad. He has, in his own way, a messianic vision."

There was a silence, then I said, "Well, his vision now extends to Emily Chadbourne. He wants her to fund all the extra feedings."

"I know. He discussed this with me."

"But why Emily?"

"Because of all the people he knows, she happens to be sitting on the biggest fortune and doing nothing about it. Also, because of you. With you here, he feels he has a foot in the door."

"But he doesn't even *like* me."

"He was the one who fought for your being asked here."

"Because of Emily," I said finally, feeling something close to despair.

"Perhaps. It may just be that he thought you'd be a terrific pastoral counselor. After all, this was before the whole homeless question became so acute."

I stood there for a moment, fighting the depression that was settling over me. Finding a job in the Church after ordination had not been easy. There are more ordained candidates than there are jobs. But being a therapist made things slightly easier. There was growing room for those who work with the damaged and downhearted. Being called to St. Anselm's was something of a coup. Now it looked as though I had, not my own shining résumé, talent and charm to thank, but Aunt Emily and her inherited fortune.

"Somehow," I said gloomily, "I feel this is probably very good for my humility."

Larry grinned. "When people say that, I know they're feeling horrible. If it's any consolation, I think you're the best ordained therapist I've ever known."

"Thanks, Larry, it does help. One tries."

"One succeeds, at least you do."

I started to leave. "By the way, how's Rafael?"

"Revoltingly pleased with himself. He thinks he's outwitted all the forces of law and order. He's also engaged to be married, and he says he has a job. He said he could only give me ten minutes."

As I turned I glanced down at Larry's desk. There, open, was the letter from the assistant to the Nobel laureate, with the Cambridge college address in black and white on top. "How's your English chum?"

"All right."

Larry sounded so odd, as though he weren't even hearing what I was asking, that I turned and looked at him. "What's going on? You sound funny."

"Do I? I wrote to him and asked him about . . . something. To look up something . . . Well, he did."

"And you're not happy with the answer?"

"No."

"You should have let sleeping questions lie," I said unfeelingly.

"How true!"

But because I was so fond of Larry, I said, "Anything I can help with?"

"No, you're a love, but there's nothing you can do. Except—don't mention to anybody that I wrote to my friend."

"Of course not."

I went straight into therapy sessions with a couple of my clients and told Josie to hold all calls. So it was four o'clock before the phone rang.

"Claire," Josie said. "Your aunt or mother-in-law or somebody has called you a couple of times. She wanted me to break in on your session, and I might have, except that she got so haughty she irritated the hell out of me. Anyway, she wants you to call her immediately, if not sooner."

Something has obviously happened, I thought to myself as I dialed Emily's number. When last heard from she was not speaking to me, in view of my—to her—unsympathetic behavior towards her adored grandchild. Obviously, something more important than that had bestirred her. I wondered what on earth it could be. I soon found out.

"Emily," I started when she answered the phone, and got no further.

The torrent of anger and reproach poured over me. "And after all that has happened, for you to expose the child in your care to the bullying of the New York police—most of whom are probably corrupt beyond understanding . . . Yes, I am talking about you," she said to someone plainly near her at the other end of the line.

"What are you talking about, Emily? Exposing Martha to whom?" I spoke sharply because my own anxiety went shooting up. I had gone to great lengths to prevent anyone in authority—except Norbert, of course—from even hearing about Martha in connection with Dick's death.

"I mean that I have always known you to be self-centered, self-concerned and selfish beyond belief about doing what was good for you rather than considering others. I am *sick* when I realize how wrong I was to let Martha, a defenseless child if ever there was one, stay in your care . . ."

This, I knew, could go on for some time, and, anyway, I was tired of it.

"Get to the point, Emily. I'll grant you all my failings. But what's happening to Martha now?"

"She is being bullied and questioned by some hulking policeman. I have sent for my lawyer, of course. But he has not had time to reach here."

"Emily, I did not, repeat not, sic the New York Police Department on Martha."

"I no longer believe you. I think now that you're incapable of the truth."

"Think what you want. Is the policeman there named O'Neill?"

"And how would I know what names these thugs may have? And how do you know that one of them is named O'Neill?" But before I could answer she went on, "But what a stupid question—of course, you're very friendly with these types, aren't you? And anyway, you were the one who told them that Martha was visiting the church when that wretched man was killed."

"Is Detective O'Neill there?" I repeated. I knew that the only way I could deal with this was to plough straight through, ignoring whatever Emily might throw at me. "Please find out."

I really didn't think she would bother to ask, but I heard her direct the question to someone near. Then she returned to me. "Your friend Detective O'Neill wishes to speak to you. When our lawyer comes, he will see to it that these dreadful men are removed, and he will also enable me to protect Martha and myself against you."

Presently a weary voice said, "Mrs. Aldington?"

"Yes. Is this Detective O'Neill?"

"It is."

"I have two questions. Just what are you trying to bully out of my stepdaughter? And who told you that she was at the parish house the morning of the murder?"

"We are not trying to bully anyone, Mrs. Aldington, and I should think you'd know that. There's a policewoman present, and we are treating Martha as gently as we do all juveniles, whether you and her grandmother believe it or not. As to who told us your stepdaughter was at the church house at the time of the murder, it was Brett Cunningham. He told us before he left to go to New Jersey."

10

I'D HEARD THE EXPRESSION "feeling kicked in the stomach" before, but never realized how apt it was. The blow was so overwhelming that I was breathless and dizzy for a moment, a reaction that indicated some measure of how deeply I felt betrayed. How much did it have to do with the previous evening? Everything. Obviously to care greatly was to give part of yourself away, and that was what I had done.

It was plain now that my misplaced liking for and trust of Brett Cunningham had extended much further than I'd realized. By itself that was a shock that took some getting used to. And in addition to everything else was guilt: guilt that because I had apparently allowed myself to become far fonder of Brett than he deserved, I had given him the damaging information about Patrick's daughter that he had passed on to the police at the first opportunity. And because of what might ensue from this, she could easily be driven out of her rather fragile hold on rational behavior.

"Oh God!" I said aloud. And then, like Henry Higgins of *My Fair Lady:* "Damn, damn, damn!"

"Troubles?" Norbert said, passing the door.

He had on his coat and hat and a muffler over his round collar, so that he looked somewhat more ordinary and less clerical than usual.

"Yes," I said. "Troubles."

"Anything I can help with?"

I paused, and then said, "No, I'm afraid you can't help, Norbert. But thanks."

"Seen Larry anywhere?"

"I saw him in his office early this afternoon. But not since."

"It's not important. Just that Josie said he had received a letter from England, and I thought he might have heard something about friends we have in common over there."

"Oh—yes. I'd forgotten you were there, too. But weren't you at Oxford?" I asked weakly, and then worried that even that much had violated Larry's instructions. Plainly, he had forgotten to instruct Josie about keeping her mouth shut.

Norbert smiled. "Oxford and Cambridge are not that far apart, geographically anyway. It doesn't matter. I'll see him later." And he ambled off.

My desk was piled high, but I shoved it all in a folder, grabbed my coat from the hanger behind the door and fled down the hall. At this hour, trying to find an empty taxi seemed futile. But I could at least get a subway.

Twenty minutes later I emerged from the subway at Ninety-sixth Street and Lexington Avenue and ran, almost literally, towards Emily's apartment. Even the doorman, I thought, looked at me reproachfully.

When I rang the bell, Trudi answered, and before I could even ask for Martha or Emily, said, "I'm sorry, miss, I've been given my instructions. You're not to come in."

Argument was, I knew, pointless. And it would be better for Trudi if I just overpowered her. So, pushing her aside, I strode into the hall, hesitated a second, then, hearing nothing, went down the long corridor leading to the bedrooms. Something told me that Martha would have retreated into one of those. Passing the rooms I knew to be Emily's bedroom and her study, I opened the next door. Sure enough, Martha was lying on the bed. As I came in, she turned her head, let out a piercing shriek and said, "No, no. Take her away. She frightens me!"

I was at the bed in two strides. "What on earth's the matter with you, Martha? What have I done to make you behave this way?"

"Take her away!' she screamed.

"How dare you push your way into my home," Emily's voice said from the door. "Unless you leave instantly, it is I who will call the police this time. Leave the wretched child to get some rest. Come out of there at once."

"I'm not moving, Emily, until I know what all this is about. And for your information, I did *not,* repeat *not,* tell the police about Martha's being at the parish house. Your great and trusted friend Brett Cunningham did that."

"I don't believe you."

"Ask Detective O'Neill!"

"I wouldn't give credence to anything he said, trying to gouge information the way he did out of Martha. I'm sending for my doctor. And I want you to leave this minute."

"Please go," Martha whimpered. "Please."

All I could see was a hunched shoulder and a face half burrowed in the pillow. "I won't move until you tell me why you are so anxious to have me go. I've never mistreated you, bullied you or, to my knowledge, been unkind—certainly not deliberately. I'm not perfect, but I think that I'm right about that."

Another shriek emerged from the bedclothes. "Leave me alone!"

"Are you satisfied?" Emily said.

Something happened to me then. All of a sudden, I felt that I had done all I could with Patrick's daughter. That it was time to stop blaming myself and turn her over to her grandmother, if that's what they both wanted. There was a large element of the manipulator in Martha, and I knew well she was manipulating both Emily and me for some purpose of her own. Well, good luck to them both. I got up.

"All right, Martha, Emily. I'll do exactly what you want me to. I'll leave you alone. Good night."

And I walked out of the apartment.

I received two calls that night, both of which I came profoundly to wish had never happened.

The first was from one of my clients, a hysterical girl with a poor job record who was possibly, for the fifth time in one year, out of a job.

"How did you get my number?" I asked. Unpublished telephone numbers were conveniences that in the past I had ascribed to snobbery or professional laziness. Within one year of becoming a therapist, I had decided that they were a necessity if I, a single parent, were to have any time with my family.

"Josie finally gave it to me," she said. "At least she didn't stop me when I looked in the church directory at her desk. But please don't be mad at her."

"Whether I am or not is no concern of ours at this moment. What is it you want, Jackie?"

What she wanted was what she always wanted, nonstop enthusiastic support untainted by any hint or suggestion as to how she might learn to take responsibility for herself. Finally, and because it did look as though she was going to be fired the following day, I agreed to meet her in my office at seven forty-five, which would give her enough time to get to her office at nine (in time to be fired, I couldn't help thinking).

I had barely hung up and gone back to the checkers game Jamie and I were having when the phone rang again.

"I'll answer it," Jamie said. "I'll say you're busy," he added. It was plain he reveled in having my undivided attention.

"Better let me know who it is," I finally cautioned.

"Hello," he said. And then: "Oh, hi. Sure!" Then he held the phone out. "It's Mr. Cunningham," he said, as though conferring a treat, and then as he looked at my face: "What's the matter? I thought you liked him?"

I was sorely tempted to tell Jamie, in a voice that could be easily overheard at the other end of the phone, to say I was busy. But Jamie's obvious approval changed that. The fight between Brett and me was none of Jamie's concern.

I started to accept the receiver from Jamie, and then said, "I'll take it in my bedroom, Jamie. When I come on the line, please hang up."

When I picked up the receiver beside my bed, I could hear the click that meant Jamie had put back the receiver at his end.

"Is it that secret?" an ironic voice asked.

"Yes," I said coldly. "I prefer my quarrels to be private."

"I suppose you're angry because I told O'Neill about Martha's being at the parish house the morning of Grism's death."

"Yes, I am." I tried to fight a sense of deflation brought on by Brett's calm acknowledgment of his violation. "And I want to tell you—"

"First," Brett's voice interrupted, "I didn't promise you not to mention it. Second, O'Neill was threatening to arrest you. And I decided, since I am as sure—or almost as sure—as you that your stepdaughter did not do this, that his knowing about it was the lesser of two evils."

"You had no right to make that decision, Brett. And as a consequence of your doing so, Martha is now at her grandmother's screaming every time I come in the room, because they both think it was I who told O'Neill. When I tried to explain to Emily that it was you, she refused to believe me, and has forbidden me the house."

"If I had not told O'Neill, he would have come and arrested you at the parish house. I don't think he really believed you committed that murder, but he knew damn well you knew something had gone on that morning, and he was determined to find out."

"So instead of that he puts pressure on a highly neurotic, very fragile fifteen-year-old girl."

"Has he arrested her?"

"Of course not."

"Then why are you so unreasonably upset? I say unreasonably because nothing terrible seems to have happened."

"Nothing except that my stepdaughter, the girl Patrick left for me to look after, has apparently freaked out."

"And it's all my fault?"

"Yes. You violated a trust. If you hadn't, I could have coped with Detective O'Neill myself."

"And you don't care that he would have arrived at the church offices to arrest you?"

"I didn't do it, so what harm would have occurred?"

"It wouldn't have done the church much good, would it?"

"And you care about that? More than you care about Martha?"

"Claire—where is your professional objectivity? Martha did not commit the crime. As I told you, I'm as sure of that as you are. Therefore, it's possible she may throw light on who did. Don't you think that's important? After all, a man, Dick Grism, died. Now that he's out of sight you seem to consider trying to find out who deprived him of his life as far down your list of priorities. Suppose it were Jamie—would you go to any lengths to prevent police even talking to him?"

His question stopped me. For a moment I didn't answer. Then I said, "That would be different. Jamie would know how to act. He could talk to anybody without flying apart."

"Do you really think Martha's that fragile? Or are you, on some level, unsure about her innocence? And isn't it possible you are overcompensating because she is your stepdaughter, and you may not like her as much as you think you ought?"

"I don't need your amateur psychology. I think what you did was a betrayal of trust. And I don't believe for one moment that you care that much how the church looks."

"Why shouldn't I care as much as say . . . Norbert does?"

"Norbert may be a little off the wall sometimes, but he's a genuinely dedicated person who follows what he feels are Christ's instructions."

"Two divorced wives might disagree with you."

"That's a typically traditional attitude—judging a man's mission by his domestic failures. Great visionaries frequently make rotten husbands. Look at Socrates. I didn't say he was husband of the year—and you of all people should be sympathetic about divorce. Your own slate isn't that clean."

I knew that my besetting sin—swift anger combined with an agile tongue—was making an unattractive appearance. If it had been anyone but Brett, I would have apologized immediately. But with him as the recipient, the words stuck in my throat.

"I'm sorry," Brett said, stiffly, after a moment. "If you'll forgive my incursion into your professional territory, I think we are using Martha and Norbert as surrogates. We're fighting about something else altogether. But I'm not sure what it is. Good night."

I stood there, hearing the click at his end, with the dead receiver at mine. Then I put it down. "He should never have told O'Neill," I said aloud.

"What's the matter, Ma? Did you have a fight with Mr. Cunningham?" Jamie asked from the door.

"Yes."

"Well, I guess that takes care of him." And Jamie walked back down the hall towards the living room. I followed him.

"Why did you come to my room?" I asked. "Did you want something?"

"I wondered why you were yelling."

"I wasn't yelling."

"Well, you were having a fight. I could tell."

"Your friend Mr. Cunningham told the police something I told him in confidence—that Martha was at the parish house the morning that Dick Grism was killed."

"You mean she did it?" His green eyes were round with horror—or was it anticipation?

"No, I don't. Of course she didn't."

"Well, then why do you care?"

"Because it made her freak out and made Emily forbid me the house."

"Guess that's why you were in such a snit when you came home."

"I was not in a snit. I told you I was upset about something and didn't want to discuss it right away."

"Anybody can tell when you're in a snit a mile off. Your cheeks get red and your eyes get bright. Why are you so mad that Mr. Cunningham told the police? And what does Martha have to do with it?"

I sighed, jumped two of Jamie's men on the checkerboard, then told him about the woman seen early at the parish house, who the police thought was I and who I thought was Martha.

"But why did Mr. Cunningham tell the police?"

"He says because he thought the detective was coming to arrest me—or at least take me down to the precinct for questioning."

"I think he did right. And if it was me, you'd have told the police in a minute and I would have told them what I'd seen."

"You're not Martha. You are, I'm happy to say, as normal and healthy as you can be, which is a great joy to me. And I'd have known without question that nobody in his right mind would think you'd do anything of the kind."

"But you think Martha did?"

"Of course not. I've told you I don't."

"Well," Jamie said, emptying the counters into the checkers box, "I think you're afraid she did. And I think she might have."

"Jamie—that's just because you're jealous of her. I don't like that in you."

"Ma—*you're* supposed to be the psychologist. I'm not saying she could have because I'm jealous of her. And I'm only jealous sometimes. But because I think she's been a little crazy lately. You're always telling me—and telling Martha—to try and think about the *facts* of things without getting them messed up with how we feel about them. Well, I think you're all messed up yourself."

And with that Jamie marched forward and turned on the television set to his favorite, and my least favorite, police show. On a less harried night I would have told him to turn it off and do his homework. This particular night I didn't. Perhaps because of what he said. But perhaps because I found the show distracted me from my own unappetizing thoughts.

After a somewhat sleepless night I arrived at the parish house a few minutes after seven the following morning. I'd left Jamie drinking his milk and eating his cereal and trying to catch up on some last-minute reading. "You're going to leave here at eight and then wait downstairs till Jerry arrives, okay?" I said.

"Sure."

"Promise me, Jamie."

"All right, I promise. Where do you think I'm going to go?"

"And don't talk to me in that tone of voice."

Silence.

"Please reply, Jamie. It's considered good manners."

"All right."

"And you'll walk Motley before."

"Yes."

I kissed his resisting cheek. "I love you."

Mumble mumble, was all I got in return.

Jerry was a slightly older friend of Jamie's who lived in an apartment house one block away and went to the same school. When I had to leave early, I called Jerry's divorced mother and she headed him in our direction. It was a pleasant arrangement, and I repaid it by having Jerry stay when his mother had to be away on business.

When I inserted the key in the main parish house door and pushed the door open, I knew, in one inhaled breath, that some of our homeless had spent the night in the lobby, and as I walked up I saw a few huddled figures on the various chairs. From the stairs leading down, I could see that the light in the big room downstairs was on, and on an impulse went down.

There were twenty cots down there, in four rows of five. The smell was, overpowering, but David Lavalle, one of our young parishioners who had spent the night on watch, was going around and waking various occupants up, handing them Styrofoam cups of coffee. I wondered if David had kept the watch alone. Usually there were two.

More often than not I found Norbert's tendency to sweep aside everyone's convenience in support of his various activist pursuits irritating. For all his charitable motives there was something arrogant about it. Yet now, seeing these few destitute who had given up all attempt to cope with the demands and difficulties of city life, a sense of pity washed over me. As far as I knew, they had committed no wrong, they were simply unable to take care of themselves, and for that reason were here, sitting, bewildered, on their cots, scratching their no doubt infested heads as they sipped their coffee.

"I don't drink coffee," one woman said indignantly. "I drink tea. Where's my tea?" She started to tip the coffee cup onto the floor. David rushed forward and stopped her.

"I'm sorry," he said. "We don't have tea."

"You should have tea," she said angrily.

He was taking the coffee back to the table when an old man reached out a hand. "I'll take it."

David, with a smile, handed it to him. "There's more," he said.

"Can I help?" I asked.

"Not really," David said. "We have to get them out of here by eight and get the place cleaned up before the day-care kids come. And clean the bathrooms."

"Can't some of the custodians do that?"

"No. It isn't their job, and they resent doing it."

"Well," I said, "the least I can do is clean a bathroom."

"You don't have to."

"I know."

Considering everything, the bathroom could have been in worse shape, particularly when I remembered that at least half of the twenty down here were former mental patients.

After that I went upstairs, along the hall towards the stairs leading up to the second floor. Somewhat surprised, I saw Josie coming out of the business manager's office.

"You're early," I said.

"I have a manuscript to type and it's got to be ready by tomorrow." Josie sometimes moonlighted as a typist and preferred to use the big office machine with its correcting device behind her on a typing table fixed to her desk.

"Are you delivering the mail already? Has it arrived?"

She gave me a sullen look. "I was returning some of Dick's books, if you must know, although I don't think it's any of your business."

"Why the hostility?"

She didn't answer, but slipped behind her reception desk.

"What's the matter, Josie? Do you think I killed Dick?"

She didn't look up. I was rather surprised to see that her eyelids were red and puffy.

I said, "I didn't realize you knew him—knew him well, that is."

"He was a nice guy, a really decent person, and I think it's rotten that he's been killed. We'd talk sometimes . . . and he lent me some books."

At that point the switchboard buzzed. Josie picked up the receiver. "It's for you," she said, and handed the receiver to me.

It was Jackie, the client whose pressing need to see me before work had got me out of bed at an ungodly hour.

"I'm sorry, Claire," she said. "I overslept. I guess I won't be there."

I took a deep breath, counted to five and tried to remember that oversleeping was frequently a result of fear, a defense against the prospect of something unpleasant and a symptom of depression.

"All right," I said.

"You're mad, aren't you?"

Jackie had enormous self-pity and only a vestigial ability to see how much she created her own problems, up to and including her fatal talent for getting fired. It was that vestige I was working on with her as hard as I could. Towards this end I decided to introduce some reality.

"Wouldn't you be, if you had come down here an hour early especially to see me?"

"I guess so. It's just . . . just that I'm feeling alienated in my own space."

"Jackie, what on earth does that garbage mean?"

Unexpectedly she giggled, giving me hope of her ultimate recovery. "I guess it means that I'm confused and feel rotten."

"Why don't you go to work instead. If you don't think about things for a while, they may look better when you get back to them."

"Okay. I guess you're right. The trouble with thinking, it almost never makes me feel better."

"That's one of its handicaps. On the whole, it's better to act your way out, rather than try to think your way out of feeling . . . what was it?"

"Alienated in my own space."

"Precisely."

"Funny, that's what my grandmother used to say."

"I bet you anything you like that your grandmother never came out with anything as meaningless and linguistically offensive as being alienated in your whatever."

"No. What she said was, do something useful and get your mind off yourself."

"It's terrible to realize that some of those old boffins might have been right, isn't it?"

Jackie giggled again. "I'll see you again next week, Claire."

She hung up and I gave the receiver back to Josie. "Well," I said, "my client's not coming. Maybe, despite myself, I'll get some desk work done."

I decided to miss Morning Prayer and work through until my next client arrived. With this admirable purpose in mind, I went upstairs to my office and started going through my "in" box. I had been filling out forms and drafting letters and reports for about three quarters of an hour when screams suddenly erupted from below, rising to a crescendo, then diminishing and rising again, wild, and with a note that brought me to my feet.

"My God!" I said aloud. "What was that?"

I started to run downstairs and then stopped halfway down. From where I stood I could see that the screaming came from one of the elderly homeless women from the parish hall downstairs, the one who preferred tea, I found myself thinking inanely. Now, her mouth a round O, she was standing in front of the reception desk with screams coming out of her mouth as though from a faulty steam engine. And she was staring at Josie's body, sprawled half in and half out of the reception area. Blood stained the floor by Josie's head and was spattered over the paneled desk and the wall behind.

For a moment I was paralyzed. Then I ran down the rest of the way. "Be quiet!" I yelled to the old woman. Amazingly, she stopped. David Lavalle and Brett came running from below. Even with my mind on Josie, the sight of Brett made my heart seem to halt, and then race, much to my annoyance. I was angry with him. And anyway, what was he doing here? All those thoughts and feelings sped through me as we bent over Josie.

"Thank God!" I said, after listening to her heart and feeling her pulse. "She's still breathing. Somebody call 911 immediately and get an ambulance."

The police arrived within two minutes and an ambulance shortly after that. Sally Hepburn, a friend of Josie's, went in the ambulance with the still unconscious Josie to the hospital.

"We ought to do something about that," David indicated the blood on the floor and the desk and the walls.

"Don't touch it!" one of the policemen stopped talking into his walkie-talkie long enough to say. "Some detectives are on their way here."

I saw Brett disappearing down the stairs again. He had left without even looking at me. "What's Brett doing down there?" I asked David.

"Down where? Oh, you mean downstairs. He was on watch with me last night."

"I didn't know he did that."

"He's a funny guy. Sounds like the world's great stuffed shirt, but does more than his share and is always there when you need him." I reminded myself again that I was angry with Brett, mostly to overcome an immediate temptation to go down and apologize to my enemy.

The front door swung open. "My God!" Norbert said, coming rapidly up the stairs. "This is really terrible. Josie's not dead, is she? At least that's the word from our friends the reporters, who have gathered outside."

"No. Josie's still alive. Either she has a blessedly thick skull or whoever hit her did not hit her hard."

The parish door opened again, and Detective O'Neill, with a couple of other men, came in.

"Rafael was not here," Norbert said anxiously. "Was he?"

"No. But I was."

His fine brows went up, and then down. "I see. Well, that still doesn't point the finger at you, Claire. So were a lot of other people, I'm sure."

But it was Rafael, not a member of his staff, that he worried about, I thought.

"Mrs. Aldington." Detective O'Neill was coming up the steps. "What happened?"

"Well, as you must know, or you wouldn't be here, Josie Beardsley got struck on the head and rendered unconscious. We called the police, who came—I must say—with great speed. An ambulance came shortly after that and took her away, with Sally Hepburn, the rector's secretary and a friend of Josie's, riding with her."

"Yes," Detective O'Neill said patiently. "I know all that. What I'd like to know is what you saw."

I became aware of Norbert, of David Lavalle and of some of the homeless standing there, and of others in the background, all apparently waiting for me to answer.

"Claire," Norbert said, "I think before you answer anything more, you should have an attorney with you. I am speaking for your own good, Claire," he went on evenly. "We all care about you a great deal—no matter what happens. Not only because you are a valued staff member here, but because you are the widow of one of my oldest friends."

Out of the corner of my eye I saw Brett coming slowly up the stairs from the hall below.

"Why don't we finish this in your office?" Detective O'Neill said to me.

"All right."

"Claire—I still think you should have legal representation with you."

Perhaps it was the weight of Norbert's words, dropping like boulders, but suddenly, in my mind, I saw Jamie. If I did get arrested, what would happen to him? Obviously, the reality of this occurring had never before struck me. Panic now came. All I could think about was my son. Martha had Emily Chadbourne. Jamie had no one but me. And Motley.

"Jamie!" I said.

"In your office," Detective O'Neill said. "Let's go upstairs."

"I most strenuously object to this," Norbert said. "This is the abuse of police practice. By herself, unrepresented, distraught about her son, who knows what Mrs. Aldington will admit to."

"Are you going to come upstairs?" Detective O'Neill said. And added, "This is only your office, not the precinct. And I have no tape on me to record anything."

"I still object to it," Norbert said.

Odd, I thought, who would have guessed that Norbert would turn out to be my defender. Not any of the people standing around Norbert, not, for heaven's sake, Brett. But I was wrong about one thing. Various people standing in the hall did pick up Norbert's statement. "Let her tell her story here. What are you gonna try and do—force it out of her?"

Suddenly Brett spoke up. "Go upstairs with O'Neill, Claire. It can't be any worse than it is, and he's right, it's not down at the police station with somebody taking down what you're saying."

"A good friend you turned out to be," David said, looking back at Brett.

Brett said nothing.

"All right, Detective O'Neill," I said. "Let's go up."

"Did you suddenly start to believe me?" he asked when we got to the top.

"Maybe. Maybe I just wanted some peace and quiet, even if it is covered with a land mine."

We went into my office and shut the door. Odd, I thought, this room that had represented to me so much peace and fulfillment now seemed full of barbed wire. "Sit down, Mr. O'Neill," I said.

He took off his raincoat and hung it on the coat rack against the wall. Then he sat down on the seat opposite my desk, because, as a matter of custom, and perhaps security, I went behind the desk and sat in my chair there.

"Okay," he said. "What happened?"

I took a deep breath. "I arrived here a little after seven to see my client Jackie Dunlap. You can check with her, she called me last night, in an overwrought state, and I agreed to meet her for an early session this morning at seven forty-five."

"What was she overwrought about?"

"Because she was about to get fired for the umpteenth time."

"What's her problem?"

"Do you really want to know what her problem is? Or shall I go on?"

"I'd really like to know what her problem is."

"Normally I would not discuss this, as it violates the therapist-client relationship. But since she's confiding in the world at large about this, I may as well tell you that her problem is that she finds it hard to turn in an eight-hour day in exchange for eight hours of pay. Consequently, she gets fired a lot. Beyond that, I won't go."

"That could be said of a lot of people."

"How true."

"All right. You arrived at a little after seven to see a client at seven forty-five. Begin with when you arrived."

"I arrived. I noticed two or three of the homeless, whom we allow on cold nights to sit in chairs, still there."

"Was Josie Beardsley there?"

"No. I saw the light on in the downstairs hall, so I went down, saw the various occupants of the beds beginning to get up and talked to David Lavalle."

"He was in charge down there?"

"When we have people sleeping down there, we always have two church members, sometimes a man and a woman, sometimes two men, who remain on watch, partly to protect the church, partly to protect the people who are sleeping. Some of the homeless are quite disturbed —as I'm sure you know."

"Yes. So you spoke to David Lavalle. Who was on watch with him?"

"Brett Cunningham. But I didn't see him there at all. He must have been cleaning out one of the bathrooms or getting cups for the coffee from upstairs in the cafeteria."

"Okay. Did anything of significance happen there?"

"Nothing that I could see. I cleaned up a bathroom and then came upstairs. At that point my client, Jackie, called to say she'd overslept. So I decided to do some desk work and went upstairs. I was still there, working, when I heard the screaming. Oh—I forgot. I saw Josie, which surprised me. She isn't often that early, except when she wants to use the office machine for her free-lance typing. Anyway, I thought she must be delivering the mail or something, because I saw her come out of the business manager's office. But she said she was returning some books . . ." I hesitated. "Her eyes were red and puffy, as though she'd been crying. I told her I was surprised that she knew Dick well enough to borrow his books, and she suddenly launched into a paean of praise about him, and how decent he was, and that he did, indeed, lend her books."

"Did you hear anything else?"

"No."

"What happened then?"

"I went upstairs to work, and about forty-five minutes later heard this bone-chilling screaming that went on and on. I ran downstairs and saw that the screaming came from one of the women who had been sleeping downstairs, and that Josie was sprawled on the floor. Somebody called the police, who were there fast, and then, as I told you, the ambulance came. That's it."

O'Neill sat there for a moment in silence, flipping through the pages of his notebook.

"I hope," I said, "that this removes any last doubt you may have about my stepdaughter, Martha. She was most certainly not here this morning."

He looked up. "What makes you so sure?"

"Listen, Mr. O'Neill, Emily Chadbourne would no more let her out of that apartment than she'd let her fly out the window. And I'd stack Emily's muscle against the police department's any day."

Unexpectedly, he laughed. "I think I'd agree with you. But, just for the sake of argument, what's to prevent her from slipping out of the apartment while everyone's asleep?"

"I can't give you a rational reason for this, but I'm convinced she couldn't do it. She wouldn't dare."

"You're probably right. But I do think—and you do, too—that she was in Grism's office after he was killed, and I would like to know very much why she was there. Wouldn't you?"

"Yes. I'll admit I haven't been as preoccupied with that as I have with fear that she—or I—might be arrested. But I'll agree that her being there is extremely odd, and if you could just reassure me that she is no longer under suspicion, I could turn my attention to it. At least I could when I don't feel under suspicion myself. But I suppose that's too much to ask for."

"You were present on the premises both when Grism was killed and when Josie was assaulted. And you were alone on each occasion at the crucial time. You saw no one, and nobody called you—or at least reached you in your office. So for neither time do you have an acceptable alibi. Surely you must realize that makes you of primary interest."

"Am I the only one who was there? Surely not! Josie was there for the first time, of course. But I can't imagine her having anything to do with Grism's death. And even if she had, why would someone try to kill her?"

"We don't know the answer to that, and we don't know whether or not she had anything to do with Grism's murder."

Suddenly, something else occurred to me. "What was Josie struck with?"

"We don't know that either. The weapon for Grism's murder—the bookend or whatever it was—hasn't turned up yet. And I haven't heard from the hospital whether the shape of Beardsley's wound would match or not."

"You mean you've never found the bookend that was used on Grism?"

"No."

"And you've looked everywhere?"

"Yes. Why, do you have an idea where it is?"

"No, of course not."

The mind is an odd thing. Had I brought up the subject of the weapon because I had seen, however faintly, the drops of blood? Or was it the other way around? My carpet was an extremely dusky rose—it had been fitted into my office long before I came and therefore represented the taste of the previous occupant. But although I made jokes about it from time to time, I didn't really object. The color blended well with a small tapestry I had brought from England and which hung over my desk. Now, as I talked, I realized I had been staring at reddish spots on the carpet. They were unevenly spaced but they seemed to be coming from . . . or going to . . . Suddenly I jumped up and went towards the paneled cupboard that was built in below my bookshelves. Stooping down, I opened the doors.

It was like seeing Dick's body: I saw the blood, the reddish stains first, dripping down a pile of pamphlets that I'd stacked on the upper shelf of the closet. Above that was something wrapped in newspaper, the lower part of which was soggy with the same reddish liquid.

O'Neill was right behind me. "Let me," he said as I reached out. He lifted the object out.

"Do you have anywhere I can put this down?" he asked, looking at me, his face expressionless.

"Here." I spread the newspaper I had picked up on the way to the office on top of my desk. O'Neill laid his burden on that, then unwrapped the paper.

Hair as well as fresh blood had stuck to the bottom of the ugly bookend.

I am not normally squeamish, but I felt my stomach heave.

O'Neill said nothing. It was I who spoke. "You looked in my cupboard before, didn't you, when you searched the parish house?"

"Yes. Or tried to. But I seem to remember that that particular cupboard was locked."

"But you got it open, didn't you? You must have had a search warrant."

"Yes. We got it open. There was nothing."

"You can't believe that I would be stupid enough to put it there if I had indeed used that to kill Grism, or hit Josie over the head."

"It would be either a very stupid or a very wily thing to do. By the way, I think I will go along with the rector. You should, perhaps, call a lawyer before we go any further."

I stared at him and repeated, stupidly, "A lawyer?"

"Yes," he replied steadily, "a lawyer."

11

O'NEILL WENT TO THE DOOR and shouted, "Joe!"

There were quick steps up the staircase and one of the uniformed police appeared.

O'Neill was wrapping the paper loosely about the bookend. "Take this, *carefully.* If you have a plastic bag big enough, that'd be the best thing. I'm sending this to prints, and I don't want anything on it smeared or destroyed. Got it?"

"Got it," the young cop said. He went over to the desk and picked up the newspaper-wrapped monstrosity as though it were a giant egg, the last of its kind. Then he walked carefully to the door, watched by O'Neill.

There seemed to be a small crowd outside my door by this time: Norbert, several of the custodians and Johnny McKnight.

"Have you seen Larry?" Johnny asked Norbert as the officer passed him.

"No," Norbert said. "I don't think he's come in today."

Even stunned as I was, I reacted to that with a little surprise. Larry was usually extremely prompt.

As O'Neill was about to leave my office, he said to me, "Don't leave town, and if you go anywhere except here and to your home, let us know where you are. And, as I said before, I strongly advise your getting counsel."

Norbert put his hand on my arm. Suddenly I felt his power and warmth and was comforted by it. At the same time I knew that with Norbert it meant nothing.

"Listen, Claire," he said. "We're on your side, whatever the story is, whatever pressures have been on you."

They all think I did this, I thought. And, as I looked around, I realized I was right. Glances suddenly dropped. People who had been standing around started drifting to their offices or downstairs.

"The vestry meeting's still on, isn't it?" Johnny asked, moving to the upper conference room.

Norbert glanced at his watch. "Yes. Almost immediately."

"We're not going to vote on that St. Cuthbert's offer today, are we?"

"Yes. I think it's time and we certainly need the money."

"But it wasn't on the agenda." Johnny sounded indignant. "I mean, is that fair? Some of the vestry who might not be here today would probably make a special effort if they thought that vote would be taken."

"You know as well as I do, Johnny, that vestrymen and vestrywomen are supposed to turn up to every meeting if at all possible. I won't give dignity to this question of turning up only when there's a crucial vote. That shows disrespect to the church and its mission."

"It may show disrespect, Norbert," I said, and heard the queer, dragging tiredness in my voice. "But it's long been known that that's what happens."

"Then we're going to have to shake them up. You won't be coming, will you, Claire?"

He would offer his support, but considering how near I was to being arrested, he was not going to take any risk involving his precious St. Cuthbert's project. Numbly, like an acquiescent child, I shook my head.

"You understand, don't you?" Norbert said.

"Am I also under suspicion here—among you?" I asked.

"My dear. I've just said we would do anything for you we could. But we mustn't confuse issues. What St. Cuthbert's money will do for the thousands—hundreds of thousands—of homeless and poor is far too valuable to endanger. I know you agree."

His eyes were like twin suns, pouring out love and approval. And what was behind those suns? I found myself wondering.

But at that point Sally Hepburn came up the stairs.

"How's Josie?" several voices called out.

"Not too sharp," Sally answered. "In fact, not good. But she's hanging in there."

"Has she regained consciousness?" Norbert asked.

"A little. But she's groggy. And they're sure not taking any risks. She's in a private room with a cop at the door. Claire, she told me to give you this—" She detached what I saw now was one of two bags hanging by their straps over her shoulder. "It's her handbag. She says she doesn't trust those safes at the hospital. Here."

"Fine," I said, and reached out my hand.

"Shouldn't it go in the safe in my office?" Norbert said, his own hand going out.

"Josie said Claire was to have it. It was about the only thing she was clear on. She wants you to call her roommate."

"Oh, yes. Okay." One of Josie's previous rommates had been a client of mine.

"Norbert, are we ready?" a voice said from the foot of the stairs.

I glanced down and saw that it was the head of the vestry, Joe Pike. Spread around him were various other members, including Brett Cunningham. As his eyes met mine, he looked away and said something to the man standing beside him, as though I were thin air and he hadn't seen me.

Well, I thought, I'm glad. Given how angry I was at him, and how little he was to be trusted, it was just as well that my feeling about him was obviously returned.

"Don't panic, Claire," Norbert said, and started down the stairs.

Johnny gave me a strange look and followed. Everybody else melted away.

The vestry meeting would last, in effect, till two o'clock, since it was a custom that the vestry and clergy would go out to lunch afterwards to a neighborhood restaurant. Well, I thought, Norbert will be there, and Johnny, and Larry, if he's in. It was the first time since I'd come to St. Anselm's that I would miss one of those meetings, and I felt a sense of loss and diminishment at being barred from the one today. The feeling was so strong, in fact, that I wondered if I had received a wound in my self-esteem. Was it geared so soon and so much to my status? A disturbing thought.

I went back into my room with Josie's bag swinging from my hand.

On the whole, I was a little surprised that she had confided the bag to me instead of Sally Hepburn, but supposed that either she was not very clear in the head or she wanted me to look up the name and phone number of her current roommate in some address book in her bag so I could inform her.

I opened the handbag and after a little scrabbling around among powder, lipstick, pencil, eyebrow pencil, comb, brush, letters and a paperback mystery, finally located an address book. But while the address book was filled, and I found also a wallet with her name and address on it, I was unable to figure out who her roommate was.

Finally I called Sally Hepburn. "Sally, do you have Josie's current roommate's number?"

"Sure. Just a minute."

I heard the faint metallic sound of an address wheel being cranked, then Sally said, "Josie's roommate is Paul Riverton, and the number is 874-9658."

"Paula Riverton," I repeated, writing it down.

"No, Claire. Not Paula, Paul. I didn't know you were that old-fashioned."

"I'm not, but I could have sworn that she talked to me about Paula once."

"Oh, well, she did, when she first came to St. Anselm's. She had the idea that all church people were ferociously strict."

"And then she discovered we were as depraved as anyone else," I finished sardonically.

"Well, yes. Anyway, Paul has a daytime number if you want it. It's 722-4853. You can try him there."

"All right."

Paul turned out to be a pleasant but taciturn young man who simply got the details of what had happened, then said he was taking off for the hospital, as he didn't trust doctors. He was going to make sure that Josie came out of her coma. "And what are the people at the church doing about it?" he asked belligerently.

"There's not much we can do at the moment," I said. "Trying to find the murderer, or at least trying to help the police to find him."

"Pigs," Paul said laconically.

"Come on, Paul. That went out ten or more years ago."

"Yeah, well. Maybe you're right. But I don't like 'em."

"You owe the fact that Josie's still alive to their speed in getting to the church."

"Yeah, well, as a rich Wasp church on the Upper East Side—what d'ya expect?"

"Nothing," I said, sighing, and hung up.

The desire to feel oppressed seemed to be catching, I reflected.

My eleven-thirty appointment turned up, releasing me at twelve-fifteen. Shortly after she'd gone Sally called. "Claire, would you take the twelve-thirty service? Larry's supposed to be doing it, but he's still out on that call."

"Okay."

Celebrating the liturgy had always either calmed me, when I was upset, or exhilarated me, when I was depressed or tired. Some magic in the ancient words seemed there, regardless of my mood.

Although it was not part of the Communion service, I found, running in the back of my mind, words from the Collect for Peace, to me one of the greatest prayers of the entire liturgy. *O God, who art the author of peace and lover of concord, in knowledge of whom standeth our eternal life, whose service is perfect freedom . . .*

Whose service is perfect freedom . . . What was perfect freedom? I wondered. My uncle the bishop, whose conservatism so irked Patrick, nevertheless could say some memorable things. Once, when I asked him the meaning of the phrase from the Collect, he said, "It means that when you do what is right and leave the results up to God, you have, in a sense, total freedom. The person who is in a constant sweat as to where his best interests lie is having always to make choices that may prove disastrous. That, to me, is servitude . . ."

If the above were true, I thought, as the service continued, then I should feel wonderfully free. But I didn't. I felt caught and, somehow, in the wrong, as though I were as guilty as everyone thought I was. Why?

After the small congregation had filed out of the chapel, I went back in and sat there, in the front row, my hands in my lap, staring at the altar and the stained-glass window behind it.

One very obvious reason for my feeling caught was my growing sense of a net closing around me. And it was an extremely unpleasant feeling.

I knew, but only I knew for a fact, that I had not committed Dick's murder or the assault on Josie. Yet the suspicion that surrounded me like a thickening blanket was now so strong that I had to make a conscious effort to speak in a normal voice. Only Sally, with her single-minded concern for Josie, had not translated that concern into a suspicion of me. The police seemed on the point of arresting and charging me. Norbert . . . Norbert's manner towards me was strongly reminiscent of the prison chaplain's towards the condemned.

I did not kill Dick or attack Josie . . .

I felt as though I were addressing, constantly, an unseen audience. If I had been a man, they would have arrested me, one side of me whispered. . . . But taking a woman priest to jail was probably more radical than they were prepared to be on anything but an open-and-shut case—or a confession.

Come on, Claire, don't be paranoid. . . .

The two sides, like two opposing characters in a play, went back and forth. But there was something else, something deeper, bothering me. It had been growing for days, but I had deliberately not looked at it. I tried to focus now on my sense of dis-ease. What hurt when I touched it in my mind . . . ?

After a minute or two I knew there were two answers: Martha and Brett, but in which order I couldn't be sure.

Sitting there, I watched the gray day growing grayer behind the leaded panes, and I thought about Martha. And the more I thought about her, the more astonishing it became that I hadn't confronted her with my belief . . . fear . . . that she had, for some unimaginable reason, been in Dick Grism's office the morning of his death. Had seen him dead, and touched him . . . or killed him? No, my mind repudiated the idea, but I forced it back. Could Martha have done it? Answer: yes, she could. She was frail, but she was certainly capable of picking up that dreadful bookend and bringing it down on Dick's balding skull.

"But I'm sure she wouldn't do it," said Claire the defense attorney.

"Oh—what makes you so certain?" asked Claire the prosecutor. "Just because you don't like to think she would?"

"All right, cut out the smart comments," said Claire the judge. "Concentrate on: if, *if* she was there, what brought her? For this emotionally disturbed, anorexic and perfectionist girl to go downtown and kill a man she'd seen only once would require a powerful motive. What is it?"

What connection had she had before with Dick? countered the opposition in my mind.

Her comment about his gross weight.

Was there anything else?

Not that I knew of.

"But there's got to be something else," I muttered aloud to myself, and then glanced around at the other rows of chairs in the small, jewel-like chapel to see if anyone was there to overhear me.

What connection did Dick have with anything other than the various aspects of church life with which he had been associated—the budget, the portfolio, the yes-ing and no-ing to various church projects? According to some of the second-guessers he must have had a buddy somewhere in a bank or brokerage house . . . no, that was a red herring. Except that Josie seemed to be his friend . . .

No, I almost shouted in my mind. Get back to Martha. What did she and Dick share? Because that was always the terrible thing about murderer and victim. They shared something, and the sharing proved lethal to one of them . . .

And then, apparently out of nowhere, came the memory of my saying to Brett . . . "only Elsie Shaftsbury." Plain, earnest, radical Elsie . . . And Brett's comment that the Shaftsburys were, in some way, connected to Dick Grism.

Martha's words were rushing in now . . . "You should never have married him . . . he was exclusively faithful to my mother . . ."

What might a man from whom most pleasures have been withdrawn —drinking, smoking, even, possibly, sex itself—do for satisfaction? What other powerful narcotic was there . . . ?

Suddenly I saw Dick's face, the greedy interest with which he listened to everything, his fondness for pretending that he could effect the impossible, just as a special favor, the rulings that had seemed to come more and more from his office, less and less from Johnny's or Larry's or even Norbert's . . . Power, the oldest, strongest and most enduring of the human appetites.

But how and why would Dick bother exerting his power over

Martha? And then I remembered her taunting tone outside the conference door as she sneered her repudiation of the heaviness Dick was powerless to do anything about.

Some realization was snapping at my neck, pursuing me, as I pretended to myself that I was looking for it . . . I had to see Martha, ask her a question.

And Brett?

Quickly I turned my mind away. I would not think about him.

Leaving the chapel, I went to the sacristy and took off the stole, surplice and cassock, and then entered the parish house through a side door in the church. Running upstairs, I flung on my raincoat, took my handbag out of my bottom drawer and snatched up my ever-present tote bag.

I went through the parish house door so fast I almost collided with a lanky, fair-haired boy of about sixteen or seventeen in windbreaker and jeans coming up the steps.

"Sorry," he said.

I smiled. "I'm afraid it was my fault."

He glanced at my clerical collar. "Is the rector in?"

"Yes. He's sort of tied up right now. We had . . . we had a bad accident inside."

"I guess that accounts for the police cars. I was wondering."

I was itching to go, but I said, "Anything urgent? Anything I can do?"

"No. Not really. I just came to see the rector to thank him for giving me a lift to Stamford the other morning." He grinned engagingly. "I never would have made it back to school on time if he hadn't given me a ride. We talked on the way. He's a pretty interesting guy. I've never been interested in a church before, but I've been thinking and I'd like to talk to him."

Norbert frequently had this effect on young people, I thought. "Well, why don't you go on in. If he can't see you now, you can make a date for later."

"Okay. By the way, my name is Dan Hepburn. I'm Sally Hepburn's nephew."

"Hello and welcome!" I said. "I know Norbert, to say nothing of Sally, will be glad to see you. I'm sorry, but I have to run now."

"See you," he called as I fled down the steps and hailed a cab.

I was halfway to Emily's apartment when I realized I had two clients to see that afternoon. Leaning forward, I started to tell the cab driver to stop at a phone booth. But no New York taxi would wait calmly while I made the necessary phone calls. The clients, I decided, would have to make out as best they could and I would negotiate my peace with them afterwards.

Just as we turned into Fifth Avenue I remembered something else: Josie's bag, the one she had sent for me to take care of. Where was it? Curiously, I had no memory at all of doing anything with it—either putting it on a shelf or giving it to someone to put into one of the church's safes when I went to take the twelve-thirty service. Where was it before that? Where had I put it when Sally handed it to me? I couldn't remember.

What is the matter with me? I thought. Never before (to my knowledge) had I been so careless of responsibility, so oblivious of other people's wishes and feelings. Now I was being untrustworthy with a bag entrusted to my care, not showing up for appointments with clients, leaving the church when we were one short of clergy and there was a vestry meeting going on . . . and where was Larry?

Of course, it was entirely possible that some member of the parish had landed in the hospital or had died and his pastoral services had been suddenly needed. But . . . in some way I couldn't pin down my mind was making a connection between Larry and Josie . . .

"Lady," the driver said. "We're here. Isn't this the right address?" Plainly, this was not the first time he'd said that.

"Sorry," I mumbled, and handed him some bills that would cover the ride and a decent tip. Then I got out.

In New York, where the rich apartment houses and condominiums line Park and Fifth avenues, I had always looked upon the doormen as uniformed props, symbols of the kind of service only a small percentage of the people could pay for. I suddenly discovered that every now and then they lived up to the implied purpose of their title.

"I'm sorry, Mrs. Aldington," the doorman at Emily's apartment house said, "Mrs. Chadbourne is not in."

"I want to talk to Martha Aldington, my stepdaughter."

His face, usually fairly wooden, became totally expressionless. "Mrs.

Chadbourne said to tell you, to tell anyone who came, that Miss Aldington was not at all well and couldn't see no—anybody."

"I'm her stepmother and I must see her. I think my seeing her will improve her health considerably."

"I'm sorry. Them's the orders. You want me to call the super?"

The second doorman walked up. They were two large, stout men, and they barred the door. For the first time in my life I encountered the kind of humiliating response that certain classes of people—the poor, the minority poor, bag ladies and vagrant men—must encounter all the time.

"Nothing personal, Mrs. Aldington," the larger and more stone-faced doorman said. I could almost see visions of large Christmas tips running through his head. Like most women, I'm an overtipper. Would I, I was certain he was wondering, ever give him another tip after this little family trouble was cleared up?

"No," I said, putting as much hauteur and ice into my voice as I could, "don't bother." And I stood at the curb and hailed another taxi. Normally I would walk home, but I didn't want to feel those two pairs of eyes watching my rejected figure retreating down the avenue.

"Let me get you a cab," Stoneface said, hurrying to the curb, whistle in hand. "Joe, put the light on."

"Don't bother," I said again, despising myself for retaliatory behavior. "I can manage."

But the red winking light above the awning had its usual magic effect on passing taxis. One pulled to the curb.

When Stoneface had whipped open the door, I stepped in, a duchess with glacial demeanor, ignoring *la canaille.*

And then, all the way down Fifth, I laughed at myself.

"What's so funny?" the cab driver asked.

"Me," I said, and sighed. At this point, I was the only thing that was.

I should, of course, have gone back to the office. But I couldn't bring myself to. The warm friendly welcoming manner of my own doormen did a little to soothe my lacerated ego. But once inside the empty, silent apartment, my spirits dropped, and the anxiety that had been stalking me like a predator rushed back.

I called the office immediately and explained about the two clients.

"You're in luck," Susannah said, having obviously taken Josie's place at the switchboard. "One of your clients called in right after you left for the service and said she couldn't make it. Her boss wanted her on hand this afternoon. I'll call the other. She isn't due for half an hour or so anyway. And, Claire—"

I'd been on the point of hanging up. "Yes?"

"There are a lot of queer stories making the rounds these days. I just wanted you to know . . . that with me you're tops, always have been, always will be. That's all." And she hung up.

I must have underestimated my distress at the suspicion my colleagues at the church seemed to feel. Because there was no other way to explain the tears of gratitude that were pouring down my cheeks.

Why was I here? I wondered as I walked from room to room of the empty apartment. What could I possibly hope to solve? The answer lay, at least in part, in the miasma of suspicion that filled the parish house. I simply could not endure it another moment. But that was only part of the explanation. The trouble was, I didn't know what the other part consisted of.

And then, as I walked like a restless cat from place to place, my eye fell on the drawer of the night table beside my bed. Abruptly I went and opened it. Martha's diaries that I had started to read were all there. Nothing that I had seen in the early entries was particularly earthshaking or revealing, and I had stuffed the little books into my night-table drawer thinking I would continue with them. But I hadn't.

This time I would begin at the end.

I should, of course, have begun with the last volume in the first place, because at least one answer was immediately apparent. The book fell open at some day in the previous August. I read:

Last night I dreamed about the woman who ran away from the car when Daddy was killed. I know now he must have been having an affair with her like that girl told me at school. But I know he wouldn't have done it if he had had a real marriage with Claire. I don't think she loves him. I think she married him for his money. I asked him once when I heard people saying that and he said no. But I'm sure he meant yes. I was only ten when he died, so he probably wouldn't have thought he should tell me. But the girl who told me, her parents were members of the parish. They said that Claire didn't really believe in what Daddy was doing. And now Mr. Grism said that Daddy was having a relationship with somebody he knew named Elsie Shaftsbury. But I know that he was only paying me back for saying that thing about him . . . about him being gross. Well, how was I to know that he was a paraplegic . . . ?

The neat writing spread over its own page and into the next day's page. It was obvious that the reason the book fell open there was that it had a news clipping folded in there. The clipping was about the death by suicide of one Elsie Shaftsbury, a teacher and member of the parish of All Angels in Fairacre and a well-known activist in peace and civil-rights causes. The news announcement went on, "Ms. Shaftsbury often appeared with the Rev. Patrick Aldington on the platforms of various activist groups . . ."

At the top of the news sheet sprawled Dick's writing: "This is the woman I was telling you about. Even the perfect have their flaws . . . yes?"

But Patrick died alone, I thought, staring down at the book. He was coming home from one of his many political meetings. This one had taken place on the empty campus of some college, unoccupied because of the summer vacation. He had been there for the weekend and, according to our local radio, had made quite a few speeches. I was home with Martha, aged ten, and Jamie, aged two. That was a reason that had become an excuse.

Before Jamie was born we had left Martha with a neighbor who had a child Martha's age. When Jamie was first born I did, of course, have to stay home. But after that, I could have either left Jamie with his favorite nanny, who would have been glad to stay in the rectory to be with him, or even taken him with me. But by that time I had fallen out of sympathy with the people that Patrick felt most comfortable with: the reformers. I grew tired of the yelling and the placards and the confrontational rhetoric, of hearing the country constantly referred to as a warmongering, bomb-dropping monster, a Judas among nations, racist, bloated and hopelessly materialistic, a well of corrupt justice . . . My memory easily picked out some of the favorite phrases, many of them left over from the days of the Vietnam War.

"You don't believe any of that, do you?" I asked Patrick once, when we were at such a rally.

"Don't pay any attention to that. It's just tactics. We're out to reform the system and to stop nuclear war."

"Have you talked to the Russians about that lately?" I asked, quoting one of the questions my district attorney father would sometimes pose.

"Somebody has to start," Patrick said stubbornly.

But I was too much my father's daughter. He had fought through World War II, not only in Europe but in North Africa and the Pacific, and he had come home to go to law school on the GI Bill. He thought the country was great and the system was fine, and he must have so programmed me to feel the same that every time one of Patrick's activist cohorts introduced his subject by a casual reference to the iniquity of his fellow countrymen, he lost me before he got well launched.

"You've been brainwashed," Patrick would often growl.

"So have you," I would growl back.

Our differences grew, rather than diminished. That was when I used the children as my reason for staying home. And that was the time that Elsie started to take my place. But she was so plain, so unlike anyone's concept of the Other Woman, that, bewitched as I was by the popular image of the seductress, I never gave her a thought. In fact, I found her funny.

Mea culpa . . .

But Dick must have known about the deepening relationship between Patrick and Elsie. We didn't know one another then, but he lived in the neighboring dormitory town in New Jersey across the Hudson, and his wife's maiden name was Shaftsbury. She may have been a cousin or a sister-in-law. It didn't really matter.

Why would a crippled man-on-the-rise bother with Martha?

Because she had struck a painful nerve. Her insensitive (and public) comment had inflicted pain in an area that provided its daily humiliation to a man who had once been proud of his body. She was known in St. Anselm's from the days of her regular attendance at Sunday school as looking back on her father as a prince among men. Well, I could imagine Dick deciding, she could have a dose of reality about him, too. It might not have been planned. If Dick still took his former hometown paper, he would see the announcement of Elsie's suicide and on impulse cut it out and send it to Martha . . . And then the words in the diary surfaced in my mind: *"And now Mr. Grism said that Daddy was having a relationship with somebody he knew named Elsie Shaftsbury."* So, obviously, he had talked to her . . . And because they had talked about it, he had, cruelly, sent her the clipping. To be one up on everyone was a mania with him. It made up for . . . for so much else. Poor Martha! She could have had no weapons to help her deal with that. And above all else, the image of her father must remain pristine. I could easily imagine her going to see Dick, so that she could be persuaded, somehow, that it wasn't true.

But I couldn't see her killing him.

All of this was speculation, I thought, staring at the gray day from the window of my bedroom. I must—I had to—talk to Martha.

Finally, I went to the phone and dialed Emily's number. As I feared, Trudi answered and announced flatly that Emily would not talk to me, nor would she allow Martha to talk to me.

Emily had always been—along with the charming, well-bred lady—a domineering old battle-ax. But this was a bit much, even for her. Something else must have happened—or been said.

"Trudi, I have to talk to Mrs. Chadbourne."

"I have told you, Mrs. Aldington—"

"Trudi, you tell Mrs. Chadbourne that if she won't talk to me, I shall tell the police that I have evidence that Martha committed the crime. They will come immediately and arrest her, and all the family lawyers in the world won't be able to stop them."

It was a complete fabrication, of course, but I put my soul into the part and my hopes into Emily's possessive mania about Martha.

I could hear the phone being put down. There was a wait, and then Emily's voice, encrusted in ice, said, "How dare you send me a message like that. You have no evidence—"

"If you were sure of that you wouldn't have come to the phone, Emily. I have to talk to Martha. I don't want to frighten or hurt her. She is hiding from me to protect her memory of her precious father. And I think she'd go to any lengths to shut out a reality about him that Dick Grism, the church's murdered business manager, forced on her.

But for her own sake, if she doesn't make some peace with this, I don't give her much chance of mental or emotional health."

"I will not listen to you. Martha has told me that you were in that man's office before her. That you killed him. She says she has proof, and I have been wrestling with myself as to whether I should tell the police. If it's a question of Martha's safety and peace of mind, I shall tell them immediately."

"What is the proof?"

"I shall not reveal that."

"Because neither you nor Martha has it."

"But one thing I have become convinced of. Martha states that you did not love her father. That you married him for his family and his money. I've heard that said before. I've always wanted to give you the benefit of the doubt. But now I know the truth. You did not love him. My Priscilla did. And Priscilla's daughter does."

"Emily, because you failed with Priscilla—you tried to stop that marriage, you know, Patrick told me—you're going to try to succeed with Priscilla's daughter. All you'll do is drive her further into her illusions. Can't you see—?"

But the phone had been slammed down. Curiously, standing there, with my life threatening to come unstuck, all I could think of was: Emily and Martha were right. I didn't really love Patrick, not the way he deserved and the way I should have. Money and family were only part of the reason. The rest was fear. Marrying Patrick, I figured that—even if the marriage were a failure—it would prevent me from ever feeling a rejected, humiliated castoff, a judgment by myself on myself that had been born one day in a London hostel.

I was standing, shocked by this discovery, my hand still on the replaced receiver, when the phone started ringing again.

12

WHEN I PICKED UP THE RECEIVER a masculine voice said, "This is Paul Riverton. Josie wants to know what you did with her handbag."

"You've talked to her?" I said. "Then she must have come around."

"Yeah. She did. She's better. But she can't talk much and the only thing she said was: what did you do with her handbag, the one that Sally Hepburn took back to give to you? She wants to make sure you have it."

I hesitated. Truth fought against an impulse not to say anything that would worry Josie, laced with a desire not to make myself look foolish.

"Well?"

"Paul, I'm sorry to say that a lot was happening at the time and I don't know what I did with it. But don't tell Josie. Not if it's going to upset her."

"Well, Christ almighty, she sends the damn bag back to you and you don't even look after it! Some church!"

I took a deep breath. "I said I was sorry. I—" But the only things I could produce were excuses. "Look—did she tell you why it was so important that I should have the bag? There wasn't any money in it, and as far as I could see there were no credit cards in the wallet."

"Does it matter *why* she asked? I don't believe this!"

"Paul—I'm sorry, I was wrong. I would like to undo the wrong. But it would help me if I knew why Josie was so anxious for me to have the bag. If she just wanted it kept in a safe place, then why didn't she tell Sally Hepburn, who had it, to put it in the main safe? And incidentally, Sally sits in the office where the safe is. If you could possibly find out the answers to these questions, instead of yelling at me, then I think it would help to achieve the purpose Josie had in mind. Will you try?"

"Okay, but I still think—"

"You're right. I was remiss. Will you find out what I asked?"

"Okay."

"And call me back."

"All right." He almost slammed down the receiver.

Well, I thought, he and Josie were two of a kind—each carrying around a huge grievance to which an uncaring world seemed constantly to add.

I opened the french windows and went out onto the little balcony that abutted onto the living room. Eleven floors below, the cars sped along the street towards Fifth Avenue. If I leaned over the low balustrade, I could see the huge gray façade of the Metropolitan Museum. Since the balcony was really more of an ornament than for use, it was mostly occupied by a variety of plants. Idly I examined the plants and noted that, what with one thing and another happening lately, they had been neglected. Deciding they could use some encouragement, I went back to the kitchen and got the watering can, shears and some plant food.

As I worked, I let my mind circle around Josie's bag. I knew from previous experience that to tackle the problem head on—to try to force my mind to remember what was in the bag and where I'd put it—would produce nothing but frustration. It was better to keep my fingers busy and my mental processes free to range. Often, during my seminary training, I had tried meditation as taught by the Zen Buddhists and the Vedantists, sometimes counting backwards from ten (Zen) and sometimes using a Christian mantra (Vedanta). For me it didn't work. All I got was a severe case of frustration, a low opinion of my spiritual capacity and, for one hideous fortnight, hives. My more disorganized Christian method of abbreviated prayer, occasional one-way conversations with the Deity, bursts of conviction about the Presence of Reality and a maundering contemplation most successfully practiced when washing the dishes or watering the plants—all these worked better for me . . .

And this time, as I pulled off dried leaves and small dead branches, I found my mind fastening on a small scrap of memory: the upper edge of a letter, stuffed in Josie's bag along with the makeup, pens, pencils and the address book. I thought there were letters, plural, in Josie's bag. But there was only one. Or perhaps it was the only one I remembered. On the upper right-hand corner of the letter was an English stamp . . . or was my memory supplying an English stamp because of Josie's request for the stamp? I tried to concentrate on the letter. Had I seen it or not? But when I tried to clear my mind so I could recall the presence of the letter, the whole thing just slid away. I straightened, dropping my hands, and attempted to concentrate. It was a mistake. Nothing came clear.

I was still chasing the phantom of the letter down the rabbit hole of my mind when the phone rang again. "She's gone to sleep and they won't even let me see her," an outraged Paul said without preamble.

"Listen, Paul, she needs rest more than she needs anything else."

"Yes, well, in the meantime, what's happening about her bag?"

"I'll call and get someone to try and find it. Right away."

"Okay, but do you mean it this time?"

I sent up one of my short prayers for patience.

"Yes, Paul. Call me back in half an hour and I'll tell you about it. Better still, give me your number and as soon as I have some information I'll call you."

"This is a phone booth in the hospital. I'm not even on the floor where Josie is. All the phones there were busy. So I'll call you."

"All right."

I put my finger on the receiver hook long enough for the line to be disconnected, then dialed the number of the parish house. Susannah answered.

"Listen, Susannah, among the various goofs I committed today was losing sight of Josie's handbag." And I explained Sally's returning with it and giving it to me. "Why she didn't tell Sally to put it in the parish safe, I don't know, but she didn't. Anyway, I put it down somewhere and I have no memory of where. Does that ever happen to you?"

"Oh yes, Ms. Therapist," Susannah said with gentle sarcasm. "It usually means your mind's overloaded."

"I know. And I can vouch that that's true. But Josie's boyfriend is railing at me over the telephone about it from the hospital. Apparently Josie came around long enough to express great anxiety about it. I told him the truth, which may have been a mistake. He has a thoroughly negative view of life and people and I've done nothing to improve it. So now I am asking you—could you go to my office, or have somebody trustworthy like Sally or Janet go to my office, and find out if it's there? Look everywhere, in all the drawers and closets."

"All right. I'll get someone. By the way, speaking of closets, did you know that Detective O'Neill allowed as how there were no fingerprints of yours on that bookend? There are a lot of prints, but they're all smudged beyond recognition, except a couple of Dick's."

"You're not telling me he is exonerating me, he's just saying they didn't get usable proof."

"Something like that."

"How come he told you?"

"Because I asked. He asked where you were and I told him you'd gone home. Then I asked him about the prints."

"Thanks, Susannah. Could you let me know whether that bag's in my office?"

"Sure, I'll look for the bag and don't beat yourself about it. You're not the only one to lose something. Larry called in and wanted me to look for some letter from England that he lost. He says it's disappeared from his desk and it's not at home. Since we get at least half a dozen letters a week from England, I asked him what it was about, in case I came across a letter from England addressed to him. But he wouldn't discuss it. He acted very cagey."

"Oh," I said. "That may be the letter I saw in Josie's bag."

"Josie's bag? What would it be doing there?"

"I don't know. I know she—or her boyfriend—collects stamps, and she asked Larry if she could have the whole envelope. She said she was going to ask Norbert for his, too."

"I didn't know Norbert got a letter from England at the same time. Although, like I said, there's nothing unusual about it. We get quite a few."

"Maybe it wasn't Larry's letter that I saw in her bag. Maybe it was Norbert's."

"Well, Norbert was asking about Larry's letter. Claire, this is getting more complicated by the minute. My head's going around. I'll ask

Norbert about it anyway . . . Well, speak of angels. Hello, Norbert, have you seen either Larry's letter from England or Josie's handbag?"

Norbert must have been standing near the phone, for I heard him reply, "What letter? What bag?"

Then Susannah replied, but her voice grew dim, as she must have turned from the telephone. In a moment she was back. "Anything else?"

"No. Did Norbert see the letter in the handbag?"

"No. He says to tell you hello."

"Tell him hello back."

I hung up. Then, increasingly restless, went to the kitchen to put on some water for coffee.

The mind is a curious thing. Frustrated on the subject of the letter, it drifted off to Martha's conundrum . . .

I had had to make the final identification of what was left of Patrick after his car burst into flames. It was a grisly and horrible task, and it was a long time before I could drive out the memory of what I saw on the morgue slab and replace it with memories of him throughout our life together. It never dawned on me that Martha had actually witnessed the crash, but it would explain her unnatural quiet during the weeks and months following his death, and the periodic nightmares that punctuated the quiet and from which she would wake up screaming. Nor, of course, had she ever, to my knowledge, said anything about seeing someone else with him in the car. Wouldn't that be considered strange for a ten-year-old? No, not really, I decided. She had always been a reserved, even secretive child. Ten years old was not too young to have vague intimations of what adult life was like and what subjects preoccupied it. So she had buried that all those years, the one scene in the story that would take away from her father's perfect, shining image . . .

And now what?

Patrick had left her to me to take care of, and while less and less did I think that I'd done the job he would have liked for me to do, I was quite sure he wouldn't want her brought up by Emily. Because Emily was incapable of leaving anyone alone. She would, without realizing it and meaning well, so control and dominate Martha that she would produce what she produced in her daughter—a rebel. But Priscilla was more stable that Martha. She could take her anger and turn it into an idealistic crusade. I had my own problems with people who knew exactly how the rest of the world should live and couldn't wait to force other people to agree with them. But Priscilla had a sturdy emotional core. Martha did not. That same anger in Martha could easily turn against herself . . .

"Oh, blast!" I said aloud.

I could, of course, get a lawyer to match Emily's lawyers. Patrick deliberately specified in his will that I was to have charge of his daughter. It would be a long, ugly legal battle, and right now possession, which was in Emily's court, was nine tenths of the law. Also Martha didn't want to live with me. She had managed to rewrite the current plot so that I was the villain, and had no trouble, obviously, in persuading Emily of its truth. Even if I won a custody battle, wouldn't it be a pyrrhic victory? Martha was nearly sixteen. How do you keep a fifteen-year-old in a place she didn't want to be in? That part of it was my fault. Somewhere along the line, or perhaps all the way along the line, I had failed.

And what about Jamie? Was I failing with him?

Curiously, my paranoia evaporated at even the thought of his name. I had no neurotic worries concerning my son. We had our battles, but we loved one another . . . It suddenly occurred to me that that was the secret of our success as mother and son. I had no particular guilt about Jamie. I adored him. He loved me. We had our squabbles and our disagreements. But we also had a lot of fun together. Some tight cord in me relaxed when I thought about it. But, however healing to my wounded psyche it might be, thinking about Jamie was not helping Martha. And helping Martha had to be priority one right now.

On an impulse I went to a two-year-old address book and dialed a number on the phone.

"Dr. Meitzner's office," a woman's voice said.

"Is Dr. Meitzner there?"

"She's with a patient."

"Would you please tell her that Claire Aldington called about Martha Aldington, a former patient of hers. And that it's an emergency." Being a therapist myself, and knowing the ways of therapy schedules, I knew it might be several hours before she got back to me.

As I turned away from the phone, another thought came out of the blue: *But I don't have several hours.*

A flicker of fear ran down my spine. As though sensing something wrong, Motley came over and pushed his nose against my hand. "It's all right, Motley," I heard myself say aloud. "Thanks, anyway." And I patted and stroked him.

I was watching the kettle boil for some coffee when the telephone rang again.

"Mrs. Aldington? It's Dr. Meitzner."

"Dr. Meitzner, thanks for calling back so soon. I telephoned to tell you, among things, that you were right. I should have left Martha with you for a while."

"What's happened?"

I told her, resisting temptation to telescope, and going into the gradual deterioration, the food lying around, the rebellion, up to what I was sure was Martha's visit to Dick, finding his body, and taking refuge with Emily, who now forbade me even to see Martha and had effectively barred the door of her apartment house.

"Why do you most want to see her?" Dr. Meitzner asked. "What I mean is, do you most want to see her to find out what she saw when she was there with your business manager's body, or do you want to see her to help her out of her obsession?"

Astonishingly, I hadn't even thought that Martha might have information as to who murdered Dick. "You may not believe this," I said slowly, "but finding out from her who may have murdered Dick hadn't even occurred to me. What I want is to get her to accept that Patrick could be fallible in some area and still be her wonderful father. As I look back on about the last, say, three years, it seems to me that all her neurotic behavior has been linked to this attempt to keep his image unspotted. Which means, of course, that if whatever happened was not his fault, then it must be mine. I must have failed him in some way. Unfortunately, in that, I think she may be right."

"Maybe, maybe not. You're not my patient, but why do you say that?"

"Martha accused me of marrying him for his money and his name, rather than because I was in love with him. I think there *was* an element of that. I also don't believe, now, that I was in love with him.

In fact, I think that's one reason why I *did* marry him. Since I was not in love with him he didn't have that terrible weapon over me that . . . well, a previous lover had."

"Was he in love with you?"

"Not in the way he was with Priscilla, his first wife, Martha's mother. I think he married me partly because I'm down-to-earth and would be better at helping him with parish chores than somebody as idealistic as himself, and partly because I think he thought I'd be a good mother for Martha."

"Marriage can be based on a lot worse things than that. In fact, in the past, most marriages had less than the romantic dream to start with. So why are you beating yourself? If you weren't romantic about him, he wasn't about you."

"True. In the meantime, how can I get to Martha? Legally, I have the right to go in there and demand her return. But I can't imagine that I'd succeed, and to go to court about it would take months. The more I think about it, the more I'm convinced that for her own mental welfare, I'm going to have to get in there right away."

"To say nothing about her physical welfare."

"How do you mean?"

"If she did see something when she visited your late business manager, then I would think whoever did kill him would take great interest in seeing her silenced."

"Of course." I felt stupid. "I was so busy worrying . . . But you're right. I have to get to her."

"I think if you can get this obsession about her father's perfection cleared up a little, she'll get a lot better. I have to go now. My next patient is waiting. Let me know what happens." And she hung up.

Dr. Meitzner was right, I thought. I had to see Martha now.

The kettle had boiled during our conversation and I had switched it off. I now poured the steaming water over some instant coffee, added milk and sipped the hot, strong stuff. The chief question about seeing Martha was: how?

I could, of course, take somebody formidable with me—somebody like Brett, who could push his way through two rock-like doormen. But, if it succeeded, I'd be talking to a terrorized Martha in the presence of her infuriated grandmother. Given Martha's confusion about reality and her fear of authority, this could easily produce nothing.

Besides, Brett had proved himself untrustworthy.

Very well then, if not Brett, who?

It was at that moment in my deliberations that there was the sound of a key in the lock and I heard the front door open.

"Jamie?" I called.

"Yeah?"

I walked out into the hall, the coffee mug still in my hand. "Why are you home at"—I looked at my watch—"three-fifteen?"

"The coach was sick. No practice. I thought I'd take Motley out for a while in the park."

I watched the reunion between boy and dog, which, judging by the intensity, seemed to indicate they had been held apart for years by unjust fates.

After a moment something seemed to strike Jamie. He looked up from his wrestling match and said, "Why're you home? You sick?"

"No, I'm trying to figure out how to go and see Martha without having to take a large man along and also without letting Emily know. They wouldn't even let me in the apartment house today."

"You mean they stood in front of the door?"

"Yes, like two images from Mount Rushmore."

"Crazy! Why don't you pretend you're a delivery boy?"

The stunning brilliance of this shocked me speechless.

"You know," I said slowly, "you may have something, you smart boy!"

"I say smart things lots of the time. Come on, Motley!"

I watched my son snatch the leash off the hall hook and shepherd the leaping, ecstatic dog out into the hall. Then I put down the coffee cup on the nearest flat surface and went off to make myself into an acceptable delivery boy.

Twenty minutes later, wearing sneakers, jeans, a shirt and a zip jacket, one of Jamie's caps and a large muffler around my neck and the lower part of my face, I looked around for something to serve as a delivery. The obvious thing was my tote bag, which I slung over my arm and to which I added some flowers snatched from a vase on the hall table and wrapped in tissue paper I found lying on a closet shelf.

Downstairs I was cheered when one of my own delivery men asked me who I was and what apartment I'd come from. Muttering something, I ran out of the apartment house, pursued by shouts from one of the doormen, went around the corner and tried to hail a taxi. Three empty ones passed without even slowing. The fourth stopped and snarled, "Where ya going?"

I gave the corner of the nearest street and Madison Avenue. With obvious suspicion, the driver dropped me down there and seemed relieved when I not only paid him but added a tip.

As with most old apartment houses, the delivery entrance was at the back of the building, half a block away from the front entrance. I offered up a prayer that the door was controlled by the doormen at the front, who, when the bell rang, would look at a closed-circuit television screen. My prayer was answered. The door was small and beside it was a bell. Above, sticking out from the corner where the door fitted into the wall, was the single eye of a small TV camera.

"Yeah, who is it?" the voice box beside the bell blatted out.

"Delivery for Eleven A," I said in a scratchy contralto, keeping my head down.

The door buzzed open, and I was in. Straight ahead was the service elevator. In case there were more cameras, I kept my head down and pushed the button beside the elevator. The doors opened and I went in. I was about to look up to see if there was a camera there, when it occurred to me that I would be looking straight into it. My disguise was obviously good (who would expect to see the Reverend Claire Aldington, usually seen in a round collar, a black rabat and a black or gray suit, dressed like a delivery boy?) but there was no use to strain it.

The next challenge would be Trudi. I would just have to hope that the disguise would work with her, too. But even if it did, how would I get in? I had no clear plan in my head, but hoped that something would occur to me.

Nothing did. Standing in the back hall, beside the now empty doors, I tried to summon up some plan of action. But my mind was a blank. Finally, I rang the bell of the back door. If worse came to worst, perhaps Trudi would understand my urgency—but I knew that was a dim hope. As an afterthought, I put the flowers in a garbage can beside the apartment's back door. They would be of no use.

"And who would you be?" said a decidedly Irish voice.

"I'm collecting for the Hibernian Society for Crippled Children," I muttered. "Just a few pence for the weak ones." I sent up a short prayer that I was faithfully reproducing the vowel sounds of an Irish baby-sitter we'd once had for Jamie.

"Niver heard of it."

"We're a branch of the Vincent de Paul Society."

"Ach, well, I give at Mass. I don't have much over."

"Just a quarter would be of help." I had to get her away from the door for a minute.

My accent must have slipped, because a swift glance upwards showed a frown on what I thought to be a normally good-natured face.

"The saints will bless you," I said, heavily back into my role.

"And why've ye the scarf around yer neck like that?"

"It's the croup."

"Ah well. All right. Wait in here. I'll get you a quarter. Now that's all, mind!"

I stood there, praying steadily that Trudi, the housemaid, would not be back in what were obviously the cook's quarters. A delicious smell came from the stove. Onions, I thought, in some kind of a casserole. My stomach gave a faint growl. As soon as the footsteps faded, I turned and pushed the button on the edge of the door that would make it possible to open it from the outside. Barely in time I stepped back. The footsteps returned. "Now this is all yer gettin'. What parish would you be from?"

"St. Francis de Sales," I muttered, mentioning the nearest Catholic church.

"Well, God bless. Ye'd better get movin' before Trudi gets here. She's a good soul, but she's a Lutheran."

And I found myself on the outside. I went to the elevator, pushed the button and, when it came, got in. Inside, I simply stayed there. Then, in a minute, I pushed the "Door open" button and stepped out again. Then I went over and listened at the back door. After I'd listened for a while, I very gently turned the knob of the door and pushed a little. When I had opened the door enough, I slid my head around. The kitchen was empty. I slipped in and listened to see if there was anyone in the pantry. Then I walked quickly along the hall. Voices from a pantry right behind the dining room indicated that Trudi and my Irish friend might be there, so I left the kitchen quarters by a door that gave into the main hall of the apartment. There, I hesitated, again listening.

From the living room I could hear, faintly, a man's voice. It was too faint for me to identify either the speaker or what he was saying, but it indicated, I felt, that Emily was there. And it might also indicate that Martha was there as well. On the other hand, she might be in her bedroom. Every step, every moment, I was in the apartment was a risk. But that couldn't be helped. I tiptoed down the hall to Martha's room and paused outside the door.

The last time I had come into Martha's room she had started to scream. There was every reason to believe that she'd do it again, and I would probably be arrested for trespassing. But I had to try. Taking a deep breath, I turned the knob and walked in. Martha was asleep on top of her bed, the cotton quilt drawn up to her waist.

Tiptoeing over, I put my hand over her mouth (just like in the movies, a cynical observer within me commented), grabbed her arm and said, "Martha, I have to talk to you. Please don't scream. Please, please, please. Just give me a chance."

I could feel her mouth moving under my hand, so I took my hand away. After all, if Martha was determined to scream, there was really nothing I could do to stop her, but my move must have surprised her, because she stared at me without making a noise. Her large eyes fixed on me with an intent, almost demanding look. Slowly, she sat up.

I took a deep breath. Where did I begin? I wondered. How could I make her willing to let me threaten her obsession? I decided to begin at the end. "Your father was a wonderful man, Martha. I think you're right that I wasn't really the right wife for him. There were certain aspects of his . . . his belief system that I wasn't part of. So he found that in Elsie Shaftsbury, whom you saw running away from his car. But that should never, ever, affect the way you feel about your father, as a father. As a father, he was perfect."

I was prepared for a variety of reactions—all of them dangerous for me: screaming, hysterics, fury, shouting. I was not prepared to have her put her face in her hands and start quietly to cry.

"He *wasn't* perfect," Martha said through her fingers. "He was unfaithful."

"Does it take away from the way he was towards you?"

"Yes. It's no use pretending that it doesn't, because it does."

What she said was true. I could talk about the separateness of their relationship until I was blue in the face, but it would be a long time before she was totally willing to accept the loving but fallible father in place of the shining hero. Various things to say occurred to me. Instead, I leaned over and put my arms around her, fully prepared for her to push me away. But she didn't. She seemed to shrink against me. "It will be all right, Martha," I said. "I know it doesn't feel that way now, but it really will."

After a while I went on, "There's something else I have to talk to you about. I know you don't want to discuss it, but I'm afraid there's no choice."

"I didn't kill him," Martha said rather limply.

"I didn't think you did. But you did go and see Dick, didn't you? Forgive me, but in trying to figure out what happened I skimmed through some of your diaries." I felt the quiver go through her. "Martha, the only reason I even found them was because I thought that box was the family home of all those cockroaches."

"Yes, I know. I'm sorry. I kept meaning to clean it out."

"Well, anyway, last August you wrote in your diary that Dick Grism had told you about . . . about your father and Elsie Shaftsbury. How did that come about? Did Dick call you?"

"No. He wrote to me. You told me to write that note telling him I was sorry I'd made that gross remark. Well, I did. Not right away, but after a while. He wrote back saying he knew people who knew Daddy and when I was next at the parish house to drop by and we'd talk. So I did. One day I was going to surprise you. But I went to his office first . . ." She stopped.

"And he told you then?"

"Not at the beginning. He just said about being in the neighboring town and having heard of Daddy and all his good works, and how his sister-in-law, Elsie Shaftsbury, went to Daddy's church and thought so highly of him. And he went on and on with that funny look in his eyes, like they were excited, and then I realized he was telling me that Daddy was sleeping with her and everybody but you knew it."

"My God—what a sadist! I'm sorry, Martha. It must have been horrible for you. What did you do?"

"I wanted to scream at him, but somehow I couldn't. I can't explain it. He was smiling, like he was eating a piece of cake. All I wanted to do was get out of there, so I ran. I didn't even think about you till I was home."

"And then he sent you that clipping?"

"Yes."

"I wish I'd known."

"I wanted to tell you, but it would have been—well, like betraying Daddy . . . You see, I had the horrible feeling he—Mr. Grism—was right. I saw when Daddy was killed. I saw the car skid and then fall and then blow up. But I also saw somebody, a woman who had been thrown out of the car when it went down the bank, get up, look at the fire and then run away."

"So that's what you meant when you said you dreamed about the woman who ran away from the car. But you were only ten. Why did you think it was suspicious?"

Martha was crying again. "Because a girl at school—her parents were in the parish—said everybody knew Daddy was having an affair. So I decided to ask him first thing after he got back from that trip and was waiting for him to come home."

"You poor baby! I wish you'd told me this sooner—got it out! Who was the monster who told you?"

"Betty Carpenter."

I remembered the Carpenters. They were among the few who didn't like Patrick or anything he did. They were also almost prototypes of the well-groomed, well-to-do suburban couple, ambitious for their children and, between their jobs and their social life, rarely at home. A housekeeper did most of the child-rearing.

"Why did she do it, Martha? Just to be mean? Were you having a fight?"

"I dunno. We'd just had a test. I got A and Betty got B-plus. Boy, was she burned! But she pretended she didn't care."

"And she then presented you with this tidbit about your father?"

Martha sniffed. "Yes."

I recognized the tactics: Don't get mad, get even. And there flashed into my mind the exhortation, read recently in church, "*Avenge not yourselves . . . for it is written, Vengeance is mine; I will repay, saith the Lord.*" For a few seconds I wondered how much Martha's life might be different today if the Carpenters, *mère* and *père,* had stayed home a little more and stuffed their offspring with that thought rather than the overwhelming necessity of getting ahead . . . But it was pointless to speculate on that now . . .

I could see more easily than ever what must have happened to Martha in the intervening years, carrying this (to her) terrible secret about her father, unable to tell anyone because it would be, in her mind, an act of betrayal. This must have been the unknown ingredient in Martha's psychological mix that Dr. Meitzner suspected. Would it have come to light if I'd resisted Martha's pleas and made her stay the extra three months at the hospital? Perhaps. Perhaps not. That, too, was wasted speculation. In any case, Dick Grism forced open the wound and poured a river of salt in it, and she did the only thing she could do to make the burden more bearable: she twisted the story around and made it all my fault: If I had been a better wife, et cetera, it would never have happened . . .

Well, a mocking voice in my head taunted me, isn't that at least partly true? Again, I conceded, perhaps, perhaps not. I would never know. But it was possible Brett was right when he accused me of parroting Patrick's words rather than believing them; that this was, unconsciously, my expiation for not loving him as much as I felt I should . . .

With this acknowledgment—I had never really admitted it before—I straightened, as though losing a burden. Until this moment I had fought against admitting to myself that I'd married Patrick for emotional security: because of, not in spite of, the fact that he didn't excite me. With Patrick I felt safe. I would not have to make a present of my inner self as I had with my previous lover. Loving him, *à la folie,* as I had, I had known the degrading power of jealousy, and wanted no part of it ever again.

But I knew now there was no such thing as a risk-free love. Both Patrick and I had learned that. And it was time to let him and the marriage, with its blessings and its failures, go. But Martha, who had lived with a father and a stepmother, both of whom were playing it safe, was still paying the debt for a little emotional dishonesty on our parts. And I couldn't let the past go until she did—along with the unreal image of her father.

I looked at Martha, who was sitting there drying her face with a tissue. Dick's death had been a curious catalyst: I saw now that just as Martha had to accept her father before she could get better, I had to accept myself before I could . . . get on with my life. Suddenly the picture of Brett in my mind was so vivid that it was as though he were in the room.

I pushed it away and took a breath. "I now understand why you felt it to be my fault."

"Yes . . . I'm sorry. But that was more after Mr. Grism was dead."

"Why did you go back that morning he was killed?"

"To shove the clipping in his face and to tell him he was wrong about Daddy, and that I knew he'd made the whole thing up to pay me back for what I'd said about him being gross."

"Was he alive when you arrived?"

"Well, he must have been, because I heard two men quarreling in his office."

I could feel my heart beginning to pound. "And you knew it was the right office?"

"Of course. I'd been there before."

"Did you hear what the quarreling was about?"

"About money. One man was yelling at the other man for selling something the church had."

"But you don't know which was which?"

"No."

"Then what happened?"

"It got louder and louder and suddenly there was a queer noise, like something hitting something sort of soft. Then there was another noise like a grunt. For a while after that there was no sound at all. Then somebody started coming out. I hid on the other side of that bookcase in the hall, although I knew if the person came that way he'd see me. But he didn't. He went the other way."

"Did you see who it was?"

"No."

We sat there for a while longer. Then Martha surprised me even more than she had. "Can I come home, Claire?"

"Of course, darling. I was afraid you wanted to live with your grandmother."

"I like her a lot, but I've decided I don't want to live with her. She's nice, but awfully bossy, and every now and then calls me Priscilla. Besides . . . Well, I miss you. And I miss Jamie."

"That's wonderful to hear."

The dim voices that we'd heard all along from the living room seemed to be getting louder. One was definitely Emily's. The other . . . I paused, waiting for the male voice to say something again. Obviously he'd been standing further away in the large hall, perhaps at the hall closet putting on his coat, because although he said something, all I could hear was a murmur. Then came Emily's voice again.

"I'm grateful to you for telling me these details, sad as they are. I will, of course, do everything I can to see she recovers. Fortunately, money does not have to be a consideration. And I will most certainly show my gratitude to the church and to you in the most appropriate way."

My fingers closed on Martha's arm as the man said, "I wouldn't be here if I did not think she might do herself harm, in remorse, of course, and horror at what she had already done when her sense of reality slipped. But I felt I had to warn you . . ."

His voice grew suddenly nearer and we heard the front door open. Slowly, as his words sunk into my head, Martha gave a little cry and clutched me. "That's the man, Claire. That's the man who was having a fight with Mr. Grism."

As I recognized the voice, I heard in my mind another voice, a boy's voice, saying, "I never would have made it back to school on time if he hadn't given me that lift . . ." And the pieces fell into place.

"It's all right, Martha," I said gently. I patted her back and then said, "I'm going out to talk to Emily."

"Can I come home tomorrow?"

I looked back at her. "You're sure you want to?"

"Positive." I was at the door when she said, "I'm sorry . . . I'm sorry for what I thought about you. It was because . . . because of Daddy . . ." And then suddenly: "I hate him."

"No, you don't. He was a terrific father. I'm just sorry that Jamie was too young to know him well. He gave you love, affection, loyalty, attention and a sound grounding in values. You knew that, as far as you were concerned, he was one hundred percent trustworthy. You could rely on him."

"But you couldn't."

"Martha—sex makes things different. I'm not saying there aren't principles there, too. But at this point you don't really know, so don't judge him."

"All right," she said after a while.

I walked out into the hall and bumped straight into Emily.

"How did you—how dare you . . . leave this house immediately."

She was backing as though I were contaminated.

"Emily, we have to talk."

"We do not have to talk. There is nothing to say. I've heard everything about your illness and the fact that you're not responsible. But I cannot have a woman who has murdered one person and tried to kill another in my house and around my granddaughter."

"That's what Norbert just told you, I gather."

She drew herself up. "If you don't go, I shall have to call the police."

"By all means, Emily. Call them."

She didn't quite expect that, but she said, "I have been counseled not to pass judgment on you" (shades of my advice to Martha, I thought!), "so I shall try not to—"

"Norbert again," I said, advancing slowly, as Emily slowly backed. "He told you that."

"Yes, he did."

"Well, I have to talk to him myself, about that, and a few other things."

"Then you had better get over to your apartment. That's where he is going. He wants to help you in any way he can, and I've told him that I will also help—financially."

As her words went on, I understood then what I had overheard from him: *"I wouldn't be here if I did not think she might do herself harm*

. . ." I had thought he was referring to Martha, but he wasn't. He was preparing the way for my . . . suicide, or a death that would be made to look like suicide. And then, quick as thought: Jamie . . . . He was home early, and would soon be back from his walk. If he were in the way, would Norbert hesitate to get rid of him? No, not if he stood in the way of achieving his obsession . . . There was, after all, the example of the Reverend Jim Jones, who also had an obsession . . .

"I must go," I said.

"Let me call a doctor," Emily said, barring my path.

"Emily, Norbert is a murderer. Jamie may be at home. I have to get there."

"He told me that part of your illness is making wild accusations."

"If you don't move out of the way I'll have to move you."

Emily drew up her erect bosom. "Don't you dare touch me!"

But for all her power, she was a frail old lady, and I had no difficulty in putting her firmly to one side. "Emily, call the police. Call Detective O'Neill, tell them I'm going to my apartment to meet the murderer . . ."

"Murderer!" Her voice echoed behind me as I ran down the hall to the front door.

As I sat in the taxi still clutching my tote bag, I examined various possibilities: Unfortunately, the doormen, well trained not to admit anyone without an announcement, might wave in a man in a round collar. Clergy were special, and their visits occasions of mercy and comfort. If Jamie were there, he wouldn't hesitate to tell the doorman to let him in. He knew Norbert from Sunday school (when I could get him to go, which was increasingly seldom). Norbert wouldn't hurt a child, one side of me argued. But Norbert was not rational, the other side pointed out . . .

I almost threw the money at the driver and ran to my door. "Did a clergyman come in here?"

The doorman looked at me with an expression that indicated both awe and nervousness. "I didn't know you'd been . . . well, upset, Mrs. Aldington. I'm real sorry. He said the church was anxious to help you." His eyes took in my jeans and zip jacket. If he made the connection between me and the delivery boy who had run out of the house,

Norbert's tales about my unstable state would fall on well-prepared ears. And Norbert, when he put his mind to it and his electric gaze on you, could convince anybody of anything.

"Is Jamie in?"

"Yes. He came in from his walk with . . ." I moved towards the elevator so fast that I missed his last words as the elevator doors closed. God help me, I prayed. Whatever happened, Jamie must not be hurt.

When I got to the door I was on the point of ringing once or twice, which would bring Jamie running (I hoped), but decided that that would indicate my fear. So, fighting for a calm manner, I slipped my key into the door and turned the key.

As Motley jumped up on me, licked me and generally indicated how pleased he was to see me after decades in the desert, I put down the bag and called out, "Anybody home?"

"Hi, Ma." Jamie appeared in the living-room door. "Mr. Shearer is here. He's waiting to see you." Jamie's voice sounded strained. I peered at him in the darker hallway. "What's the matter, Jamie? You sound funny."

"Yeah. Fine, I guess."

I switched on the hall light, even though it was broad daylight outside. But I wanted to see Jamie's face. In a low voice I asked him, "What's Norbert been telling you?"

"He—he said you were sick . . . in the head," Jamie said. And stopped. Norbert's tall frame appeared in the doorway of the living room. "Hello, Norbert," I said as calmly as I could.

"Hello, Claire. It's good to see you. I was wondering if we could have a private talk."

For a second I hesitated on the brink of saying that I had no secrets from Jamie. But I abandoned that. Jamie must be safe, and I had no certainty that a man who had killed one person and tried to kill another would boggle at dispatching a small boy who might prove inconvenient.

"Of course. I was going to ask Jamie to do something for me anyway. Jamie, would you go to the grocer and get me some milk, some apples, some of your cereal and a couple of cans of Motley's dog food? I meant to pick it up on the way here, but I forgot."

"Couldn't you ask them to send it?"

"One of their delivery boys is sick. I phoned them from a booth on the way here, but they asked if I couldn't send you."

"They don't know who—"

"Jamie!" I put some bite in my voice. "Please do as I ask. And don't embarrass me!" This was slightly dirty pool, because it was strong medicine. Since the time when I had thoughtlessly scolded the six-year-old Jamie in front of others for some lapse in grace, we had had a bargain, he and I, that we didn't embarrass one another in public.

He went bright crimson, folded his lips and said, "*All right!* Come on, Motley!"

As I watched him go, I felt as though he were taking with him some vital organ out of my body. "Jamie!" I said as he reached the door.

"What?" The single word was anything but gracious. He was mad as hell and intended for me to know it. I didn't blame him.

"Thanks," I said, ashamed of the quaver that showed in my voice.

"Okay." It was a barely audible mutter. I stood there, listening to the familiar sounds, the slap of the leather and steel of Motley's leash against the wall as Jamie took it off the hook, the faint sound of his parka zipper, the opening of the door, the noise of Motley's toenails on the parquet and then the closing of the door. It had never before occurred to me what wonderful sounds they were.

"He's gone," I said, and became aware of how frightened I was. I could, of course, go myself, make a dash for the door. If I made it, I would be safe—for now. But how long would I, or Jamie, or Martha, or various people at the church be safe with this murdering maniac and his messianic crusade? And surely, I told myself, Martha or Emily would call the police . . . Martha would be able to resolve Emily's doubts and dislike of me enough for that.

"Sit down, Norbert," I said.

"No. I think I'll stand." His back was to the light. Behind him was the french window and the little balcony.

I couldn't see his face and was gripped with a strong feeling that if his expression was hidden, I would not know what might happen. "Come on, Norbert," I said, walking towards the empty fireplace to my right. "Let's sit down." And I moved so that I was level with him. If I walked a few feet nearer to the window, then he'd have to turn. So I kept on walking. It was only then, when I faced him with the afternoon light streaming over my shoulder to fall on his face, that I realized what a stupid thing I'd done. Nonsense, I told myself. Don't be paranoid. There's no danger. Anyway, I'm not that kind of idiot-heroine . . .

"Where's the letter?" Norbert asked.

"What letter?"

"The one you asked Susannah to find, the one that people all over the parish house are moving heaven and earth to locate." He paused and smiled. "The one that was in Josie's bag."

"As you know, I don't have it. What was in the letter anyway?"

He smiled. "Don't be disingenuous. You know what's in that letter, which is why you're so rattled about losing it."

"I don't know . . ." And I realized I didn't. All I knew was Larry's distress and the strangeness of finding it, not in Larry's office, but stuck out of Josie's bag . . . Josie's bag! I thought, appalled. Once again I had forgotten all about it. So that was what sent Norbert on his chase to Emily's. He thought I had it.

"What's in the letter, Norbert?" I repeated.

He smiled. His eyes, brilliant and far-seeing, as blue as summer lakes, were on me.

"Why should I tell you?" he asked.

"Because if you won't tell me, I won't tell you where I think it is."

He paused and licked his lips. "Just some busybody friend of Larry's in England, confirming that I had been hospitalized twice while I was there."

"Psychiatric hospital?"

"Of course. Nobody over here knew. It was done through relations in England and was considered a family matter. Nothing very troublesome. But in view of everything that happened, it might be."

"I'm surprised the Ministry's Commission didn't turn it up somehow. Surely they wrote to people there."

"Possibly. But you know how reserved the British can be about things they consider private. Besides, there never was anything to it. Just fools making a mistake." He smiled, and another little chill went down my back.

"How did you know what was in the letter? Did Larry tell you?"

"No. Larry's friend is also my friend—we all three went to the same

Oxford college. And the friend, who has a positively medieval sense of honor, wrote and told me what he'd written to Larry."

"I see. By the way, where is Larry today?" A nasty worm of fear crawled inside me as I asked that. Until now it hadn't occurred to me that anything could happen to him.

"I really don't know. I sent him out on a fictitious parish call so I could find his letter. Unfortunately, Josie had taken it, and before I could remove it from her bag, somebody came along."

"Why on earth would Josie have Larry's letter about you?"

He stared at me, pondering perhaps whether or not to answer my question. I knew when he started to answer that, in his mind, my end was already assured. Otherwise he would never have replied.

"She was fond of Grism, you know. Towards the end they were quite chummy. I got hold of Larry's letter when he was out of his office—I arranged for him to be called out suddenly to see somebody in the reception lounge, and counted on his well-known untidy habits for it still to be there, and it was. Unfortunately, I, too, stupidly left it open on my desk. Evidently Josie, who sometimes goes around in the late afternoon collecting outgoing mail, saw it. The stamp on the envelope nearby may have drawn her attention. All this is conjecture. All I know is I had left it on my desk. When I went into the parish house the next morning I saw the letter in Josie's open handbag on the reception desk and heard her trying to call the police. I heard her say, "You're looking in the wrong place for the murderer . . ."

"And you hit her."

"Of course. It may sound, well, ruthless. But arresting me would not help Grism or Josie, and would impede my plan for taking care of the poor. Nothing can stop that. Unfortunately, I heard someone coming before I could get her letter. I ran upstairs to your office and put the bookend in your cupboard, then went down the back, through the church and around the front again."

"My cupboard," I said slowly. "Why there?"

"Because, of course, suspicion was pointing in your direction anyway. I just wanted to give it a little push." He was so calm it frightened me half to death.

"Where was the bookend all this time?"

"First in my office safe and then at home."

"Wasn't that a bit risky? Who else knows the combination of the safe?"

He smiled. "Dick Grism, who wouldn't be using it, and Brett. But after all, he's no friend of yours, is he? I could easily tell him, if he found it, that I was keeping it there to prevent your being further incriminated."

"So you took it home, then. How did you happen to have it with you?"

"One of those wild coincidences. I'd cleaned it up very carefully and was bringing it back in. My plan was simply to replace it in Dick's office and let them discover it."

"Very handy for you." If he took in my sarcasm he didn't show it.

"Yes, wasn't it?"

"You didn't think they'd trace it back to you?"

"The police? My dear Claire, you flatter them! Anyway, when I got back to the front door, I could hear the screaming from where I was standing outside, and knew that there was nothing I could do. I suppose that's why she wanted you to have the letter. You were the chief suspect."

"You're crazy, Norbert, you know that."

"Most religious geniuses have been called crazy. What do you think would happen to Jesus of Nazareth today if He suddenly appeared."

"That's blasphemy. And I don't remember Jesus killing anyone, let alone two or three. You did kill Dick, I take it." It was a statement, not a question.

"The stupid man started questioning me about my order to sell some of our capital holdings. Threatened to tell the vestry. I engineered his appointment to the job because I thought he'd be so flattered—socially—that he'd be a good boy and not make a fuss. Apparently I underestimated the power of his middle-class values . . ." Norbert smiled.

"Very well founded on the Ten Commandments, one of which, I seem to remember, was Thou Shalt Not Steal."

"But as a priest yourself you must know that the New Dispensation wipes out the Old. The people must be fed."

"But the church and its property are not ours, Norbert. They belong either to the diocese or to the congregation." I knew my scholastic and practical arguments were pointless, but they were taking up time until the police would arrive . . . if they would arrive. "And what about Josie? She's going to be all right. And Larry? They both know what's in the letter. And it's only a matter of time before they learn from that boy—Sally's nephew—that you were in New York early enough to kill Dick Grism."

"Yes. He's a bit of a nuisance. I didn't want to give him a ride, and of course I didn't know that I was going to kill Grism and have to make a quick return journey." The blue eyes fixed on me. "I take it you talked to him, too."

"Yes. It didn't hit me at first. But when Martha was telling me how she overheard your voice yelling at Dick that morning, and then we heard you in the hall, I suddenly knew what the boy was talking about. To get back to school in Stamford on time it must have been before eight. I had assumed he was one of the four students you said you brought down in the later, official, trip. But when the pieces fell together I realized he wasn't old enough to be at Yale. He was talking about high school."

"Yes, he was at Yale, looking the university over, and came up and introduced himself."

I looked curiously at Norbert. "Aren't you afraid he might come and blow your cover, your alibi?"

"Oh no. If he says anything, I shall simply say that I remembered when I was leaving Stamford that I'd forgotten some vital something in New Haven and decided then and there to go back. There's no problem there. I have always been led. When and if a crisis comes I shall know what to do."

"You mean you were led to hit Josie on the head."

"Josie was like you, my dear. A troublemaker. However, I should not have hit her—or hit her harder. It enrages me to see a semi-literate typist getting in the way of the work I have to do. God's work. But after all, when I have the letter, it will be her word against mine, and she's nothing but a receptionist."

"And Larry? He's a bit more than a receptionist."

"I will take care of that as it is revealed to me. I can handle Larry. I can also see to it that he's so discredited no one will believe him."

"No," I said. "I don't think you can do that. He's too well liked and admired."

"You see, I am right. You would make trouble. If you had just kept quiet—but you couldn't. You had to go around making waves, as the younger people say. I brought you to St. Anselm's because of Emily Chadbourne and her money, and I think I convinced her just now that your mental state was such that your suicide would not come out of the blue."

"Norbert, even to oblige you, I'm not going to commit suicide. I'm not the type."

"Oh yes, you are. The terrible strains you have been under, the emotional breakdown of your stepdaughter—all united to push you over the edge." He strolled nearer to me. And then I saw what he had in mind. How could I have been so stupid as to help him achieve what he wanted—my apparent suicide? Desperately I tried to move. But his powerful arms were around me in a second. The french window, already half open, was easily kicked aside.

"A fall from an eleven-story balcony would be accepted immediately as suicide," he said, still in the same hypnotic, gentle voice.

I opened my mouth to scream, but his hand was on it, and when I tried to bite he ground his palm into my face, pushing my lip against my teeth so I could taste the blood.

"It's a merciful death," he said.

As his palm slackened, I flung my head to one side. "You're mad!" I screamed at the top of my lungs.

His long, powerful legs were pushing against me. I could feel the stone balustrade at my back. And then, all at once, there was a snarling sound, a huge growl, and Norbert's hold abruptly slackened. As I squirmed aside, I saw Motley's teeth sink into his shoulder where it joined the neck and heard a man's voice shout, "Stop right there, or we'll fire!"

But it was too late. Norbert's tall body wove a little dizzily above the low balustrade, then he plunged over.

"Did you see what Motley did?" Jamie's loud voice finally penetrated the rest of the noise going around. I looked down. My offish son, who disliked public display of emotion, had his arms around my waist. He hugged me. "Did you see him, Ma? He *saved* you. He ought to get a medal."

"I agree," I said weakly. My voice was behaving peculiarly and my knees were shaking. "He's a hero. I'll get in touch with the ASPCA or whoever it is that gives out dog medals."

"You can also thank your son," Detective O'Neill said. "He went down and dialed 911 and kept yelling until we got here. Then he let us in."

I gave Jamie a hug. "Two medals," I said. "I thought you were mad at me."

"I was. But I thought about it and decided there was something funny going on—Mr. Shearer kept saying you were queer in the head, which you're not, and you breaking the contract about not putting me down in front of people, so when I went downstairs I called the police from the house phone."

"I said you were smart. I didn't realize how much!" I looked then at Detective O'Neill. "Norbert?"

"Dead. By the way, can we take this letter?" He was holding the letter I had seen in Josie's bag, and which I had sent half the parish staff looking for.

"Where did you get it?"

"Your tote bag. Josie's bag was in there."

"Are you telling me that after all the panic and fuss I put Josie's handbag into my own tote?"

He smiled a little. "You must have shoved it in without thinking. Anyway, somebody remembered your putting it there. So I looked in your tote bag, which was in the hall, while we were waiting for Shearer to convict himself."

"You mean you were here?"

"For most of it, yes. I told you, you owe one to your son, who called us. By the way, that was the third call. The first was from Mrs. Chadbourne. She was in something like a state of shock. She was convinced you were the murderer, but her granddaughter finally persuaded her otherwise."

"Who was the second call from?"

"Brett Cunningham. He called as soon as he found out where Shearer was going. You know, if it hadn't been for him telling us about your stepdaughter, we might have taken you in that night."

I didn't say anything for a moment. "I was very angry with him."

"Yeah, well, I figured that. You owe *him* one, too."

Later, after the noise and confusion was over and Norbert's body had been removed and the police and reporters had gone, I called Brett at his apartment.

"Detective O'Neill says I owe you one."

"You owe me nothing." He sounded at his curtest.

"Brett, stop sounding the way I thought bankers always sounded. I'm trying to say I'm sorry. I wondered if you would like to come to dinner. It's going to be delicious leftovers."

He paused. "I've always liked leftovers." Another pause. "I suppose your son is going to be there. Not that I don't like him," he added hastily.

"Sometimes he spends the night with his friend Jerry, and Martha isn't coming home till tomorrow," I said. And felt instantly wanton.

"I have, from time to time," he said thoughtfully, "had ideas on how we could get all those worlds together at once—Jamie's and Martha's and ours. Would you be interested in hearing them?"

"Yes," I said. "I would. I haven't felt this way since . . . well, since I received a letter in a London hostel. I'll tell you about it sometime."

"Tell me about it tonight. A sort of miniseries, but shown all in one session, with intervals, of course."

"All right," I said. "I'll do that."

It occurred to me that, for the second time in one day, but for entirely different reasons, my knees had a strange, watery feeling.